Books by Michele Chynoweth

The Faithful One

The Peace Maker

the
FAITHFUL
ONE
— A NOVEL —

MICHELE CHYNOWETH

Ellechor Publishing House, LLC

Ellechor Publishing House
2431 NW Wessex Terrace, Hillsboro, OR 97124

Copyright © 2009 by Michele Hartlove
2011 Ellechor Publishing House Paperback Edition

The Faithful One/ Michele Chynoweth. ISBN: 978-0-9826242-6-5
Library of Congress Control Number: 2011937041

Ellechor Publishing House, LLC
1915 NW Amberglen Pkwy, Suite 400
Beaverton OR 97006

Printed in the United States of America

www.ellechorpublishing.com

Acknowledgements

For their love and support, my parents Mike and Doris Dietz; for their encouragement and advice, my husband, Bill Chynoweth, Rev. William J. O'Brien, Robin Axtell, Ann Cambre, Debbie Kingham and the late John Kluge; for their help in making this a better, more accurate story, Kevin Mahoney, Esq., Mildred Horodynski, Phd, RN, the late Gwen Van Scoy-Linzy, Christiana Health Care and Temple Adas Shalom; and for giving me the idea in the first place, my Higher Power Whom I choose to call God.

Michele Chynoweth

With love to my children,
William, Michael, Kendra,
Morgan and Bobby -
Never give up on your dreams.

Michele Chynoweth

"The Lord giveth, and the Lord taketh away."
- The Book of Job 1:21

Chapter 1

Life is good.

Seth Jacobs reflected on the idyllic September afternoon outside as he adjusted his tie before the hallway mirror while awaiting his limousine. It was the type of day that made you grateful just to be alive – clear, crisp, with temperatures in the mid-seventies and puffy, white clouds billowing across a bright cerulean sky.

There, perfect, Seth thought, surmising his outfit. He still had a tan leftover from summer that contrasted nicely with the starched, white shirt collar around his neck and the charcoal tuxedo, which had been tailored well to fit his large, muscular frame, bringing out the golden highlights in his silver-flecked, light brown hair.

Hearing the sound of a vehicle approaching, Seth quickly shifted his attention from the mirror to the foyer.

The limo driver pulled the sleek, black extended Cadillac into the entrance of the Jacobs' estate, maneuvered up the long, circular drive and parked, letting out a soft whistle as he stretched his lanky figure out of the driver's seat. He had chauffeured many wealthy people in his time, but never before had he seen anything like the breathtaking home that lay sprawling before him.

Perched atop a manicured hill like a crown jewel was

the Jacobs' mansion. The stone and stucco exterior and architectural lines gave it the look of a magnificent European chateau adorned with an arched entrance, floor-to-ceiling bay windows, and first and second floor verandas. The landscaped mansion was surrounded by a wooded backdrop as far as the eye could see. It was like a Hollywood dream home tailored to fit the more rustic look of Massachusetts.

The driver stood waiting, continuing to stare. Although he was six-foot-four, he had to crane his neck to view the entire forty-room mansion. He couldn't see what lay beyond, but it was public knowledge that the two-hundred acres behind the house sported an Olympic-sized swimming pool, several gardens, and forests that buffered the estate for miles.

Seth's approach startled him from his reverie.

"Ahem, you must be my driver?"

"Good evening, uh, Mr. Jacobs, sir." The driver recovered by clearing his throat, taken off guard by the impeccably dressed man who stood nearly as tall as he.

"Relax, what's your name?" Seth extended his hand.

The driver hesitated for a moment before shaking it, appearing flustered that the famous multi-millionaire had made such a friendly, down-to-earth gesture.

"James, sir."

Seth laughed warmly, sending slight crinkles fanning out from his sea-blue eyes. "Well, I might have guessed. Okay, James, let's go."

With Seth safely tucked inside, the limousine wound its way through the New England countryside and into downtown Boston, where it proceeded to get hopelessly snarled in traffic. James attempted to meander through it before he was forced to come to a complete stop, stuck just within the city limits.

Boston's highway system was once again under major

construction and traffic was a nightmare.

It was already five o'clock and Seth was due at six. He was hosting the black-tie-only, thousand-dollar-a-plate fundraising dinner for U.S. Senator Robert Caine, a rising star in Massachusetts who was seeking the Democratic nomination for President in the upcoming election.

The dinner, of course, was being held at the Perfect Place, one of a series of now-famous restaurants owned by Seth Jacobs. With all of Boston's many fine eating establishments, it was still second to none, located at Rowes Wharf, the city's most prestigious waterfront district.

Seth checked his watch for the tenth time in two minutes. Traffic was at a standstill. *At this rate, it will take over an hour to get to the restaurant,* he thought.

"James, no offense, but I won't make it if we sit here much longer. I think I'll take the T."

"But sir, the way you're dressed, it might be dangerous," James protested.

Seth held firm. "Don't worry, I won't hold you responsible." He smiled and handed the driver a fifty-dollar bill. "Thanks, James."

Seth jumped from the limo and headed for the nearest stop of the underground metro, known in Boston as the T. *At least I'm moving*, he thought as he rounded the building on the corner of the next intersection and scrambled for the station. Seth boarded the Blue Line, which he calculated would get him to Boston Harbor in about ten minutes, just in time to make a last-minute check on everything before cocktails were served.

The Senator's dinner will be a culinary coup d'état, Seth thought proudly, taking his seat on the train.

Dining at the Perfect Place was always an occasion in itself, whether one dined alone, with family or friends, or with an intimate partner. One had to make reservations weeks, sometimes months in advance to get a table. But everyone knew the wait was always worthwhile.

Seth wanted his customers to enjoy their dining experience whether they were nine or ninety-nine. Each of his restaurants had a different decor but the same name - a name that Seth hoped reflected the experience within.

That experience included several signature attractions: a location on prime waterfront property, whether it be on a river, lake or ocean, a scenic indoor waterfall, paintings and sculptures by the finest local artists, a variety of appropriate dinner music from grand piano to string quartet, several strategically located fireplaces and the most important feature of all - the finest and freshest cuisine from around the world.

All of the restaurants in the Perfect Place family - Seth hated the word "chain" when it referred to his restaurants - were owned by Jacobs Enterprises, the company Seth formed when he was just getting started in the restaurant business at the young age of thirty. He had built his restaurant "family" one at a time and there was now a Perfect Place in every state in America.

There were no menus at the Perfect Place, which also made it unique, as well as both perplexing and delightful to first-time visitors. Daily specials were suggested by the wait staff, or patrons could order whatever they wished. Seth had decided people should be allowed to eat and drink whatever they preferred at the moment, whether it was lobster stuffed with caviar accompanied by Dom Perignon, or a good hamburger, fries and a shake. Everything was prepared to order by the finest chefs in the world.

Seth was by far the best-dressed and best-looking person on the train despite the fact his tux was disguised under his overcoat. He was forty-nine years old and felt at his prime, at the top of his game, and it showed.

Since he loved food in all of its wonderful varieties, Seth had to work to keep fit and trim for his size. He exercised early each morning in the spa in his penthouse on the seventeenth floor of the Custom House Tower, Boston's oldest but still premier office skyscraper.

He allowed his employees to use the multi-room suite and spa when they visited, or sometimes gave away private stays complete with airline tickets as incentives or rewards for jobs well done.

Seth valued his employees and believed he could always learn from them, especially those who were gifted. He also tried to be readily accessible to them, just to listen or to dispense ideas and advice even if it was by phone or computer.

Stories spread about how Seth Jacobs had helped various employees, building a loyalty among his staff unmatched in the restaurant industry.

There was the time Seth had been leaving the Perfect Place in New York City and found Billy, a frightened, black fourteen-year-old runaway, rummaging through the trash bin in the alley behind the restaurant. Billy had run away from an orphanage in the Bronx where he had been sexually abused by one of the wards. He would have been headed for life on the streets dealing drugs had Seth not caught him in time and offered him food, shelter and a job to pay for it after listening to his story.

He had found a foster home for Billy and offered him work after school as a busboy to keep him off the street and help him save some money of his own.

Bill Brown was now thirty, married with two children, and managed New York City's Perfect Place restaurant. He was one of Seth's most faithful employees and a good friend.

And there was Miss Carla. Raised in a mixed marriage by

her alcoholic mother and abusive father and living in tenement housing in a Louisiana ghetto, Carla was neglected unless she was being beaten, and was ridiculed by other schoolchildren as a "poor little white nigger." She grew up tough and mean and ended up getting by on her own as a teenage prostitute. Seth saw her hooking one night in New Orleans and picked her up. But instead of paying her for her services, he asked her to waitress at the Perfect Place which he had just opened in the French Quarter. If she could stay "straight," Seth promised he could match her income and help her get her life together.

Seth helped Carla discover the beautiful girl with the café latte skin underneath the pancake makeup and rough street exterior. Carla started as a waitress, but Seth later discovered the girl could sing. The Perfect Place in New Orleans was now known for its famous Friday night musical entertainment featuring Miss Carla, who belted out jazz and blues in a sultry, sophisticated soprano that melted men's hearts. But if guys tried to pick her up, Miss Carla knew how to say no.

Seth also helped many an aspiring cook or sous chef become world-renowned culinary masters.

In return, his entire staff – now numbering more than nine hundred – admired him, and many loved him, even though they worked thousands of miles away. Seth made sure he met each and every employee at least once, which meant he did a lot of traveling.

But his wife and kids seemed to understand the sacrifice, and they loved him too.

Tonight I'll be back before they fall asleep, Seth hoped.

Unfortunately he had to attend the Senator's dinner without his wife Maria, who had come down with a stomach bug that day. *Too bad,* Seth thought. Maria loved to get out and mingle.

At least his teenage daughter Angelica had cancelled her Saturday night date to the movies and stayed home to play nursemaid to her mother. She hadn't seemed to mind much when her father asked her for the favor. He couldn't very well have asked his sons Adam or Aaron. Both were still at Dartmouth, hopefully celebrating Harvard's soccer victory. Aaron was just a sophomore at Seth's alma mater but was already a lead player on the varsity team. Adam, a senior at Harvard, had gone with his brother to the away game.

Adam never seemed to be jealous of his younger brother's athletic prowess, secure with his own academic abilities. Seth was proud that all three of his children seemed to have a healthy self-esteem.

I'm lucky I have such good kids, Seth mused as he looked out the T window and saw the late day sun reflecting its coppery light off the glass and chrome office buildings on the downtown horizon. Looking closer, one could see the scarlet glow cast on shorter, historic brick and stone landmarks, church steeples dotting the scene and majestic trees showing off their fiery autumn colors.

Boston never looks more inviting than in the fall, Seth thought while he watched the city speed by in his mind's eye as the T plunged underground.

Seth reflected on his beloved city and all its special attractions this time of year. He knew the large grassy expanse known as Boston Commons, the nation's oldest park, was full of squirrels gathering their harvest, college kids, joggers and a mix of humanity who sought to stretch their muscles or just get some fresh air.

It was still warm enough for boaters and fishermen to be out in the Massachusetts Bay and Seth smiled, remembering how his family was looking forward to next weekend's upcoming Charles River Regatta they attended together each year.

It was warm enough to still catch a Red Sox game at Fenway Park. And the perfect climate - not too hot or cold - for tourists and townsfolk alike to dine al fresco in Quincy Market or wander through its outdoor emporium filled with arts, crafts, souvenirs, and food vendors hawking everything from fresh produce to just-caught seafood to homemade fudge.

Schoolchildren from near and far would be planning trips to Boston's plethora of historic attractions, to experience the Boston Tea Party or walk the Freedom Trail and hear stories of the Battle of Bunker Hill, Paul Revere's ride and the Boston Massacre that had been told countless times.

Seth especially loved Boston because the city was always so alive and seemed to have it all – a fascinating and eclectic combination of old and new architecture, an All-American legacy and European flair, and so much history, culture and scenery. One could never get enough in his opinion.

He had so many memories, both as a child when his family would visit on weekends from their home in Providence, Rhode Island, and as a father who delighted in soaking in all of the city's events and attractions with his own children.

I'm lucky to live in this city, Seth thought as the T raced through the black bowels of Boston's underground, and then churned to a grinding, screeching, unexpected halt.

Chapter 2

The lights in the subway flickered precariously, casting just enough light for its riders to survey the damage.

The train itself hadn't crashed, but had braked suddenly, causing rail and undercarriage damage. But its contents - namely, about one hundred and sixty passengers - had crashed within its interior onto floors and into walls, doors, poles and one another.

Above the cacophonous din an elderly woman moaned in pain as a toddler wailed in his mother's arms. Some passengers started babbling hysterically while others dazedly assessed the situation.

A man's voice over a loudspeaker managed to pierce through the clamor. "This is your conductor speaking. Please take your seats and don't panic. The Blue Line has run across an obstacle in its path and is experiencing technical difficulties. We will send medical personnel to each car as soon as they arrive on the scene. Until then, we ask that all passengers remain seated unless you are a registered nurse, licensed doctor or a certified paramedic. In that case we ask that you please assist anyone in need of aid until help arrives. We will keep you posted as to when the Blue Line will resume its course or if boarding another train to reach our destination will be required. Thank youuuu." The robotic voice almost sounded like a recording.

The thirty passengers in Seth's car, who had taken their seats and listened impatiently to the loudspeaker, simultaneously resumed their nervous chatter. Everyone glanced at each other as if to ask, "What do we do now?"

No one in Seth's car seemed to be a nurse or doctor. At least no one stepped forward to help the old woman sitting on the floor, her head flopped forward, still moaning. After searching the assembly of helpless, embarrassed and apathetic faces around him, Seth bent down on one knee next to the woman, lifted her chin and asked her what was hurting.

"My leg," answered the lady, a heavyset woman obviously of modest means. She wore a house dress and thin brown coat. Her wispy gray hair and watery gray eyes that nearly disappeared in the wrinkles around them made her appear to be in her seventies.

She looked at Seth with mistrust as he silently removed his expensive wool overcoat and gently placed it under her leg. It was cut, bleeding and already swelling around the ankle. He gently took off her shoe and bloody sock and wrapped her foot in the cashmere lining, which he had unzipped and separated from the outer coat. Then he gave her his kindest smile. "I hope that helps until a doctor can take a look at it."

Gratefulness replaced the mistrust in the old woman's tired eyes as she looked at the handsome man kneeling beside her. He flashed her a nearly perfect white smile that brought forth charming dimples. The elderly woman cocked her head to one side and squinted her eyes up at him. "Haven't I seen you before? Aren't you one of those models I've seen in my magazines?"

Seth chuckled. "No ma'am, I'm not a model. Just a restaurant owner."

The woman reached out and touched a gnarled finger tentatively to Seth's gold wedding band. "Too bad you're married. Good looking and charming to boot. You would make a great catch for my daughter Lucille, who if she waits much longer, is going to end up an old maid for sure. Pity too. She's a beauty."

"I'm sure she is if she looks anything like her mom."

"Pshaw!"

"What's your name?" Seth wanted to know who was in his care. It was his nature to ask.

"Ruthie. Ruthie O'Hanlon. And thank you Mister uh..."

"Jacobs. But you can call me Seth."

"Thank you Mister Seth."

Once he had sufficiently comforted the woman, who now lay resting her head back against a seat with her eyes closed, Seth took out his cell phone to call Henri, his maître d', to inform him of the T's delay. He noticed with dismay that his cell phone had no service underground. *Oh well, nothing to do now but sit back and pray the subway gets fixed in time for me to get to the Senator's dinner for dessert, or at least in time for his speech.*

Seth checked his watch. Over an hour had passed and, while a paramedic team had arrived to help passengers with physical injuries, there had been no word on the Blue Line's condition.

Finally the monotone conductor's voice came over the loudspeaker once more, welcome even in its ingratiating banality.

"We are sorry to inform you that the T has not yet been fixed and, due to the position of the Blue Line on its tracks, another line cannot transport you at this time. An engineering crew is working on repairs and we will keep you informed. We are anticipating approximately another hour delay. We will be providing everyone with a snack and beverage shortly and apologize for the inconvenience. Refunds and a courtesy certificate good for a one-month, unlimited-use T ticket will be given to each passenger upon arrival at your destination. Thank youuuu."

Well, there goes the Senator's dinner," Seth thought, feeling cold, hungry and a bit dejected and irritated.

Then he looked at the doleful faces around him and realized, standing there in his tux, that he must look quite smug and rich. He felt like neither right now. Just uncomfortable in his dressy clothes.

Taking a few more stolen glances at the other passengers, wondering what walks of life they came from suddenly made Seth feel fortunate, and his mood lifted.

I have so much for which to be grateful, he realized.

He decided to make the best of a bad situation and snuggled into his seat to ponder the riches of his life. *It's a way to pass time without my cell phone, a good book or even a magazine to read,* he smiled to himself, his thoughts drifting back to the breakfast table that morning.

It was a typically busy Saturday with all of their various schedules, so it was rare that the entire Jacobs family was gathered for breakfast, and Seth reveled in the fact that all five of them could enjoy one another's company, if only for an hour or so.

The morning sun streamed into the French doors and bay windows of the cavernous morning room where they ate together, giving an amber cast to the wooden beams overhead and flooding the room with warm, soft light.

It was Seth's favorite room, not only because of the expansive windows which afforded a breathtaking view of the hills and woods beyond, but also because of the everyday yet special times his family had spent here.

"Daddy, how do you think I look?" Angelica Jacobs asked as she bustled into the morning room where her father and brothers sat awaiting the breakfast their mom was cooking in the adjoining kitchen. At seventeen, she was the youngest of Seth's three children and still the baby of the family.

"Too much makeup, skirt's too short, heels too high." Seth mumbled his characteristic response between sips of coffee without looking up from the sports section of the *Boston Globe*.

"Dad!" Angelica stood, hands on hips, exasperated. She wore a little makeup, low heels, a blouse and knee-length skirt and her long dark hair in a ponytail. It was her first day at her part-time job as a bank teller. "This is conservative compared to my friends, but I need to make a good impression."

"You look..."

"...like an angel," Adam and Aaron Jacobs finished sweetly in unison. It was their father's favorite line for their younger sister.

"She does." Seth raised his eyes from the paper and appraised his daughter. Meanwhile his sons rolled their eyes and snickered, teasing Angelica as they often did. But she knew, like playful lion cubs, they teased her affectionately and would band together to defend her if needed.

Maria handed a steaming platter of pancakes over the stone half-wall that joined both rooms, adding to the spacious effect of the home.

Her cheeks were flushed from being bent over the stove and her dark eyes sparkled with the joy of presenting her family with the results of her labor.

But the sparkle faded a bit as she watched her sons wrinkle their noses and stare with dismay at the flat brown disks they forked onto their plates.

Seth cautiously took a bite and looked disparagingly at his sons, who responded by bursting out in laughter.

"Good try, Mom." Adam stifled a laugh which caused Aaron to guffaw and nearly snort out his milk.

"Adam, Aaron, that's enough," Seth rebuked them, feeling sorry for his beautiful wife. He knew she had given her best effort but would never be a Susie Homemaker no matter how hard she tried.

"It's okay, they're right." Maria laughed at herself after pretending to be offended. "I wouldn't eat these either. But I did try."

Maria had tried on many occasions to cook for her family. While she did a fairly good job replicating some of her mother's native Italian dishes, she knew cooking wasn't her thing, and happily relinquished the duty whenever possible to Seth, who had become a master at it. This morning he had slept in for a change since it was Saturday and he knew a late night lay ahead.

Seth stood and crossed the room to kiss his wife's cheek. "Thank you, dear, for trying. Besides, you're quite good at what's important." He whispered this last sentiment into her ear.

"What's that, Dad?" Aaron asked. "We didn't hear you..."

"I was just saying how your mother used to be a fine waitress." Seth grinned as he untied the apron from his wife's waist and playfully swatted her behind. "Now you go have a seat and let me take over."

In a few minutes they were feasting on stacks of fluffy, golden pancakes cooked to perfection.

Adam finished the last syrupy bite and stood to leave. Headed into his senior year with med school looming, he had a full course load with a major English paper due.

"Where are you off to already?" Seth couldn't hide his disappointment that their family time had to end so soon.

"Gotta get to the library before all the good research books are taken. And I'd suggest you come with me, little brother."

Aaron was still seated at the table polishing off his fourth pancake. "For God's shakes, Adam, whatsha rush?"

"Please don't talk with your mouth full, Aaron," Seth admonished his younger, more cavalier son. "I think Adam's right; a little library today wouldn't hurt."

"But I thought we were going to hang out at Phi Kappa Phi for a little while. Y'know, invite them to the game?" Aaron raised his eyebrows mischievously.

"Oh, must be a sorority," Angelica observed as she carried her own plate to the sink, walking with her back straight and nose in the air like a princess, as if to show she was above her brothers' crudeness. "Really Aaron, don't you ever think of anything besides girls?"

"Hurry, let's get out of here before you have to answer that." Adam grabbed his brother's arm and dragged him out of his chair. "Thanks for breakfast, Mom, Dad. Can we be excused?"

Aaron grumpily followed. "Do you have to be so perfect?" he growled at his older brother.

"You could use a lesson on manners from Adam." Seth also stood to help clear the dishes. "And if the library is so painful, you could stay to clean the kitchen."

"Uh, the library sounds great." Aaron perked up and, after giving his mother a quick hug in passing, pushed Adam through the kitchen and down the hallway toward the front door. "See ya."

Seth shook his head as he watched the two boys leave.

He would never get over how different the two were from one another, not only in looks but in their personalities and character.

Although neither brother hung out in any particular clique in college, Adam was like the student council president to Aaron's popular jock. Seth's oldest son was independent, studious, punctual, organized and brainy. He had a few close friends, loved music, had a steady girlfriend and wanted to be a doctor one day.

His younger brother was adventurous and a little disorganized, but smart when he applied himself. He had a lot of casual friends, dated around and liked to make people laugh. He thought he might become a professional soccer player one day, although most people told him he'd make a great comedian.

Although they had their differences, the brothers shared a mutual respect for each other and usually enjoyed one another's company. And they shared a mutual fondness for their baby sister.

Enveloped by her brothers' protectiveness and her parents' doting, Angelica was like the prom queen, somewhat spoiled with a slight defiant streak. But she too loved the rest of her family and was especially close to her father, whom she looked up to the same way now as she did when she was three. He was her hero and she wanted to help him run his restaurants one day. In her book, school and her job were just the means to an end; boring but necessary until she could get a business degree and prove herself.

All three children were blessed with their parents' looks— Adam and Angelica with their mother's dark Italian beauty and Aaron with his father's lighter-colored, rugged handsomeness.

But even Angelica, in her blossoming youth, is no match for her mother, Seth thought, missing his wife's warmth and humor now as he pulled his jacket more closely around him and snuggled deeper into thought on the torn vinyl seat of the subway.

Chapter 3

Maria Giovanni met Seth Jacobs for the first time when she waited on his table in the little Italian restaurant her parents owned and operated in Providence, Rhode Island. She was eighteen, restless, wanting to break free from her big Italian Catholic family, and gorgeous.

Most girls would have fawned over the athletically-built, attractive young man with the Paul Newman eyes seated in the booth before her, especially if he smiled at them the way Seth was smiling at her right now.

To Maria, he was just another customer, and she gazed at him with indifference, or at least so it would have appeared to the casual passerby.

But Seth saw something more in those smoldering, smoke-colored eyes, the way her dark brows arched disdainfully and the way her red, pouty lips pursed in defiance. Like a captive wild animal that begged for freedom.

It drove him crazy from the moment he saw her.

"What would you like?" Maria asked, not hiding her impatience with her job.

"What do you recommend?" Seth feigned innocence, holding out his menu, wanting her to stay, trying to engage her in conversation.

Maria shrugged. "Anything Italian is good," she said shortly.

Are you Italian? Seth wanted to ask, but thought he better not come on too strong. Besides, he could figure that one out, even if her nametag didn't say Maria.

"Surprise me," Seth responded with a grin.

"Whatever you say." The young waitress grabbed his menu and headed for the kitchen. Seth watched her walk away. *Long, slender legs,* he noticed. *Curves in all the right places. Thick, wavy hair the color of bittersweet chocolate. Bewitching.*

Maria returned with a heaping platter of linguini smothered in a red garlic sauce with sausage, onions and peppers. She also sat before him a glass of red wine, some homemade bread and olive oil for dipping and an overstuffed cannoli.

"Can I get you anything else?" She gave him a polite half-smile.

Your number, Seth thought. "Could you sit and share this with me? I'm afraid I'll never eat it all by myself."

"I'll get you a doggie bag." Her smile widened in amusement, this time reaching her eyes, before she turned and sauntered away.

Seth left her a twenty-dollar tip and a note that read, "Maria, thanks for the surprise. You're right. Anything Italian is good. Give my regards to the chef. Sincerely, Seth Jacobs."

Seth stopped in Giovanni's for dinner at least once a week after that. On his fourth visit he finally got up the nerve to ask her out.

"May I take you out to dinner?" Seth had asked after Maria came to take his plate. He hadn't expected her answer to be so simple.

"Sure, as long as it's not Italian," Maria answered, flashing him a brilliant smile.

"Tomorrow, then, I'll pick you up—seven o'clock?"

"Okay." She picked up his tip and seductively waved goodbye. Seth waved back, hardly noticing that he spilled red wine on his tie as he did so.

Maria was aware of the effect her looks had on men—even a man like Seth Jacobs, who was as handsome as she was beautiful.

Growing up she constantly had to fend off advances from boys starting as early as sixth grade. She had matured a little early for her age, which hadn't helped. Luckily, she had always been able to call upon one of her older brothers to assist her.

The youngest of five boys and two girls, Maria had moved to America from Sicily with her family when she was just two years old. She had been raised by hard-working parents who struggled to make ends meet in their modest three-bedroom flat in New York City by operating a bakery in the vacant shop below.

Maria had grown up surrounded by the delicious smells of home-baked breads and pastries and it was a constant struggle in her teen years to keep her girlish figure. Poor as they had been, her family had always eaten well.

The Giovannis moved to Providence when Maria was five. Her parents had explained that they wanted to move away from the noise and congestion of the big city to a better place to raise their family. They also had some cousins who lived in Providence beckoning them to move there.

In fact, Providence was home to a large number of Italian families, so they ended up feeling right at home. Their cottage in the suburbs seemed like a mansion compared to their New York apartment and the Giovanni bakery grew to become a full-scale, premier dining establishment.

But as she grew to become a young woman, Maria became restless waiting tables and tired of living with her big traditional Catholic family under her domineering Italian father and smothering Italian mother. She longed to move back to a big city.

And she now saw Seth as her chance.

Seth drove Maria into Boston for their first date, where they ate at a quaint French cafe he had heard about through his college friends. They described it as romantic, a real "chick" place where a guy was sure to get a girl "in the mood," if a guy could afford it. Seth used half of his meager savings, not to get Maria "in the mood," but to treat her to the very best.

Over a bottle of Cabernet Sauvignon, Seth politely asked Maria a few questions about her life in general and she soon found herself opening up to this attractive young man.

Maria ended up telling Seth of her dreams of getting out of Providence, breaking free of her family and starting out on her own, away from their protective wings.

"What do you want to do?" Seth asked. "What do you want to become?"

No one had ever asked her that before so Maria had never given it much thought. With her family's strong Sicilian roots, she grew up being told that women were destined to become married, have children and support their husbands in the family business, whatever that turned out to be.

While Maria had no plans to get married anytime soon, she didn't know what talents or skills she possessed, other than waiting tables. "I don't know," she answered, flustered.

"With your looks you could do a lot of things." Seth immediately noticed the red in her cheeks deepen. "I'm sorry. I meant that as a compliment. As in, you could be a model or actress. Of course, your intelligence and charm may get you somewhere as well. Maybe you could be a scientist, a writer, an astronaut, the President; of course, part of life's challenge is to discover what talents lie within and how to use them to become the best person you can be."

"Pretty wise words from a guy who's only twenty-two." Maria's face broke into a genuine smile. "You know, Seth Jacobs, I'll be honest with you. At first I decided to go out with you because I thought you might be my ticket out of Providence."

Seth frowned.

"I know, pretty terrible of me. I'm sorry. But my whole life guys have seen me as just another looker and haven't really gotten to know the real me. I thought you might be just another guy looking to get some. But now I realize you're a real gentleman, someone I can talk to, confide in, maybe even become friends with..." Maria became tongue-tied and she picked at her food in humble embarrassment.

Seth saw her discomfort and, hearing the first strains of a violin, stood and gallantly offered Maria his hand and asked her to dance. Maria discovered that, in addition to his handsomeness, politeness and intelligence, Seth was a graceful dancer.

She had been used to dancing with her Italian cousins, who moved energetically, albeit rambunctiously and awkwardly, at many a wedding or celebration, or with sweaty, clumsy high school boys. In contrast, Seth moved her adeptly across the floor to a waltz and then more slowly, holding her close, to a slower, classical tune.

When Seth delivered her to her doorstep that night promptly at ten and asked if he might kiss her, Maria offered her lips willingly and it was she who parted them so they both could explore.

One year later, they were engaged.

Unlike Maria, Seth had found his own talents did lie in the culinary arts, which probably stemmed from his parents. But Seth was more ambitious than his mom and dad, who had been content to run their Jewish deli in Providence. The Jacobs family had also moved there from New York City after finding the Big Apple too expensive, noisy, and congested.

In addition, Eli and Rachel Jacobs had moved because Jewish delicatessens were a dime a dozen in New York. In Providence, the Jacobs were much more successful because theirs was the sole deli amid a throng of mostly seafood, American and Italian eateries. The Jacobs' Deli carried not only kosher food but also a variety of Jewish soups, salads, sandwiches and fresh-baked breads and desserts that had people from all nationalities lining up during their lunch hours.

Seth had been the only child born to his devout Jewish parents, who had fled their native Germany when they were just teenagers to escape the Nazi regime. After they were married and had set up "home" in a tiny apartment in Manhattan, they had been told by a doctor that they could bear no children because Eli had a low sperm count. Despite the doctor's dour diagnosis, the Jacobs prayed for twelve years that God might grant them a child.

Finally, their prayers were answered when Seth was born.

To Eli and Rachel, he was a "miracle baby" and because of that, they believed he was destined for greatness. So they selected the Hebrew name Seth, meaning "appointed one."

Eli and Rachel had both worked at the only jobs they could find when they emigrated from Germany to New York, he as a dishwasher in a deli and she as a seamstress for a coat factory, before they could scrape together enough savings to start their own restaurant. They had been open for business just two years when Seth was born and were struggling to make ends meet, so they weren't able to spoil their only child as they would have liked.

Instead they showered Seth with all of the educational privileges they could afford, reading to him day and night, buying him used books and mustering enough money to send him to the local Hebrew school.

Thirty-five-years-old, overweight and suffering from high blood pressure, Rachel had a difficult childbirth and was told that, due to the strain that had been put on her organs during her pregnancy and labor, she could never bear another child. It might kill her.

But Eli and Rachel didn't care when they heard the news that they could bear no more children. They had a healthy baby boy and together they got down on their knees and thanked God each night for their little family.

Although the Jacobs remained faithful to their Jewish upbringing, they were grateful to be living in the United States and attempted to slowly change from their orthodox ways to a more assimilated American Jewish way of living. They still kept a Kosher home and observed the Sabbath and major Jewish holidays. But they were aware and tolerant of other faiths around them, especially in Providence, where there weren't many Jewish families.

Since all of the members of their extended families had either died in Germany or still lived in New York, the Jacobs mostly kept to themselves, sharing holidays with a few friends they had met in Providence who attended the same temple with them.

Growing up, Seth was a bit isolated and became very studious and ambitious at an early age. He learned a lot of his cooking skills from his mother and a few business skills from his father, who had to learn them on his own. Seth was also quite an entrepreneur in his youth, selling lemonade, arts and crafts and other sundry items on the street corner. Following Seth's Bar Mitzvah, his father allowed him to work in the deli, first as a dishwasher and busboy, then as a waiter and finally, as a cook.

Cooking, by far, was his favorite job. Seth actually

perfected some of his family's recipes, like the matzoh ball soup, by adding more spices and a little bit of sweet potato for flavor.

Seth saved every dime. When his parents proudly announced on his eighteenth birthday that they had saved enough money for their son to go to the local community college, he surprised them with his own announcement that he had applied for and received an academic scholarship to Harvard where he wanted to study for a business degree. Seth told his parents that, by his calculations, with the scholarship, their college savings and his own money he had saved he would have just enough – if he also worked a part-time job – for tuition, books and room and board.

Both Eli and Rachel were so proud that they sat down at the kitchen table and wept.

It was during summer break just before his junior year at Harvard that Seth met Maria in Giovanni's. The following summer, he asked for her hand in marriage.

Seth took her back to the French café in Boston and proposed on one knee, a modest diamond ring and a long-stemmed red rose in hand. Maria rewarded him with an enthusiastic yes.

"But what about you finishing college?" she asked.

As usual, Seth had thought it all through. "I figured that I would finish college first, then we would get married, maybe move here to Boston, and I could attend the Cambridge School of Culinary Arts nearby. I could work part-time, and together with your salary as a waitress, we could afford it all, and maybe even save a little for our own family one day. I'm sure you can find a great job at any of Boston's fine restaurants…"

Maria interrupted, pouting. "What about pursuing *my* dream?"

"What dream is that?" Seth tried not to sound flippant or

condescending but he wasn't aware that his new fianceé had set forth any career goals. Her silence confirmed his assumption. "Well, when you discover it, then I'll help you pursue it with all my heart."

Maria still frowned.

"Besides, wouldn't you want to get away from our families and tiny little Providence and move here?" he added, stroking her cheek. "There's so much to see and do. We can go sightseeing and sailing…"

"And dancing and shopping," Maria finished with a smile on her face and gleam in her eye.

"Alright." Seth relented to her gorgeous smile. "But don't take us broke before we even get started, dear."

"It's a deal," she agreed.

Chapter 4

In line with his traditional upbringing, Seth asked Maria's parents, Isabella and Antonio Giovanni, for their daughter's hand in marriage when he took Maria home that evening.

The Giovannis had met Seth on several occasions in their restaurant and had liked him from the start. In private discussions they agreed that Seth would be the perfect man to try to tame their impetuous youngest daughter, and they looked past the cultural and religious diversity of the two. Seth seemed to have all of the qualities of a good husband in their book. He was bright, ambitious, well-to-do and polite. The fact that he was handsome and interested in their line of work were bonuses.

Seth's parents, on the other hand, had a more difficult time accepting the engagement when their son told them about it the following day.

"We don't even know her," Rachel Jacobs protested in her typical Yiddish accent. She put down her latest sewing project, stood to her full five-feet-two height, and started pacing.

"She's Italian—and Catholic for heaven's sake," Eli grumbled from his recliner, where he listened to a Red Sox game on the radio. Even though they had a television set which Seth had given them as an anniversary gift, they rarely watched it, turning it on usually just to see the nightly news. "Sounds like a bad mix to me."

Seth had told them all about Maria, accentuating her positive qualities and downplaying her wild streak. "Her parents are the same as you are—very decent, hardworking, religious people with good morals and values."

"But they're not Jewish," Rachel and Eli chimed together.

"So what, there's a law that says I have to marry a Jewish goyl?" Seth mimicked his parents' heavy Jewish accent. "Oy vey! I've picked a Shiksa to be my wife! I'm doomed!"

"Alright young man, that's enough disrespect." Eli turned off the radio and stood to put his arm around his wife. "We're just looking out for the best interests of our only son."

"Believe me, Pa, once you meet her, you'll see Maria is in my best interests." Seth grinned and stood from the couch where he had been sitting. "In fact, I was hoping to bring her over tonight to meet you."

"Oy veh!" Rachel held her hands to her face. "I'll never be ready in time! What am I going to fix for dinner?"

"She'll like anything you fix, Ma." Seth wrapped his arms around his mother's thick middle and gave her a fond squeeze. "As long as it's not Italian."

Over a huge spread of food, including a corned beef brisket, potato pancakes, steamed vegetables, fresh-baked Challah bread and apple cake, all of which Maria sampled with pleasure, the Jacobs talked with their son and his fianceé about their plans for the future.

Eli marveled at Maria's beauty, trying to be discreet, but as he helped his wife with the dishes afterward in the kitchen, Rachel scolded him. "I saw the way you looked at her," she chided.

"You're not jealous, my little latke? A man can't help but appreciate beauty like that. But don't worry. I was looking at what was inside too. I think that Maria is okay."

Rachel smiled warily. "Jealous! Huh! I'm not worried about you. I'm worried about Seth. Beautiful women like that tend to wander if you know what I mean."

"Well, they look happy enough together to me."

"Alright, okay." Rachel gave in. "At least she's not after Seth's money, since he doesn't have that much, so she must be pretty smart to see what a real catch he is. I'm sure she realizes our Seth is going to be somebody someday."

"And our boy is not that shabby in the looks department either." Eli was proud of his offspring, who looked a lot like him except for the gray hair and glasses that had come with age.

"Humility is not your strong point, is it my love?" Rachel teased back. "But you're right. They do make a handsome couple."

Eli and Rachel came back into the dining room with coffee in time to see Seth and Maria sharing laughter and holding hands.

"Ah, it's good to see a young couple laughing together." Eli set the tray he was carrying onto the coffee table, and proudly stood puffing out his chest like a parrot. "Your mother and I give both of you our blessings on your marriage, and even though we're from humble surroundings, we'll be happy to help get you started any way we can."

"Thank you!" Maria's eyes brimmed with tears over the acceptance of her in-laws-to-be. The four of them hugged each other warmly.

"Yes, thank you Dad, Mother." Seth was secretly glad his parents had decided not to hold Maria's Gentile heritage against her.

Maria and Seth set their wedding date for June first, two weeks after graduation.

Seth graduated summa cum laude with a business degree

from Harvard and was enrolled in The Cambridge School of Culinary Arts.

The Jacobs and Giovannis both wept for joy as he crossed the stage to receive his diploma.

Maria beamed and ran to him to hug and kiss him, turning the heads of more than one of Seth's colleagues. She was dressed in a red suit that set off her chocolate-colored tresses.

Maria, Seth and both sets of parents went to dinner afterward to celebrate the graduation and their upcoming marriage. The wedding plans were all in place. Now all they had to do was pray for good weather and God's blessing.

Seth and Maria had chosen to get married outside and had received permission to use Harvard Yard in the center of the University.

The weather couldn't have been better. The sun shone brilliantly on the Jacobs' wedding guests, all seated in white chairs lined in rows on either side of a runner that led up the Yard to an arched trellis covered in dark green ivy and white roses.

Because he was Jewish and she, Catholic, the Yard had been the perfect choice, since there was no compromise between church and temple. A priest from the Giovannis' church and a cantor from the Jacobs' synagogue jointly presided, and the ceremony included one custom from each of their respective religions. First, after drinking from a cup of wine, Seth offered it to his new bride, then smashed the empty goblet beneath his foot, a Jewish tradition meant to bring luck to the couple. Then Maria and Seth took separately lit candles and together lit a joint candle, a Catholic tradition signifying their unity before God. And while the vows Seth and Maria wrote themselves were somewhat non-traditional, they were very much from the heart.

As everyone cheered and threw rice, the two walked down

the runner as man and wife. After a quick change into more casual clothes, they rejoined their guests for the reception, a buffet supper under a huge canopy in the Yard next to where the wedding took place.

As the sun set, a trio played dance music and the group partied until midnight under thousands of twinkling miniature lights strung under the canopy's vaulted ceiling.

It was a night they would always remember.

Seth and Maria left the reception a little early and drove to a quaint bed and breakfast in Boston to start their three-day honeymoon. It was the best they could afford with their combined savings, but they both believed it wouldn't have made a difference if they were in Hawaii; they were together as husband and wife, and that was all that mattered.

Both of them had waited to make love with each other until their wedding night and Seth wanted it to be as romantic as possible for his beautiful bride.

He arranged to have a bottle of champagne chilling in their suite, a huge bouquet of white roses to greet them and dozens of candles lit throughout the bedroom.

Maria gasped in delight when Seth carried her over the threshold and gently let her down.

"Oh Seth, this is wonderful!" she gasped, looking around at the flowers and candlelight. "Why don't I go change into something more comfortable while you open the champagne?" She gave her new husband a wink and disappeared into the bathroom with her bag, closing the door behind her.

Seth stripped down to his boxers, popped open the champagne and brought two glasses into the bedroom. He turned off the lamps so that the candles' luminescent glow alone softly lit the room.

Maria came to him dressed in a sleeveless, long, white

silk gown with lace trim and stood next to the bed nervously, expectantly.

Seth was moved beyond words when she told him she was still a virgin.

He had never asked, allowing himself to think she was even though he wasn't sure. After all, they were in America and it was the start of the eighties.

But here she was, shyly revealing her secret virginity like an ethereal angel.

She slowly parted her white gown to reveal a negligee underneath made entirely of sheer white lace and sat down on the bed next to him, her long brown legs crossed before him as she waited, for the first time in her life, unsure of herself with a man.

He knelt down on the floor before her, said a quiet prayer of thanks for this beautiful creature that was now his wife, and tenderly took them both to a place somewhere very near paradise.

Chapter 5

Less than a year later, Maria found out she was pregnant with their first child. Her Catholic upbringing had ingrained in her that birth control was wrong, so she had relied on the rhythm method she had learned about from her mother.

But sex had been so new and exciting to her, and Seth was such an eager partner, that she must have counted incorrectly one month.

She found out after two weeks of being nauseous every single day. At first she figured she had come down with a bad stomach flu. But one of her new friends at the upscale restaurant in downtown Boston where she waited tables led her to suspect otherwise, and a home pregnancy test confirmed the fact.

Her doctor told her the baby was due on Christmas day.

Despite her sickness, and after her initial feeling of shock subsided, Maria was excited and couldn't wait to tell her husband the news. She picked a day when she was off work to tell him, and after her nausea went away, spent the afternoon carefully trying to duplicate the meal she had brought him that fateful day he had ordered "something Italian" and they had met for the first time.

She broke the news to him after dinner in their little apartment.

"Oh my God!" Seth shouted with delight. "We're going

to have a baby!" He jumped up from the table and pulled Maria to her feet to give her a hug. "Oh, honey, that's great!"

Then a slight frown came across his face and Maria watched Seth's brilliant blue eyes darken like the sky when a storm was approaching.

"What's wrong?" she asked, as Seth released her and started pacing. "I thought you'd be happy."

"Well, I'm just hoping you're happy." He looked at her hesitantly from across the room. "Here you've been waiting tables to help put me through school and you've never had a chance to find what you really want to do and now...well, this changes everything."

Maria crossed the small eat-in kitchen and put her arms around her husband. "Actually, I surprise myself that I'm so happy," she replied with tears in her eyes. "I always thought I wanted to wait to have children. But now, even if I found the perfect calling, no job could ever make me feel as happy as I do now. We're going to have our very own family, Seth! Speaking of which, wait until *our* families find out! They're going to be so excited and...Seth, what's wrong now?"

The clouds had not left his eyes as Seth broke free from Maria's embrace and began to pace the room again.

"I'm just wondering how we're going to manage. How are we going to afford all this? Don't get me wrong. I've always wanted to have children. I just never thought they'd come so soon and...well, I guess I'll quit school and find a job myself so you won't have to wait tables in your condition."

"My condition?" Maria's voice rose in incredulity and she stepped back to look her husband squarely in the eyes. "Seth, you can be so smart and yet, like a man, so dumb when it comes to women's affairs. I'm healthy as a horse and after this morning sickness goes away, I'll be perfectly fine. Now that I'm on the dinner shift I don't even go in until after lunchtime.

I'll probably be able to work right up until the baby is born. And I'm sure they'll be able to switch me from waitressing to doing something easier, like being a hostess, once I get too big. Besides, I'm making great money. We've already saved a few hundred dollars. What's a baby going to add to our bills? You stay in school, Seth Daniel Jacobs, and that's an order. Besides, you said you only have a little less than a year to go before you apprentice as a sous chef. Knowing how ambitious you are, you'll be making money as a chef before we know it. I have faith in you. We'll be fine, so quit your worrying."

Seth stopped pacing long enough for Maria to grab him by the belt and pull him close to her. She pressed herself against her husband's broad chest and started unbuttoning his shirt. She felt Seth getting aroused and she impishly grinned at him.

He couldn't help himself. His wife was so beautiful, especially now. *It's true what they say about women glowing when they're pregnant,* he realized. And he knew what she was offering. Maria had been a quick study in the bedroom and was usually as eager to please him as he was her.. Still...

"Maria, is it okay for you to...for us to make love in your condition?" he asked.

"There you go again!" she cried in mock frustration. "Of course it's okay, silly. He, or she, is just a tiny thing, about as big as a grain of rice, and well protected. See, you didn't know it, but I've actually been reading up on all of this. So the only condition I'm in right now is an excited one."

Maria finished opening the last button on Seth's shirt and slipped out of her T-shirt. Seth hungrily drew her to him and kissed her full lips, breathing hard with desire. He lifted her up into his strong arms and carried her into the bedroom, laying her gently on the bed, and they made love just like they did on their wedding night, at first tenderly, then passionately, with abandon.

Seth remembered the day Adam was born like it was yesterday.

How perfect his face was, how tiny each finger and toe, how Maria cried tears of relief and joy as she radiantly held him in her arms. *Gazing at them was like looking at a painting of the Madonna and her child,* Seth thought.

It wasn't the belief of his Jewish religion, as it was of Christians, that Jesus was the Savior, the Lord. *Right now I just believe this little baby boy is a Godsend.* He looked down on the tiny gift of love in his arms, his son, born like the Christ child on Christmas day, and said a silent prayer of thanks.

Before children, he and Maria had celebrated both Jewish and Christian holidays together, attending their families' respective gatherings.

They decided to raise their children in both faiths and let them decide for themselves which to choose when they grew older. *Perhaps they would find a combination,* Seth thought. At least they would have faith in God, would be raised by two families who loved them, and would have values and morals that were handed down by generations. It would be a good foundation.

Aaron followed Adam by a little less than two years, and Angelica followed by another two years after that. While their hands and lives were overwhelmingly full, Seth and Maria counted their blessings. Maria had relatively smooth pregnancies and childbirths and all of their children were good babies, growing up healthy, give or take the normal coughs and colds that came with Massachusetts winters.

After he graduated from the Culinary School of Arts, Seth used his business degree and cooking skills to get a job as sous chef at The Catch, a popular seafood restaurant on the water in Boston Harbor. He learned from one of the best chefs in the country how to prepare food for tables of one to one hundred and he learned how to run a restaurant that could seat two hundred people at the same time.

Seth loved the restaurant business and even though it was exhausting work, he often showed up early and stayed late just to soak in as much knowledge as he could. He learned tips on how to set a table more attractively, how to garnish entrees, how to make guests feel special, and how to make foods sound delicious before they were even tasted.

Presentation, he learned, was a key ingredient.

And so, when the maitre d' had a heart attack, Seth was able to step in and take charge, receiving a much needed raise just after Aaron was born. It gave Maria and him the money they needed to move from their tiny apartment in downtown Boston to a Cape Cod style house in the suburbs. They had been bursting at the seams in the apartment so the house seemed huge, giving each of the boys a room of their own.

When Angelica was born, the boys moved in together, but they didn't seem to mind. Bunk beds, pillow fights and reading books together late at night were great fun.

When Charles Ryan, the owner of The Catch, approached seventy, he asked Seth to take over the restaurant.

"This place has been my life." The elderly man coughed, emitting a brittle, crackling sound. "But you can't take it with you, you know."

"Don't talk like that, Pops." Seth spoke the old man's nickname fondly.

"You are like a son to me, Seth." Pops leaned forward on his cane as he gave in to another coughing spell, then sat back on the bench the two men shared at a waterfront table on the outside deck of The Catch. The lunch crowd had come and gone so they had a few moments to rest and gaze out at the dozens of sailboats, barges and yachts that filled the harbor. "You have earned the right to take over. And since I have no children, it's only natural.

"I want this old gal to stay in the family." Pops Ryan looked with rheumy eyes at Seth, but his look was far from soft. "And I know you run a tight ship. I know you care. All I ask is that you run her with respect and keep her name the same. You know, my grandfather gave her the name over seventy-five years ago. And it ain't been worn out since."

"I am deeply honored sir." Seth stood and shook the older man's hand. "But I will need to discuss this with my wife first." He promised he'd get back to Charles Ryan the very next day.

The discussion that night with Maria turned out to be their first major argument in their seven years of marriage.

Seth had thought long and hard about Charles Ryan's proposal before bringing up the subject that night after the children were asleep.

Owning The Catch would be a dream come true…for most people.

"Just not for me," he told Maria as they sat at the kitchen table sipping tea and eating a piece of fresh peach pie, one of the many desserts Seth had brought home from work over the years. "I already have a dream. I've been meaning to tell you about it, but I wanted it all to be worked out up here first." Seth pointed to his temple. "It would be a restaurant of my own, that I start from scratch. That way I can create it, it can be my very own place and I can see my own ideas come to life."

"Well you can do that at The Catch, can't you?" Maria asked. "Make a few changes here and there. Seth, if you start new, on your own, you'll have to invest your own money. You're only thirty years old, for God's sake."

"Well, we can look at it as a thirtieth birthday present." Seth tried to lighten the mood but was only half joking. *I've worked so hard all these years, it's about time I work for my own goals, my own dream,* he thought, feeling a little self-righteous.

"In case you haven't noticed, Seth Jacobs, we don't have that kind of money!" Maria's Italian temper began to flare and she gestured more wildly with each sentence. "It's gone toward doctor's bills, mortgage payments, diapers, clothes, food. We still only have about five hundred dollars in our savings account. Mister Ryan is handing you a restaurant on a silver platter and you'd be crazy not to take it."

"Sometimes, sweetheart, you've got to take risks in life to see your dreams come true." Seth tried hard to be patient. He knew Maria's fears were real and he sympathized with her. But he also knew in his gut, in his heart, that this was the right decision. "I've thought this out and we could get a loan. We've got good credit. And I could get our families to help."

"I don't want their help!" Maria's voice rose in exasperation. "I don't want to take risks! I want to keep this house on this street, I want our kids to go to college, and I don't want to be poor. Things are finally looking up for us and you want to throw it all away!"

Two-month-old Angelica started to cry from her crib on the second floor. "Now look what you've done," Maria snapped and climbed the stairs to comfort their daughter. Seth heard a door close loudly from above and realized she wasn't coming back down to talk further.

He stayed up most of the night sitting at the kitchen table, pondering what to do. Mister Ryan needed an answer. And he wouldn't make a second offer if the answer was no. *In fact, he'll probably be furious,* Seth thought.

He prayed into the night, asking God for guidance.

Chapter 6

And the rest, as they say, is history, Seth smiled to himself, still sitting stuck on the subway as the ensuing seventeen years flashed before him.

Hard work had given way to much happiness, Seth recalled. He had declined Mr. Ryan's offer to take over ownership of The Catch, much to Maria's chagrin the next morning.

After begging his wife to support him, Seth hit the pavement, asking twelve banks for a business loan. One finally acquiesced.

Maria did too after she realized her determined dreamer of a husband would not be deterred and she had no choice but to be loyal to him and pray for the best.

Seth bought an abandoned warehouse on Rowe's Wharf just as it went on the market and started building his dream within. The grand opening was met with critical acclaim by the news media, and the word soon spread that the Perfect Place lived up to its name.

Charles Ryan sold The Catch to a stranger and harbored no ill feelings toward Seth. In fact, he told Seth he admired the young man's spunk, and after a series of warnings, wished him luck.

"I know you'll do well, son," he had said as they parted company. "I just hope I'll live long enough to see it."

Old Pops Ryan lived long enough to attend the Perfect Place's Tenth Anniversary Grand Gala, which coincided with Seth's fortieth birthday.

More than two hundred and fifty guests filled every niche of the Perfect Place in Boston that night – business associates, employees, relatives and many, many friends.

Each of the Perfect Place restaurants, then located in thirty-five of the United States, held simultaneous parties. It was as if all of America were celebrating.

With his adoring wife and three children at his side, Seth gave a speech during the gala and it was simulcast at each of the Perfect Place restaurants.

When he finished with a heartfelt "thank you" to all those gathered, the parties culminated in fireworks. Cheers erupted within the Perfect Place restaurants, in other bars and restaurants, and in homes across the country as people watched the news coverage on their television screens.

They were cheering the hard-earned success of a man who was respected by thousands of people, welcoming the happy story of a man who went from rags to riches but didn't forget the little people. Seth Jacobs had managed to stay likeable despite his fame and glory.

Just then, the T's engines started churning, the lights flickered back on and the sounds of metal clanking and screeching back to life filled the grateful ears of the Blue Line's passengers.

Even the familiar, monotone voice cackling over the speaker was a welcome sound. "Good news, ladies and gentlemen," the conductor boomed. "The Blue Line has been repaired and is back on track and should be arriving at its next destination shortly."

The entire crowd on board, their spirits bolstered by the

news, chimed in cheerfully with the conductor's final words: "Thank youuuu."

The train emerged from the darkness of the underground up into the blackness of night. Nearly three hours had passed since the derailment. With each stop, passengers hurried from where they had been held captive, racing for their destinations, payphones, loved ones and freedom.

As soon as he disembarked from the train into the station, Seth pulled his cell phone from his suit jacket pocket. He saw it was working, then noticed he had five voice messages. All of the calls were from one place – The Perfect Place. He clicked on the number and called. The restaurant's automated voicemail greeted him. *Completely annoying,* he thought. *That's something that will have to be changed. People should be greeted by a human being, not a machine.* Seth dialed Henrí's cell phone.

After a few rings, his trusted servant and friend answered, but Seth could barely make out his words through the shouts in French blaring out of the receiver.

"Henrí, calm down, it's Seth. What's wrong?"

"Vot's wrrrong?" Henrí's native French accent with its rolling r's always became more pronounced when he was agitated or upset. "Monsieur, please come quick. Vee have a disaster here. Everyone's sick, as you say, throwing up, the place is in an uproar, I don't know vot to do…" Henrí's words dissolved into sobs, and in the background, Seth heard the sound of glass breaking and a cacophony of shouts. Medical personnel yelled words like "pulse" and "stat" and restaurant staff members, or maybe customers, were hollering "clean this up" and a slew of loud profanities.

"I'm on my way." *No sense in talking to him when he's in this state.* Seth ended the conversation. *Better to get there, stat.* As he quickly walked out of the station, he hit the speed dial for home.

His own voice on voicemail answered. He redialed twice. Still the voicemail. *Where are Maria and Angelica?* he wondered. *Probably in bed already since Maria was sick,* he reminded himself. *Oh well, I'll check on them again later after I deal with this mess.*

Since the harbor was only a half mile from the T stop, traffic was still snarled, and since he was in great shape and needed to expend all of the energy he had pent up from sitting so long during the delay, Seth decided to jog to the restaurant.

Ten minutes later, he sprinted down the pier to the entrance of the Perfect Place, through the heavy wooden front door and up a short flight of marble stairs to the French doors of the main dining room.

Just before he reached the doors, he nearly slammed into the bulky frame of Henrí, who was shouting nonsensically in English/French gibberish and gesturing wildly, his face flushed.

Henrí, normally calm, cool and collected with his suave French airs and impeccable grooming, was perspiring profusely. His tuxedo was disheveled and he looked at Seth at first as if he were seeing an apparition, then grabbed him by his lapels as if he were a nomad seeing a mirage in the desert, or a drowning victim seeing a lifeguard.

"Henrí, I'm sorry I'm late," Seth began until he saw the headwaiter's glassy stare and open-mouthed gape. "Show me what's wrong." Seth took the middle-aged, balding man, who was about a foot shorter and at least several inches rounder than he, by the shoulders and shook him a little, trying to knock some sense back into him.

Henrí pointed through the French doors as if in shock, still unable to speak.

Seth peered over Henrí's shoulders through the glass panes onto a sight he had never seen before, and in years to come, prayed he would never lay eyes on again. Taking a deep breath, he opened the doors.

He looked into the chandeliered main dining room and saw a hundred or so well-dressed men and women in different states of sickness, their faces contorted in varying degrees of pain.

Puddles of vomit glistened on the Italian marble floors Seth had had imported from Venice.

Seth cupped his hand over his mouth to try to stifle his own nausea, which threatened to gag him, brought on by the sight and stench of it all.

An elderly woman, dressed in a silver sequined gown and standing just a few feet away propping herself with her hands on one of the many linen-covered tables, doubled over before Seth and threw up, splashing her insides on his new Gucci shoes.

Henrí now whimpered behind him in his garbled French/English.

"Caviar...mais non! Je ne ses quoi! Unbelievable!"

Seth turned and again shook Henrí by the arms. "Henrí, where is Senator Caine?" Seth shouted above the sounds of people moaning and writhing in pain.

Henrí again pointed, blubbering, unable to make much sense.

Seth's eyes followed his pointed finger to the head table at the far side of the room. Seth approached it, winding his way around bodies, some lying on the floor, some hunched over, some doing their best to help others who were in more pain than they.

The Senator lay still on top of the table, his enigmatic hazel eyes closed, his normally tan face a wan gray. Two of his aides, handkerchiefs held to their faces, were talking on their cell phones.

"What's going on here?" Seth demanded of the two, the

only people in the room who apparently weren't sick. "I'm the owner of this place and I just got here. Can you please tell me what is going on here?"

"All of the people seem to have a severe case of food poisoning," one of the aides responded. "We've called 911 and ambulances are on the way. The Senator must've gotten it pretty bad. He seemed to be in so much pain that we gave him a sedative, which knocked him out cold."

Just then a loud series of sirens screamed through the pandemonium and about two dozen paramedics started rushing through the French doors, fanning out among the people, kneeling down, checking pulses and talking into hand-held radios.

"Over here, hurry!" Seth shouted to the nearest one. "This is Senator Caine. He's passed out. He doesn't look so good."

The paramedic, a young man who looked no older than a teenager, held two fingertips to the Senator's wrist, checking for a pulse. Then he barked at the paramedics nearest him. "We need to do CPR, stat! I can't find a pulse!"

Seth stumbled backward in disbelief, watching the nightmare play before his eyes.

The paramedics cleared a circle of space around the senator and huddled over him, administering CPR. Then one, holding paddles to the senator's chest, yelled, "Clear!" Volts of electric made the senator's body vault convexly into the air again and again until the paramedics seemed satisfied they had at least revived him.

Then he was carried out on a stretcher, over and around the clusters of people being tended to by other paramedics.

More stretchers arrived and more bodies were carried out until just a handful of people who were able to sit upright were left, along with Seth and Henrí.

"I am so sorry, monsieur," Henrí babbled, crying into a napkin, seated at one of the tables, unable to stand any longer. "The only thing I can think of was the caviar. Everything else was cooked."

"Come on Henrí, we're going to get to the bottom of this."

An hour later, after he had managed to get some help to clean up the dining room and escort the remaining guests to awaiting taxis, Seth sat in his office in the Perfect Place with a ghost-white Henrí crumpled in a chair before him.

He started dialing a number on the phone, but a scene on the television in his office made him drop the receiver onto the desk.

"Henrí, turn up the sound." Seth waved at Henrí with one hand and pointed to the television above with the other.

Flashing across the screen on a Special News Report, which interrupted some sitcom, was a picture of Senator Caine, looking his best in a recent head shot. "...I repeat, U.S. Presidential hopeful Senator Robert Caine died just minutes ago in Massachusetts General Hospital from complications resulting from food poisoning he contracted at a dinner in his honor tonight at the Perfect Place restaurant. Sources at the hospital say it is too soon to tell what the complications were pending a coroner's report..."

"Oh my God," Seth whispered, dumbfounded.

"Hello? Hello?" the voice coming from the receiver on the desk distantly shouted.

Seth picked it up like it was a snake and clicked off the talk button so the voice would stop.

The phone immediately started ringing again. Seth looked at it uncertainly, then answered.

"Seth Jacobs," he answered impatiently. He desperately needed to think.

"Mister Jacobs, this is Rebecca Williams from Channel Four news," the female voice chirped on the other end. "We're calling in regard to Senator Caine's death...we'd like to come there and interview you for a follow-up story to air on the eleven-o-clock news if it's not too late..."

"Listen, Miss...uh...Williams," Seth said, trying to hold his irritation in check. "Now is a very bad time. Please call back tomorrow after things have settled a bit."

"Well, can I ask you a few questions then?" the bright female voice asked politely. "What food caused the Senator to die so unexpectedly, and how are the other people who attended the dinner?"

"I don't know and I have no comment." Seth hung up the phone, cutting off Miss Williams' voice trailing from the receiver with another question.

As soon as he hung up, the phone rang again. Seth looked at Henrí and shook his head. "Let's get out of here before these news reporters track us down, so we can find some answers in private," he said, his mind racing.

The two of them left the office and were turning out the lights when they were met at the front entrance by two investigators who were there to follow up on the initial police report.

"Not so fast, gentlemen," the larger of the two officers said gruffly. "Where are you both off to so fast?"

"Hello officers," Seth said politely, introducing himself. Henrí just stood by wringing his hands nervously. "My maitre d' and I were just trying to get out of here and go someplace more quiet, like my house, to escape the media and make some phone calls to try to make some sense of all this. In fact, now that you're here, I'm thinking maybe you can help us investigate this whole mess."

"Well it just so happens that's what we're here for," the

smaller of the two officers, who looked like Barney Fife straight out of a Mayberry RFD episode, said in a high-pitched, snide tone.

Seth dismissed him and addressed the larger officer, a beefy man who towered over him by at least a head, but seemed a little less confrontational than his partner.

"I guess you'd like to come in, then?"

"Yes, Mister Jacobs, that would be a good idea. I'm Officer Jason Worthington and my partner here is Officer Todd Snodgrass. "We'd like to ask you and your maitre d' some questions. We'll just ignore any phone calls or knocks on the door if you'd like to avoid the media."

"Please," said Seth with relief. "I'd like to get to the bottom of this as much as you."

Seth proceeded to explain how he had arrived late to the dinner and described the scene that awaited him. Henrí sat quietly until Officer Snodgrass threw him off guard.

"Well, Henry, exactly why do you think it was the caviar that made everyone so sick?" he asked in his ingratiating voice, mispronouncing the headwaiter's name by using the American version. *Probably on purpose*, Seth thought, trying not to smile at the ludicrousness of it all. *Maybe I'm just punchy from being so tired. Or maybe it's just that news reporters and cops bring out the worst in me.*

"Monsieur, le caviar was ze only menu item not cooked," Henrí sniffed, obviously offended by the scrawny, pinch-faced rookie. He talked slowly and emphatically, as if to a child. "En plu, it is ze only product we received from overseas zat day. It is likely that it became...contaminé'...contaminated...a mon opinion."

"In your opinion," Officer Snodgrass clarified, taking notes.

"Oui," Henrí said stiffly.

A brilliant thought dawned on Seth. "I'm sure some of our other restaurants received shipments of the same caviar," he said. "If they had reports of illness, we would know for sure, since they wouldn't all serve the same menu items along with it as we did here in Boston. If we call them we can kill two birds with one stone. Not only can we find out if the caviar is to blame...with the three-hour time difference on the west coast, maybe we can prevent some of them from serving the stuff and making more people sick."

"Perhaps you should be a detective," Officer Snodgrass snickered sarcastically.

"I think it's a great idea," Officer Worthington said, ignoring his partner's comment. "Give us a list of numbers and we'll divide it up to save time."

About three dozen phone calls later, Seth and the officers came to the same conclusion. The caviar was to blame for more than five hundred cases of food poisoning across America.

With their phone calls, the three had managed to warn the restaurants on the west coast, which were just about to serve dinner.

From their notes, the detectives and Seth determined that food poisoning had occurred in each of the Perfect Place restaurants along the East Coast, and several in the South.

After hearing the numbers, Seth wearily held his head in his hands. By now he too felt sick to his stomach.

"Boy, are you in for some lawsuits," Officer Snodgrass joked.

"Todd, a man has died here, a Senator for crying out loud," Officer Worthington snapped in disgust. "There might even be more deaths as a result of all this. Not to mention hundreds of people are seriously ill. Why don't you try to be a little bit more compassionate?"

Then he turned and faced Seth.

"Mister Jacobs, you've obviously been through a lot here

tonight and I'm sure tomorrow will bring its own problems. Why don't we get you and Henrí home?"

The two nodded and Officer Worthington called separate cabs for each of them. "We'll lock up for you and make sure the restaurant is barricaded with police tape," Officer Worthington said.

"Yeah, it looks like the Perfect Place won't be opening its doors for a while," Officer Snodgrass offered glibly, still smarting from his partner's remarks and miffed at the lack of respect he had been shown by Seth and Henrí.

"We'll call you both in the morning," Officer Worthington added. "We'll need both of you to report to the station tomorrow to give a statement on what occurred. Good night, gentlemen."

"Yeah, don't forget to say your prayers," Officer Snodgrass sneered. "Sweet dreams."

It was midnight before Seth's taxi pulled up in front of the Jacobs' residence.

But it could only get as close as the entrance to the circular drive.

The entire pavement was filled with police cars, their sirens casting a red glow on Seth's house beyond.

People swarmed like ants along the front lawn. Through the darkness and the sirens' eery glare Seth could make out several police uniforms and three television crews.

Surprise, surprise, Seth thought glumly. *These people must love working overtime.*

Little did he know a real surprise awaited him.

After paying the cab driver, Seth climbed out of the taxi and starting walking up the front lawn. He was still several yards away from his house when he heard someone scream his name.

"There he is, Seth Jacobs!" a female voice belonging to a TV reporter shrilled.

Seth was instantly surrounded by police officers and reporters shoving microphones in his face. He held up his hands to shield his eyes from the camera lights.

A Boston City Police officer stepped ahead of the rest of the pack and swatted the microphones away like irritating flies.

He pulled Seth by the arm, barking at the others to get back, and led him a few feet from the crowd.

"Mister Jacobs, I'm afraid there's been an accident," the stocky police officer said sternly in his Boston Irish accent.

"I know, Senator Caine has died," Seth said tiredly, trying not to let his frustration slip into his tone. He had had enough already. *Just let me get home to my family and let me get some sleep,* he inwardly pleaded.

"No, Mister Jacobs, there's been another accident," the officer explained. "I'm sorry, but your sons have been involved in a car crash. They were flown to Mass General. Your wife and daughter had police escort them to the hospital. We can take you there."

They were the last words Seth remembered before falling unconscious at the officer's feet.

Chapter 7

Whew. Seth awoke to the burning of smelling salts in his nose and a dull ache in his head.

He felt movement under his prone body, and realized as he slowly opened his eyes that he was lying on the backseat of a police car as it maneuvered through the city toward Massachusetts General Hospital.

"Hey, he's up," said a young black police officer who had been sitting beside him, waving the smelling salts in his face. "Welcome back to the living."

"Thanks," Seth said, rubbing his red-rimmed eyes with his thumb and forefinger. "What happened?"

"You passed out, man," said the black officer. "Too much bad news in one day, I guess."

Seth recognized the driver as the Irish officer who had greeted him at his house with the bad news.

Your sons have been involved in a car crash.

"How close are we to the hospital?" Seth asked, panicking.

"It's straight ahead," the Irish officer said, flashing his siren to clear the way for their arrival as the huge, multi-story hospital loomed in front of them.

Seth still felt wobbly, so the young black officer held him up by the arm until they reached the receptionist's desk beyond the main entrance.

"I'm okay," Seth said, pulling his arm free, his terror giving him a newfound strength. He briefly felt embarrassed he had fainted but realized he hadn't had anything to eat in ten hours, the past seven of which had dealt him several shocking blows. "Where are my sons, Adam and Aaron Jacobs?" he asked the receptionist, who directed him through the Emergency Room double doors.

There he found Maria, her olive skin almost as white as a hospital sheet, sobbing into Angelica's arms.

Angelica turned her tear-stained face gratefully toward her father and the three embraced.

Seth couldn't ask his questions fast enough.

"What happened? Where are they? How did...where..." His voice trailed off as his daughter tried to explain.

"Daddy, calm down, Mother needs us to be strong," she said, trying her best to act like an adult in the midst of her parents, who were seized with childlike panic. "The boys were in a car accident coming home from the frat party. Aaron was driving and the car ran off the road and hit a tree. They said Aaron is going to be alright, but...oh Daddy, Adam...they're not sure...we don't know..." Angelica couldn't hold up her adult act any longer and slumped into the chair next to her mother, crying into her hands.

A chubby nurse, sweating and red-faced, burst through the operating room doors into the ER waiting room just then and quickly scanned the hopeful faces around her.

She knew Seth Jacobs as soon as she saw him, although his appearance was a far cry from his magazine photos. He was hunched down on the floor at his wife's feet, his hair and clothes a wreck, his face smudged and his eyes red.

"Seth and Maria Jacobs?" she asked just to be sure.

The three of them quickly rose to their feet, hovering over the nurse so that she had to back away a foot to speak to them.

"Your son Aaron is in serious condition and is recovering

in the Intensive Care Unit," she said in a matter-of-fact tone. "He has some bad cuts and bruises and a fractured arm but no internal injuries. Adam, I'm afraid, didn't fair so well," she continued, clearing her throat as if a bit of emotion had clogged her air passage. "He was admitted in critical condition with internal bleeding and a head injury. He's still in surgery so all we can do now is wait."

"Can we see them?" Seth asked, trembling.

"I think you can see Aaron," the nurse answered. "Wait here."

A few minutes later, Seth, with one arm supporting Maria and the other around Angelica, followed another nurse through the hospital's corridors to Aaron's room in the ICU.

Tears streamed down from his bruised blue eyes that peeked out above the bandages covering his cuts from the windshield's glass shards.

He reached out bandaged hands to his father, mother and sister, who took turns hugging and comforting him. "Shhhh, it's okay," they said. "You're going to be alright. We were so worried. We love you, Aaron."

"Stop." Aaron managed to silence their voices with his own raspy one. His words came out halting and forced but clear. "Please don't say that. This was all my fault." He suddenly got a wild look in his eyes. "Adam…how is Adam?"

"We're not sure, sweetheart," his mother said, gently stroking his cheeks as she sat beside him on the hospital bed. "They still don't know yet. We came to see you first."

Shame and guilt made Aaron turn his face from his family, and tears welled in his eyes and trickled down his bandaged cheeks. "I'm sorry Ma, Pa," he cried, sobbing into his pillow. "It's all my fault. Oh Adam, I'm so sorry…" his voice broke.

"Aaron, what do you mean?" Maria asked.

Just then two police officers, one male and one female, filled the doorway.

God, more police officers! Seth felt like saying, exasperated. *Haven't I had enough of you?*

"What do you want now, officers?" he asked instead, trying to keep his temper in check.

"We'd like to ask Aaron a few questions about the accident." Officer Megan Adkins, a tall brunette in her forties, approached Aaron's bed, flipping open her notepad.

"Well, I think it can wait," Seth responded angrily. "As you can see, he is in no condition right now."

"That's not what the nurse said." Officer Chad Smith, who was an inch shorter, ten years older and a lot less sensitive than his female partner, stepped forward. "So if you can excuse us for a few moments..."

Aaron turned his head back around to face his family and the police. His son's face was now wet with tears but the wild look had been replaced with one of meek surrender.

"It's okay, Dad." It seemed to Seth that his nineteen-year-old had suddenly changed from the brash college sports star he once was to a fragile kid, his voice quavering just above a whisper. "They have a right to ask. And I need to get it out."

"Well, you have a right to an attorney before you do." Seth took a deep breath and turned to face the officers, squaring his shoulders. "Officers, we would like to speak with our son first. We'll call you in once our attorney arrives."

The officers exchanged glances, then silently turned and left the room.

Confused, Maria backed away from the hospital bed and sat down in a chair along the wall in the room. Seth ordered Angelica to go for coffee and sodas. *She doesn't need to hear this,* he thought.

After she left, the hospital room fell silent. They could actually hear the buzz of the monitors and the drip of the IV.

"Do you want to tell us what happened tonight?" Seth

tried to keep the anger in his voice at bay, facing the hospital bed with his arms crossed.

"I don't know if he's ready, Seth. Are you sure you're up for talking about this, honey?" Maria came to her son's defense. "You need your rest."

Aaron laid his head back on his pillow and closed his eyes, then opened them and straightened up in the bed, as if ready to face whatever was about to come his way.

"Yes, I'm sure. If I don't, it's just going to keep replaying in my head like some horror movie that keeps going on and on." He swallowed as his parents waited. "I was on such a high after scoring the final goal today at the game. We beat Dartmouth four to three in their own stadium." Aaron allowed himself a small smile, then his expression became serious again.

"My teammates were all whooping and hollering, carrying me around the field on their shoulders. They handed me up one of the bottles of champagne they'd popped open, so I took a few chugs. Then I had another half-bottle in the locker room.

"One of the Dartmouth players invited us to a party at his frat house, so after we all got dressed, I found Adam and we went. The place was pretty wild. And I was the center of attention. Someone put a beer in my hand the minute I walked in, and it was like every time I finished, another guy would hand me a new one. We were reliving the game, the big plays, getting down on the other team, and I guess I lost count of how many drinks I had.

"Later, the lights were dimmed and the rowdy music changed to something soft, and this girl I'd had my eye on came up to me and asked me to dance. Her name was Riley. She was really pretty, a cheerleader, and a junior. Any other time she probably wouldn't have given me, a sophomore, the time of day, but just then I guess I was a star. She started coming on to me..." Aaron glanced at his mother to make sure he wouldn't get in trouble for his choice of words. "...and next thing I know, she's asking if I want to go upstairs to be alone. By then I guess I wasn't thinking straight and I let her take my hand and start leading me to the steps. She handed me this pill, saying it was Ecstasy and would get me 'in the mood.' At first I told her no, I didn't need anything. She said she had taken one, that everyone was taking one, that it wouldn't hurt and would just make me relax. I'd heard of it and thought it was pretty harmless. So I thought, what the heck, and swallowed it down with my beer.

"Then Riley takes out a joint from her purse and tells me we could really have some fun smoking it together, and starts kissing me and stuff. I told her no, to put it away, I didn't do drugs and we didn't need it.

"Just then Adam walked up to us. He started giving me a hard time, asking me how much I'd had to drink and did I do any drugs. I was really mad that he was interrupting our good time so I let him have it. I was sick of him being such a worry-wart. I told him to go get his own girl and leave us alone. Only probably not in those words. I think I was pretty nasty."

Aaron took a deep breath and continued.

"Adam insisted I go home with him right then and there. Well, that really set me off, but he grabbed me by the arm and wouldn't let go. I tried to get away but Adam's pretty strong and I was feeling pretty out of it by then, so I let him drag me away from the girl and out the door.

"But once the night air hit me, it was a different story. Adam insisted on driving, but I was really angry once the cold woke me up. I wasn't going to let him boss me, so I managed to snatch the keys from his hand and push him off me. He fell down, which gave me just enough time to jump into the driver's seat and start the car.

I told him get into the car or I was leaving without him, and revved the engine to prove my point, so he didn't have a choice but to get in the passenger's seat, and I took off."

Aaron paused again and fresh tears started from his eyes. "The rest is blurry. I was totally out of control, driving too fast, arguing with Adam. I didn't see the tree until it was too late. The next thing I know I was covered in all these little pieces of glass. I looked over at Adam…the dashboard was crushed against him and he was crumpled up against the door, so I leaned over to look at his face…" Aaron sobbed out loud. "Oh God, what have I done? I'm so sorry. Adam…"

Maria sat quietly, dabbing her eyes. In the silence that enveloped them, Seth felt his fury fade into compassion.

He looks so much like me, but we are so different, Seth thought, feeling both sympathetic and frustrated with his youngest son. *He's got so much potential that it seems like he has to keep proving himself, and it always lands him in trouble. Maybe because he's the middle child, we didn't give him enough attention. It's almost like any attention, even the wrong kind, will suffice. Perhaps somehow this was our fault. But I know we tried our best.* Seth recalled something an old friend once told him: *"You can only do so much as a parent. The rest is up to the child."*

Kind of like God is with each of us. Seth pondered this in the empty silence that seemed to stretch across the room as each of them became lost in their own thoughts. *He loves us unconditionally, so He gives us the world…gives us so much…even our own will, hoping for the best. He expects nothing in return but our own happiness. That's why it's so hard when we keep taking wrong turns, causing ourselves to be unhappy.*

Seth looked into Aaron's eyes, his unconditional love for his son melting the rest of his anger into grief. He heard a small voice in his heart say, *Just like God catches each of us when our willpower leads us astray and we fall, you must comfort this son of yours and love him now, when he needs you most.*

He took Aaron's hand and his own tears fell onto the bandages there.

The knock on the door broke the silence. It was Officers Smith and Adkins. Officer Smith held papers in his hand and spoke first.

"We have received the results of blood tests taken on Aaron." His voice was clipped, his words to the point. He addressed Seth and Maria, as if Aaron was a small child unable to comprehend his words, or as if he were not even present. "They confirm that there was alcohol and the drug Ecstasy present."

"What exactly is this Ecstasy?" Maria came out of her trancelike grief, jarring Seth and Aaron to attention.

Officer Adkins answered, looking sympathetically at Maria. "I've got two teenage kids of my own, so I know it sounds scary, and in fact, it can be. Ecstasy is a drug that's very popular with young people today. Makes them feel high, like they're on top of the world, energetic, passionate. It comes in the form of a little pill and is a synthetic drug usually made up of MDMA. Stands for methylenedioxymethamphetamine. It's a combination of a stimulant, like speed or amphetamines, and a hallucinogenic, like LSD. Unfortunately, it can have side effects similar to those caused by cocaine, and has caused heart attacks and even death. Coupled with alcohol, it can be very dangerous."

"And it's illegal," Officer Smith glibly added. "By the way, we received a warrant to search Aaron's clothes taken here at the hospital, and we also found marijuana in his coat pocket, which means he was found to be in possession of drugs as well. That means that we're going to have to file charges against him."

"Now wait a minute!" Seth barked, not liking where this

was headed. "I demand you wait until we have our attorney present!" He glanced at Maria for support, but his wife was too busy crying and shaking her head at hearing more bad news, wondering aloud how their son, her baby boy, had gotten mixed up with alcohol and drugs.

"Marijuana?" Aaron asked, confused. "I know I didn't have any, and I don't know how it got in my pocket." He looked around the room in bewilderment, searching for understanding. Then enlightenment dawned on his face as he apparently remembered Riley and the joint she had offered him.

"Be quiet, Aaron," Seth gave his son an icy stare, feeling anger well within him again.

"We wanted to let all of you folks know what we've turned up so far," Officer Adkins said. "But we realize you have the right to have your attorney present before we question Aaron, so we'll just leave these papers here for you and your attorney to review." Her voice was kind, maternal. Unlike her partner, she seemed to care that this family was in pain, one son facing criminal charges and the other lying in critical condition in another hospital bed, no one sure if he might live or die. "We'll be back tomorrow..." she looked up at the clock on the wall. Its hands showed two a.m. "...I mean later today. That will give Aaron a chance to rest and you folks a chance to see Adam." She tapped Officer Smith on the shoulder and motioned for him to exit the room. Even though he was ten years older, she was still the senior partner.

As they turned to leave again, Angelica and a nurse burst through the door.

"Mom! Dad! Adam is coming out of surgery! They said come quick!"

Aaron watched as his parents scrambled out of their chairs for the door. They looked back to make sure he was okay.

"Go!" he said as loud as his choked voice could muster.

Seth, Maria and Angelica practically had to jog to keep up with the nurse, who hustled down several corridors and two sets of stairs before entering through the ER doors.

She stopped before the nurses' station, where a doctor approached them, removing his mask and wiping the sweat from his brow.

"Seth." The doctor removed his surgical gloves and embraced Seth's hand in both of his own.

"Oh my God, Ben, it's you! Thank God you're here! But how…?"

"I called him while we were waiting here for you," Maria told her husband. "Once I knew how serious the accident was."

Angelica stood mutely, looking with wonder from one parent to the next. Seth recovered from his initial shock and quickly introduced the doctor to his daughter. "This is Doctor Benjamin Grason. He's an old friend of ours."

Benjamin Grason shook Angelica's hand. He was tall like Seth but a little stockier, and his dark hair had nearly all turned gray, as had his bushy eyebrows and goatee. He was slightly older than Seth but his face had aged much more than his friend's, the sickness and suffering he had seen over the years leaving their marks. "We worked on Adam for the past few hours. He's in stable but critical condition, still unconscious. But it looks like he'll make it."

"Oh, thank God!" Maria collapsed against Seth, holding a fist to her mouth to stifle a sob.

"But I do have some bad news."

Seth felt his whole body go numb with cold.

"It appears Adam may be in a coma." The soft-spoken doctor guided all three of them to a row of chairs in the nearby ER waiting area and motioned for them to sit. They were in shock and sat down without a sound, staring at him, dumbfounded by what they had just heard.

"Adam suffered head injuries in addition to a broken right collar bone, leg, jaw and ribs and had some internal trauma to his liver and spleen. The impact was on the right so that's where his body suffered most of the damage. His lung collapsed from the broken ribs, but we've inserted a chest tube so he can breathe. He also suffered a great deal of blood loss both through the accident and surgery. That, together with the concussion, may have caused him to remain unconscious. We can't tell yet at this point if he has suffered any brain damage..."

"Nooooooo!" Maria suddenly couldn't listen to anymore and she burst into a wail. Seth put his arms around his wife's heaving shoulders as if trying to literally hold her together, hoping that if he held her tight enough, he could keep from falling apart himself. Remembering Angelica, who quietly wept in a chair on his other side, he reached over and brought her head to his shoulder, absently stroking her hair. Doctor Grason knelt before Maria and took the bereft mother's hands in his own.

After their sobs subsided a bit, Doctor Grason spoke again. "Adam will be transferred in a few hours to a patient room in the ICU, but you can come see him in a few minutes in the ER. I'm sorry, but we did the best we could. Now all we can do is hope and pray."

After several agonizingly slow minutes passed, Seth, Maria and Angelica approached the bed where Adam Jacobs lay still. At least a half-dozen tubes crossed his upper body, their ends attached to various pieces of machinery, and drips ran from three different fluid-filled bags.

His family steeled themselves to look past his face - which was almost unrecognizable, covered in bandages except for his lips which were swollen and bloody - to try to find recognition in his eyes, now hidden under lids that were black and blue. The three of them encircled him, hovering, praying for his eyes to open. They didn't.

Chapter 8

Seth and Maria kept watch at Adam's bedside around the clock, sometimes together, sometimes taking turns. Angelica took turns too, transferring from school bus to city bus to head straight from her last class to the hospital. She gave up any social or extracurricular life she had to be with her family.

The three of them prayed, read the Bible and the Torah and often just sat silently, staring at Adam's face, hoping for his eyes to open.

Often while one stayed awake, the other two would try to sleep on a cot set up in the room or on the sofa against the wall. But sleep didn't come easily. They were afraid Adam might awaken when they weren't watching, and petrified he may never awaken at all.

Minutes stretched to hours and hours to days. The third morning of their watch, Doctor Grason asked to meet with them again. He wore the same serious expression he had when he first told them of Adam's condition.

After checking all of Adam's vital signs, he led them down a hall into a family consultation room and sat down with them at a table in a remote corner.

"I'm afraid you're not going to want to hear what I have to say, but I always tell my patients and their families the truth," he began. "And since I know you, Seth, I feel like I can tell you like it is. While Adam's injuries are healing, he is still dependent on the ventilator to breathe." Benjamin Grason took a deep breath. "We still need to run a few more tests, but unfortunately it seems that Adam is in a coma."

Seth felt his face contort in pain. It felt like his eyes were sinking back into their sockets, and his mouth opened but no sound came out. He was frozen, in a state of shock.

Maria had the opposite reaction, letting all of her emotions out in one huge outburst of grief and rage. And Angelica quietly wept, simultaneously leaning on her father and trying to comfort her hysterical mother.

Once Maria quieted down, wrapped in Angelica's comforting arms, Doctor Grason stood and motioned Seth aside. He told him he would prescribe a sedative for Maria, and that this would take time to digest. "Families of comatose patients often find the situation harder to bear than if a child actually dies," he said. "They can't move on until they know for sure which way things will turn. It may take weeks or months or even years. There's no way of knowing. And of course, you must ultimately decide if and when we terminate the life support machines." Seth felt like he had been dealt another blow to the stomach, and he nearly doubled over in pain. His friend reached out and gave him a hug. "Seth, I know you're a strong guy and you'll be able to pull your family through this."

"Ben, please tell me you'll do everything you can to try to bring my son out of this coma."

"You know I will, buddy. Why don't you all go home and get some rest. And of course, we know you have to...um... take care of Aaron too."

Seth hadn't forgotten about their other son. They had visited him in between their watches over Adam, had kept him informed about his brother and had tried to comfort him despite their growing anger and dismay over his actions.

They had also hired an attorney, Michael Powers, who had been present during subsequent visits by Officers Adkins and Smith. Both had questioned Aaron on two more occasions. Each interrogation lasted longer than the one before it as the young patient became stronger.

Michael Powers was known as one of the best defense attorneys in the country. Fortunately he lived and practiced in downtown Boston, when he wasn't flying across the country to represent one of his famous clients in Los Angeles.

He was the criminal half of the law firm Rogers and Powers. His partner, Jerry Rogers, handled the firm's civil cases. Between them, they represented several of the biggest names in Hollywood and on Broadway, some of the richest business people and many well-known politicians.

Seth had known Michael since the two of them attended Harvard. Michael was a few years Seth's junior, but the two had become friends by working on the school newspaper. Seth had been on the managing end of the paper, while Michael had written a political column. Once Seth went off to the Culinary Arts Institute and Michael entered law school, the two parted ways for awhile.

But Seth remembered his old friend when it came time to hire an attorney for one of his employees who had gotten into a minor scrape with the law several years ago. At the time, Michael was struggling to start his own practice and welcomed the business Seth threw his way. Over the years the two had rekindled their old friendship and gotten together as often as their hectic schedules allowed for a round of golf or fishing. Unlike Seth, Michael had remained single.

The day Maria and Seth received the news about Adam's coma was the same day Aaron was to be released from the hospital. Officer Adkins broke the news to Aaron, his parents and his attorney as gently as possible that the college sophomore was being placed under arrest for the possession of drugs, driving while intoxicated and reckless endangerment. If his brother were to die, he was informed the last charge would escalate to vehicular manslaughter.

Since the accident had occurred just over the Massachusetts line in New Hampshire, the case would be remanded to that jurisdiction.

While Michael had prepared his friend Seth for the arrest and the charges, even he wasn't prepared for the course of events that took place during Aaron's arraignment the next morning in Hillsboro Superior Court.

Seth and his family tried to ignore the onslaught of cameras that were shoved in their faces as they picked their way, shielded as best as possible by Michael, through the throng of reporters and bystanders that crowded the courthouse steps, jostling and out-pecking each other like a flock of angry seagulls fighting over crusts of bread.

This was just the latest piece of news that seemed to be plaguing the owner of the Perfect Place conglomerate and it fed right into the media's hunger for more.

Michael and Aaron stood side by side in suits before the oak table in the courtroom, with Seth and Maria seated in the first row behind them. The attorney's olive skin and black hair, which he inherited from his Greek ancestry, contrasted with Aaron's fair complexion, which was particularly pale under the circumstances. Except for the cast on his forearm, which was mostly concealed by his suit coat sleeve, and a few small scratches on his face, Aaron's injuries looked as though they had almost all healed. He appeared the typical – albeit tired – healthy, wealthy six-foot nineteen-year-old.

"All rise," the bailiff called, and everyone stood.

Judge Ronald R. Henry took his perch and peered down

at the two men from his wire-framed spectacles. The judge was known locally for his erratic judgments, but although he had done his homework, Michael hadn't realized how irrational this judge could sometimes be. Depending on his mood, or the time of day, or whether he had had a good lunch or not, "Big H", as he was called, could find favor or could deal a blow to a defendant's entire future. The looming judge stood six-foot-eight and weighed a little over three hundred pounds. He was in his late fifties, although he looked much older with his white tufts of hair that encircled his balding head, his glasses, and the stern expression that constantly pinched his pudgy face. He managed to conceal much of his weight under his robes, which, together with his large nose, had the effect of making him look like a giant hawk or bald eagle ready to swoop down on its prey.

The relatively small courtroom was packed due to Seth Jacob's notoriety.

Headlines had appeared in every newspaper across the country each day for the past several days: "U.S. Senator Treated to Caviar, Food Poisoning;" "Presidential Hopeful Dies in Perfect Place"; "From Bad to Worse – Accidents Follow Seth Jacobs;" "Two Arrests in One Family? Police Looking at Father and Son;" and "How Much More Can Jacobs Family Take?"

Seth Jacobs and his restaurants were now at the mercy of the Federal Bureau of Investigation and Food and Drug Administration, which were investigating the series of food poisoning cases, since they crossed state lines and involved the death of a U.S. Senator. The Perfect Place restaurants all remained closed pending the investigation.

Adam Jacobs remained at the mercy of the machines to which he was hooked up, still in a coma.

And now Aaron was at the mercy of Judge Henry.

With the crowd, the courtroom became heated, literally

as well as figuratively, enough to cause beads of perspiration to form on the presiding judge's forehead. Judge Henry didn't like to sweat.

The judge hadn't had time for lunch, and had had only a bagel for breakfast, so his stomach was grumbling.

Two weeks ago he had found himself the subject of a newspaper editorial claiming he was bigoted against women because he had ruled in favor of the ex-husband in an embattled custody hearing.

And now here he was presiding over a media-fest, and reporters were his least favorite group of people.

To make matters worse for Aaron, Judge Henry didn't particularly like Michael Powers and his big-shot ways. And he certainly wasn't fond of Seth Jacobs.

Raised in a tenement house with four brothers in Manhattan's Lower East side, Ronald Henry had had to claw his way up to the bench he now sat on today. From what he knew, Seth Jacobs had been handed everything on a silver platter. And his children had been born with a silver spoon in their mouths.

Ronald Henry believed the fates had smiled on Seth Jacobs…at least up until now.

His brow furrowed as he read the charges from his perch. "Does your client wish to plead guilty or not guilty?" Judge Henry asked Michael.

"Guilty to the charge of driving while intoxicated, Your Honor," Michael responded. "Not guilty to the charges of possession of an illegal substance and reckless endangerment."

"Do you agree with your attorney as to those pleas?" The judge directed his gaze at Aaron.

"Yes, Your Honor," Aaron said, his face flushing in embarrassment.

"Good. Then do we have a request for bail from the

state?"

The assistant state's attorney, a pale, thin, young man with glasses, answered. "The State of New Hampshire requests bail be set at one million dollars."

A collective gasp was heard throughout the courtroom.

Michael sprang to his feet and was so surprised he nearly barked his retort.

"The defense strongly objects, Your Honor. There is absolutely no reason for bail to be set so high, given the relatively small nature of the charges, the spotless character of my client and the fact that there was no willful wrongdoing. For God's sake, Aaron Jacobs did not intend to harm his own brother. I respectfully submit that the defendant be freed on his own recognizance to the home of his parents, Seth and Maria Jacobs."

Michael's remark sent the assistant state's attorney springing to his feet. "Your Honor, Seth Jacobs is currently under investigation for his own alleged criminal activity," the prosecutor said, his voice raised.

"Objection!" Michael Powers shouted. "The alleged activity to which the prosecutor refers has absolutely nothing to do with this case!"

"Quiet!" Judge Henry yelled, slamming down his gavel with exasperation. "There will be no more outbursts in my courtroom! Continue."

"It is because Aaron harmed his own brother that the State finds his acts so negligent," the prosecutor said. "Adam Jacobs remains in a coma because of Aaron Jacobs' actions. And, may we remind the Court that there are multiple charges involving drugs and alcohol here as well?"

"You don't need to remind me." Judge Henry sighed, rubbing his temples. "Mister Jacobs, please stand."

Aaron stood, holding his breath, awaiting his fate. The

Judge peered at him, biding his time, making him wait, before he spoke in a deliberate baritone.

"Mister Jacobs, it says here you were driving with an alcohol level of one-point-nine, more than twice the legal level to be on the road. You are also under the legal drinking age, and you were found in possession of an illegal substance." The judge adjusted his glasses, then looked up at Aaron with a stern expression. "Seeing as you are an adult and you are facing several serious charges that may, in fact, escalate if, God forbid, your brother should die, I remand you to the custody of the Northern New Hampshire Correctional Facility for the weekend. I will hold a bail review on Monday. Court's adjourned."

Instead of a gasp, there was now dead silence as the judge's harsh ruling left everyone stunned, including the prosecutor. The only sound that could be heard was an eerie wail, like an animal caught in a steel trap, reverberating from the courtroom's stoic walls.

It came from Maria Jacobs. Seth held her tight but she broke her arms free, holding them out toward her son, making the same sound over and over.

Michael Powers staggered to his feet in astonishment. "Judge Henry, this is clearly an aberration of justice," he protested, but the judge, who was already proceeding off the Bench, cut him off.

"Mister Powers, I suggest you keep quiet unless you want to be found in contempt of court, which would leave your client without an attorney for a future time when he will really need one." With that, Judge Henry turned and with a final "all rise" from the bailiff, he left the courtroom, his robe flying behind him in his apparent hurry to be gone.

Chapter 9

No one would have guessed how much Aaron really would need Michael Powers' expertise in days to come.

While Aaron was placed into the minimum-security New Hampshire jail versus the state prison, the cell to which he was confined was still an eye-opening experience.

His bunkmate was another young man who was probably about the same age, but looked older because of his Marine-style crew-cut and the fact that he was severely overweight.

Bud, as he was called for his fondness of the beer by the same name, kept to himself and was usually found sitting on his cot with a scowl on his face, just staring at nothing in particular.

For the first two hours, Aaron lay face up on his cot, trying to rest, but sleep was impossible. He opened his eyes and looked over at Bud, who sat grimacing at him. The big guy was hunched over in his bunk like his big frame had been stuffed in there and was now uncomfortably stuck.

Aaron busied himself studying the gray cinder block walls and stained gray ceiling, and then finally spoke, as if talking to himself. "This place sure is ugly," he murmured. "It's so ugly in here the rats probably don't even want to hang around."

He received no response, so he continued. "They should hang a few posters in here. A little J Lo, Britney…hell, they could hang a picture of somebody's grandmother in here to brighten up this joint."

Aaron heard Bud make a funny sound. Like a hmmphf. Then laughter bubbled from the big guy sitting on his bunk, slowing growing from a hum and hiss to a howling guffaw.

The two of them laughed together for a minute, before they became quiet and Bud resumed his glum façade.

Aaron decided to try opening up to Bud, telling a little about himself and why he was in the "slammer."

"Why you in here?" Aaron asked, trying to keep his English simple and not too collegiate sounding.

"Stole stuff," Bud replied.

"Need the money?" Aaron asked, trying to come off as nonchalant.

"Yeah. My daddy left when I was just a baby. My old lady had to make money hookin' but she was always running out, spending it on drugs to keep her from goin' crazy. I was just tryin' to help her out."

"Sounds like neither one of us belong in here." Aaron reached out a hand which Bud engulfed with his own enormous one. "So, you got any friends in here?"

"Nah. Most of 'em make fun of me. How fat I am, and that I'm dumb and stuff. Course, I don't pay no attention, 'cause I could pound any of 'em. Plus I'm good at getting' favors for 'em from the guards."

Aaron figured behind his big-bear exterior, Bud was really just a teddy bear. "I'm sure you could," he said smiling, still flexing the hand which Bud had tightly gripped in his ham-sized fist.

Bud smiled back.

Then the siren sounded and it was lights out.

After breakfast the next day, they had free time in the yard.

Aaron followed his fellow inmates, lined up in their blue-gray uniforms single file, past two hulking guards and out a metal door into the yard, an asphalt square with two basketball hoops and little else.

It was gloomy and cold for an early October day in New Hampshire. A storm loomed on the slate-colored horizon and a fine mist started to fall, dampening the already downcast spirits of some and prickling the already edgy tempers of others.

It was the kind of day that wouldn't take much to start a fight.

Aaron minded his own business, leaning up against the tall, metal fence and watching a dozen guys play a pick-up basketball game.

Several others huddled for a smoke and most dawdled like himself, loners.

Out of the corner of his eye, Aaron saw a huddle break up and the six guys who were in it advance to the far corner of the yard where he saw Bud, smoking a cigarette.

Bud looked up, but it was too late to avoid the semi-circle of guys closing in around him.

Aaron began to stride toward the gathering, casually at first and then quickly, noticing Bud was in the middle.

He approached the group just as he saw his huge cellmate hunch over in pain. One of the inmates, a lanky, rough-looking Mexican they called Sanchez, stood with his fists clenched, hovering over Bud, waiting to take a second jab. "That's for mi amigo, who you cheated out of cigarettes the other day, fat-boy," Sanchez hissed.

"And there's more where that came from if you do it again," one of the other inmates added.

"Bud, you alright?" Aaron boldly called over their shoulders.

His cell mate straightened and looked at him, his big gray eyes reflecting a helpless fear Aaron hadn't seen there before. The semi-circle of men turned to face him.

"Why, what you gonna do 'bout it, rich boy?" Sanchez advanced on Aaron menacingly, with catlike grace and speed. He stood and flexed his well-defined brown muscles, which were laced with ugly scars cutting across leathery, tattooed skin.

"Nothing," Aaron answered.

But Sanchez wasn't finished. He wanted to play.

"Oh, the rich boy is 'fraid to fight." Sanchez grinned, revealing uneven, smoke-stained teeth, an evil gleam in his eyes. And with that, he spit straight in Aaron's face.

Aaron wiped the spit from his cheek and continued to stand his ground as the Latino pranced around him like a panther, waiting to pounce on his prey.

Bud remained hunched over, frozen in his corner. Aaron stood alone, his back to the basketball game in progress, the two guards on shift in the yard not paying any attention to the small group teasing the big guy in the corner. They were lazy and didn't get too concerned unless a big yard fight broke out.

While they knew Bud was a coward, Sanchez and his allies didn't really know Aaron. They weren't aware that he had the powerful muscles of a trained athlete, nor that he had a black belt in karate.

Aaron and Adam had both taken karate as boys. While Adam had dropped out as a blue belt, wanting to pursue other interests, Aaron was encouraged to stay in it. His parents believed he needed the discipline, and he had actually liked the feeling of courage and power it gave him.

He had competed in several tournaments, earning a few trophies along with his black belt before moving on to become involved in high school sports and the social scene.

So like Bud, Aaron too was deceiving in his appearance.

All Sanchez and his buddies had heard was that Aaron's last name stood for wealth and class, two things they jealously resented. And they knew they wanted to bring him down a peg or two, maybe mess up his pretty face a little bit.

Sanchez stood looking amused for a moment more and then jumped on him in a flash, but not fast enough to avoid Aaron's foot, which delivered a crushing kick to the Mexican's ribs. Sanchez, bent in two, groaned, clutching his middle.

"I'm warning the rest of you, I have a black belt in karate." Aaron raised his open hands in a karate-style defensive gesture.

Sanchez couldn't catch his breath, but the others started laughing in disbelief.

"Yeah, right," the one who appeared to be Sanchez' sidekick said. "Let's see another move, karate kid."

And when he received no response, the hulking, muscular black man prodded Aaron by attempting to punch him in the stomach. Aaron deftly blocked the punch and the guy came at him again, this time angrier and harder. Aaron returned a swift, two-punch blow that sent the big black inmate reeling backward.

Sanchez, meanwhile, caught his breath and, angered by the blow to his ribs and his pride, advanced again on Aaron, this time accompanied by the four others. They jumped on him, punching and kicking, but Aaron managed to deflect their assaults.

Aaron saw a metallic gleam cut through the air as Sanchez pulled a small knife and wielded it skillfully at waist level, the others surrounding him to protect him from the guards' attention.

"Aaron, look out," Bud called, mustering what little courage he could to support the only inmate who had ever befriended him.

Sanchez and his group turned around again to face Bud.

"Fat boy doesn't know when to keep his mouth shut." Sanchez swiftly advanced and held the knife-point to Bud's protruding gut. "Let's see if the pig will bleed." And then he slid the knife along the front of Bud's shirt, leaving a red gash in the blue-gray material.

Aaron heard Bud's yelp and turned with fury on Sanchez, defending his new friend. Sanchez and his buddies converged again on Aaron, and the fray, along with Bud's cries, finally brought the guards and the rest of the inmates in the yard scrambling over.

But it was too late. With six guys on top of him, including one with a knife, Aaron defended himself the best way he knew how, using his memory and skills in karate. He had never had to use them in real-life defense before and because of that, he had never realized how powerful they could be.

When the guards managed to break up the crowd, Sanchez lay motionless on the asphalt.

Bedlam ensued as the rest of the inmates quickly crowded around their fallen friend, jockeying for position to see what had happened.

One of the guards called for help over his two-way radio and the other knelt beside Sanchez, checking his vital signs. Soon more guards were in the yard trying to break up the mob.

The second guard yelled, "Get an ambulance."

"Guess we're in some trouble." Bud cradled his jowls in his large hands, his elbows resting on his knees that stuck out of his cot where he sat, his oversized frame wedged between the two bunks.

Aaron sat across from him, staring at the floor.

"Well, you probably aren't, but I sure as heck am." Aaron

looked equally glum. "Did you hear anything out there?" He pointed his thumb toward the hallway outside of their cell, which was quieting down as the inmates settled in after dinner.

"Nah, I just gave 'em all a mean look and they left me alone." Bud scowled. "Plus there were extras around just in case." He referred to the additional guards that had been placed in the mess hall that afternoon to avoid another outbreak.

Bud had just returned from the inmates' main dining hall, where he had gone to eat supper after being bandaged up at the "med," the detention center's medical office staffed by a visiting physician and nurse. The cut he had suffered was only a superficial laceration and was able to be patched up there.

Both for his own protection and that of the other inmates, Aaron had eaten from a tray in solitude in his cell, ordered by the warden to confinement.

Now he and Bud made small talk, awaiting the news that Sanchez was dead or alive. "By the way...thanks," Bud offered as they sat waiting, raising his chin up to look into Aaron's eyes. Aaron thought he saw tears in the usually vacant, almost colorless eyes that looked at him from across the room.

"No problem," Aaron said with a grin. Somehow this big lug managed to make him smile despite the huge amount of trouble that awaited him. "I never meant to kill Sanchez. I just didn't want to see you get killed. I guess I never realized how powerful a weapon my hands could be. Guess the Sensei was right about all that karate stuff after all."

A series of catcalls, hisses and four-letter words signaled the warden's approach before they even heard the click of boots coming down the hall.

Warden Joe Johnson stood in front of their cell and looked first at Bud then at Aaron, letting his intent gaze linger for a moment on the rich kid. "It's time to face the music, Mister Jacobs." The warden took out his large, jangling ring of keys and opened the cell door, motioning for Aaron to stand and get cuffed by the two guards who stood as backup behind him.

"Aaron Jacobs, you are being brought to my office for questioning regarding the death of Sanchez Dominguez."

"Sanchez is...is dead?" Aaron looked up at the warden in disbelief as he slowly rose from his chair.

"I'm afraid so." The warden was stern in his appearance, with receding, marine-cut hair and large wrinkles around his mouth and on his forehead that had deepened with time and stress. He was also a huge, muscular man that was intimidating, not only by his physique, but by his deep voice which had a resonating, bass timbre that commanded attention.

"Sanchez was taken to the local Medical Center but they weren't able to save him. They said the blow you delivered to his temple hit a pressure point that caused his brain to hemorrhage and there was nothing they could do. I'm sorry, Jacobs. I know you're a good kid who made a big mistake trying to do the right thing. But this is out of my hands."

Aaron stood silently, fighting tears as the guards handcuffed his wrists and led him out of the cell.

"This isn't fair!" Bud hoisted himself off his bunk, his hands clenched in fists. The warden turned and, without saying a word, gave him a glare cold enough that the young inmate, even though he was bigger and taller, crouched back down onto the cot again.

"Your attorney is waiting for you." Warden Johnson closed the cell gate and locked it as Aaron, cuffed and flanked by the two guards, stood meekly waiting for further direction.

"Good luck!" Bud stumbled to the cell door and clenched the bars in his chunky fists. He ignored the mimicry that stirred from nearby cells and watched until the procession of the warden, Aaron and the guards, disappeared down the hall and around the corner.

Aaron found himself sitting across a table from Michael Powers once again, but this time they were being watched by a prison guard who stood in a corner. They were sequestered in a small sound-proof room that served as the prison's conference center two doors down from the warden's office.

"I'm sorry about what happened, Aaron." Michael noticed the desperation in his client's face. "I'll do the best I can to get you out of this mess, but I've got to warn you, we have a huge issue to face now. In New Hampshire, murder by an inmate while serving a sentence of life without parole is punishable by the death sentence. Now I know you haven't even been sentenced yet for the first set of charges involving the accident with your brother, but if he were to die…"

"Oh my God, Michael!" Aaron buried his face in his hands. After a minute he looked up, forlorn. "I guess it doesn't matter what happens to me anyway. I deserve whatever I get. What I did to Adam…"

"That's not true, Aaron, it was an accident. I'm sure what happened in the jail yard was too." Michael reached out his hand and grabbed Aaron's wrist, forcing his young client to look back at him. "You've got to be strong. For yourself, your parents and for Adam."

"So I guess Mom and Dad are furious with me now?" Aaron's eyes teared as he looked up at his attorney.

"Actually, Aaron, they told me to tell you they're very proud of you. They would have liked to see you themselves, but you're only allowed one visitor at a time. And we've got work to do."

A few minutes later, two Suffolk County Sheriff's deputies brandishing handcuffs entered the tiny conference room. One grabbed Aaron by the arm, hoisting him up out of his chair while the other spoke. "Aaron Jacobs, you are under arrest for the murder of Sanchez Dominguez. You have the right to remain silent. Anything you say can and shall be held against you in a court of law..."

Unfortunately for Aaron, Judge Henry was back from his weekend vacation, and things hadn't gone well.

First, his wife had called to tell him that her visit with her mother had gone awry and that she would be home earlier than planned. His mother-in-law had supposedly been on her deathbed, but had complained as usual that her health was worse than it really was. Therefore he had to cancel on his mistress who usually relieved him of some of the weekly stresses he faced.

By the time Monday's docket was placed in front of him that morning, Judge Henry was already fuming.

Then he saw Aaron Jacobs' name again before him. But it was not for the bail review hearing that had originally been scheduled for the auto accident and drug and alcohol charges involving Adam Jacobs. It was a newly scheduled arraignment hearing on charges related to the death of one Sanchez Dominguez.

His brow furrowed for a moment when he read the charges. Then, as people in the courtroom who were watching him would later comment, his expression changed from a sour frown to a strange, malicious grin.

With a murder case now on his hands, the prosecutor requested Aaron's bail be revoked.

"Well, Mister Jacobs, I thought at first that you were here for your bail review hearing after spending the weekend in jail. I guess anything can happen in a day or two. Because you are now charged with aggravated assault and murder in the death of Sanchez Dominguez, charges that carry with them the possible sentence of life in prison. Because you already have an arrest on reckless endangerment with the possibility of vehicular manslaughter still looming, that sentence could possibly escalate to the death penalty. Are you aware of this Mister Jacobs?"

"Yes, your honor."

"Therefore, I have no choice but to detain you in prison with no bail pending the outcome of both of these cases. I remand you to the maximum security New Hampshire State Prison for Men pending trial." And the gavel's crack echoed through the silent courtroom.

"Your honor, this is outrageous!" Michael, who was standing next to Aaron to hear the judge's ruling, pounded his fist on the defendant's table before him. "This..."

The defense attorney was interrupted by the booming growl of the judge. "Mister Powers, I once again advise you to hold your tongue before you say something you and your client will regret."

The court erupted in a cacophony of sound. Aaron wordlessly turned around with a pleading, helpless look to search the courtroom for his family.

His parents and sister, looking drawn and haggard, wept as they hugged him goodbye.

"I'm sorry," Aaron sobbed, as his father clutched him to his chest.

"We love you, Aaron," was all Seth could get out before his son was ripped from his arms by the bailiff and shuffled away by guards. Maria and Angelica both wailed but their cries were lost in the din of the crowd.

Once Aaron was gone, Michael approached the three, who were huddled together holding each other like orphans. Michael put his arm around his friend's shoulders. "Seth, I'll do whatever it takes to help Aaron see his way out of this as quickly as possible."

Seth looked back, gray circles of grief under his eyes.

"You have to, Michael. I can't lose both of my sons."

Chapter 10

The winter had been especially harsh and long.

Seth was dealt another blow when his father had had a freak accident falling on the ice that coated Providence that winter. Eli Jacobs had been carrying groceries into their modest house and slipped on the driveway, falling backward, his head slamming onto the hard, icy concrete. He died after suffering a severe concussion.

Seth's mother was beyond bereft at the death of her husband, the man she had married as a teenager and spent sixty-five years of her life with. He had been the only lover, friend and companion she had ever really known.

And so, one month after the Jacobs family buried Eli, they had to turn around and bury Rachel, who died from a massive heart attack in her sleep on Valentine's Day eve.

Doctors told Seth his mother's weight, age and the health problems she had suffered during the course of her life, including the stresses she had experienced in pregnancy and childbirth, all contributed to the coronary attack.

Seth believed his mother had suffered a broken heart that had finally just quit wanting to work anymore, but felt guilty his own birth had contributed to her downfall.

He took his parents' death hard and the funeral sapped a lot of strength and energy from him. It took all the will he could muster to rise from bed each morning and get through the day dealing with the needs of his immediate family and his suffering business.

While Seth was not held criminally responsible for the death of Senator Caine, the FBI investigation of the Perfect Place found that there had been deliberate tampering with the caviar that had caused the food poisoning, although it was still unknown who had been responsible for it.

As a result, all Perfect Place restaurants had remained closed for several months pending the investigation. The restaurants had taken such a hard financial hit because of the lost business and stain on their reputation that only a handful were predicted to survive.

Every day Seth locked himself into his library at home to crunch numbers, make phone calls and worry about the financial stability of his restaurant family. Employees were let go every day – employees he had come to know and care about.

Besides his visits to see Adam and Aaron, Seth normally only came out of his office for dinner. He and Maria usually ate in worried silence, or would argue over what was to become of them, an argument that never had any resolution.

Spring arrived still bleak and cold in the Jacobs' household.

It had been three long months since Aaron had been sentenced to life in prison for the death of Sanchez Dominguez, with the death penalty looming if his brother were to die. Michael Powers was still working on an appeal but told the family the chances were slim. While Judge Henry had not presided over the sentencing, he had weighed in heavily with his opinion on the matter.

And it had been almost six months since Adam had gone into a coma. There had been no change in his condition, but his family never gave up hope, taking turns visiting him daily at the assisted care rehabilitation center. He had been transferred there once the insurance money ran out and the hospital would no longer keep him.

Angelica tried to work her visits to see her brothers around school so she could get in several times a week. It was a grueling schedule for all of them.

One late March evening, unable to bear sitting at the dinner table across from her parents one more night, Angelica begged off with a migraine and lay across her bed behind closed doors.

As Maria disappeared into the kitchen to clear the dishes and Seth sat alone at the dinner table rubbing his tired, sore eyes, Angelica finally came out of her bedroom. She descended the winding staircase onto the large, carpeted foyer, and stood quietly at the ornately arched entranceway to the formal dining room.

Seth didn't hear or see her coming, his head bent and his hands holding his forehead. Sensing his daughter's presence, he slowly raised his eyes to look at her. What he saw, however, was not the lithe, raven-haired teenager who stood with her arms crossed and her brows furrowed, but his sweet, loving little girl.

"Snap out of it, Dad." Angelica unfolded her arms and stormed into the room, her hands clenched with frustration. "I can't stand to see that look on your face."

"What look, honey?"

"That look that says, 'everything's alright.' It's not alright and we need to face reality."

Seth didn't recognize this grownup, hostile version of his daughter and it took him a minute to refocus. The consternation and anger in his daughter's eyes pricked his heart like a cold needle.

Angelica must have seen her father's face crumple.

"I'm sorry, Dad." She approached him and stood next to where he sat at the head of the long mahogany table. "I know you and Mom have been through a lot. With Adam still in a coma and Aaron in prison..."

Seth held his hand straight out, motioning for her to stop. "I don't want to talk about your brothers."

"That's just it, Dad." Angelica's voice softened. "We never talk about them. It's almost as if Aaron and Adam are both dead or something..."

"Angelica! Don't you ever say that again!" Seth was filled with fury until he saw tears on his daughter's cheeks. "Please, Angelica, don't talk like that."

"But Dad, that's what I mean. By not talking about it, I feel like I'm an only child around here. Or worse, that I don't exist. You don't even see me anymore. It's like you look through me. It's gotten to the point that I can't stand to be around you or Mom anymore because I get too depressed. I feel sorry for my brothers, but I need you too. Then I feel guilty for feeling this way. It's like our whole family has been ripped apart and my life is ruined. And I'm only seventeen, Dad. I have a life to live."

Seth felt an overwhelming fatigue bear down on him, looking at a daughter whom he failed to recognize anymore. And he felt helpless to help her because he had become so engulfed by his own grief and despair.

"What do you want, Angelica?" His voice sounded strained and unsympathetic to his own ears, even though his heart did reach out to her. *I do love her,* he thought. *I just have nothing left to give her right now. And if I do, I don't know how to give it.*

"If you don't know, Dad, just forget it." With a teenage air of pride, Angelica turned and clicked along the hardwood floors out of the dining room.

"Angelica, wait!" Seth's heart went out to his daughter,

but it was too late. She was gone. *I'll talk to her in the morning when she's feeling more receptive,* he thought. *We'll spend the day together and I'll show her how much she means to me.*

Seth was so out of touch with reality and time, though, he didn't realize tomorrow was a school day, not a Saturday.

Angelica retreated to her bedroom again and was sitting on her bed brooding when her cell phone rang.

It was her boyfriend, Caleb Elia.

"Hi, Angelface, I just wanted to call and see how you're doing."

"Not so good, Caleb." Angelica sniffled back the tears that had broken forth anew at the sound of his voice.

"Oh, wow, I'm sorry. You want to talk about it?"

"It's just the same old hopelessness." Angelica had confided her growing misery to Caleb over the past few months and he had always been there for her. "I guess I'm feeling sorry for myself like a spoiled, rotten brat," she added, grabbing a tissue from her nightstand.

"You have every right to feel sorry for yourself. You've been through a lot lately. What you need is to get out of that house and have some fun, and I have a feeling tomorrow night's going to make you feel better."

"Why, because it's Friday?" Angelica teased him, knowing the real reason at which he was hinting.

Caleb had asked Angelica to go to the movies with him. "Hey, do I see a smile on that beautiful face?"

Angelica was smiling now and lay dreamily back on her pillow to enjoy the conversation. "You always manage to make me feel better, Caleb."

"My pleasure. See you tomorrow night?"

"Hope I make it 'til then."

"You will. You're my girl. Sweet dreams, Angelica."

Seth and Maria were finishing their dinner, or rather, picking at their food at the far end of the long dining room table the next night when Angelica approached them to say she was heading out on her date with Caleb. Her parents stared blankly back at her, their wooden expressions reflected in the polished mahogany.

"You forgot?" Angelica crossed her arms, a look of frustration on her face.

Caleb was picking her up and she wanted to be ready at the door when he arrived so he didn't have to come inside and talk to her parents.

She hurriedly said goodbye and was headed for the foyer when Seth stopped her.

"Angelica, hold on, what's the hurry? Why don't you have Caleb come in for a while?"

"We'll be late for the movie, Dad."

"Are you sure it's not that you're embarrassed to be seen with us old folks?"

"Speak for yourself, dear," Maria said.

"By the way, Caleb asked if I could stay out a little past my curfew so we could get something to eat after the movie. Is that okay?"

"I don't think it's a good idea, honey." Seth wiped his mouth with his napkin.

"Mom?" Angelica turned to her mother, exasperated.

"You heard your father."

"Why are you two so overprotective?"

"Do you really need to ask that question, Angelica?" Seth answered tiredly. "You know what we've lost. We don't want to lose you too."

"Well, you're going to if you don't let me have some freedom!" Angelica retorted.

"Angelica!" Maria snapped, standing to confront her daughter. "Don't ever say that again!"

"I'm sorry. It's just that I feel you don't trust me."

Seth and Maria exchanged glances. "Okay, but just an hour past," Seth said reluctantly. "Be careful."

The doorbell rang. Angelica waved goodbye. "Thanks!" she said, smiling over her shoulder as she walked out the front door.

"Hey, why didn't you ask me in?" Caleb asked as he helped Angelica into the passenger seat and slid behind the wheel of his old Pontiac. "You embarrassed to be seen with someone driving such a hunk of junk?"

"Caleb, you know I'm proud of you saving and buying your own car. Actually it's the other way around. I feel like everyone that sees the way I live ends up thinking I'm this spoiled little rich kid." She looked up at the mansion on the hill as they rode away.

She could see the silhouettes of her parents moving slowly about, like ghosts, through the front picture window draped by heavy Parisian lace curtains. A dark shadow hung over them, cast by the massive Austrian crystal chandelier that hung from the living room's vaulted ceiling.

Her parents had traveled around the world, Seth more than once, and brought home collections of some of the finest art, sculptures, fixtures and furniture.

Seth's favorite room, the library, was worth a small fortune alone with its marble fireplace and leather furniture, both imported from Italy, its cut crystal lamps from Paris, its antique roll-top desk from London and its handmade Donegal carpet from Ireland.

"Back to earth, Angelica." Caleb snapped her out of her reverie. "You forget I've already seen your house and I'm not intimidated."

"I know. It's just that lately with all that's happened, Mom and Dad are kind of morose and I think the house seems more like a mausoleum than a home. It's not that I didn't want to have you in, it's that I wanted to get out of there."

Caleb took her hand. "Consider me your knight in shining armor, come to whisk you away from the evil castle."

After the movie, Caleb suggested they get burgers and shakes and take a drive up across the Charlestown Bridge over to a bluff that overlooked Boston's Inner Harbor.

The *U.S.S. Constitution*, its frame outlined in tiny white lights, a variety of boats docked at the harbor reflecting off the water, and the city skyline as a backdrop made for a breathtaking view. It was unusually warm for a spring night in Boston and the night air was still balmy, so Caleb left the windows down as they sipped the remainder of their malted milkshakes.

Caleb and Angelica had found this secret parking spot one day while sightseeing after Caleb had arrived in Boston from his native land of Syria two years ago. Caleb's father was consul to the U.S. for his country and had been stationed in Boston to head Middle East relations in northeastern America.

Caleb had entered Angelica's high school when both were sophomores. They had become instant friends and she had eagerly volunteered to show him the sights of her fair city. Their friendship quickly blossomed into something more and they had remained a couple into their senior year. Yet both of them had restrained themselves from sexual intimacy beyond what Angelica would call "third base" because of their strict religious and family values.

But the combination of the unexpectedly sultry spring air,

Angelica's vulnerability, her need to feel love and abandonment from all of her anxieties, and the pent-up drives of a seventeen-year-old boy were too strong a combination for either of them to resist this night.

Milkshakes finished and a slow rhythm and blues song playing on the radio, the two sat on the Pontiac's cracked but roomy front seat, Caleb with his arm around Angelica, her head resting on his shoulder. Her long, dark hair fell softly across his arm. Angelica turned to Caleb and looked up at him with liquid brown eyes, and he kissed her long and hard.

Angelica removed her jacket and let Caleb touch her beneath her blouse, then slip his hand beneath her short, ruffled skirt. He stopped abruptly, pulling his hand away.

"I'm sorry, Angelica, I got caught up in…I don't know what."

"Don't stop, Caleb." Usually, Angelica would have agreed that they stop, insisted on it in fact, so she wouldn't tease him past the point of no return. But this time, she gently put his hand back where it was.

"You don't know what you're doing." Caleb winced in frustration. "You're driving me crazy and I don't want to do anything you don't want…"

"Shut up and kiss me Caleb." Angelica interrupted him with her mouth, causing him to moan in pain and pleasure. "I want you, Caleb," she said in between kisses. "Tonight. I love you."

"I love you too…oh God, Angelica, you have no idea how much." Caleb pulled away, his breathing short and ragged. "But…are you sure this is what you want?"

"I'm sure. I want to feel you love me. Make me forget everything else." And she was on top of him, leaving him little choice.

Chapter 11

"Look at them," Maria said to Seth one day, parting the heavy drapes behind Seth's desk in the library.

Seth turned around and squinted as the bright sunlight streamed in. After adjusting his eyes, he peered out the bay windows that overlooked the huge swimming pool in their backyard.

It had been months since Seth had permitted himself to wander out to the pool. *It wasn't the same without the boys*, he had thought over and over when he considered taking a swim, even on a hot day like this one.

Now he watched with Maria as Angelica and Caleb playfully splashed each other, took turns going off the diving board, then approached each other in the pool, heads together talking. Angelica put her arms around Caleb and Seth turned away to face the mountain of paperwork on his desk in the dimly lit library.

"They look like they're in love." Maria smiled. "I like Caleb. He's smart and well-mannered, not to mention very handsome. And he seems to treat our daughter well. What do you think of him?"

Seth, preoccupied with his paperwork, didn't answer.

"Did you even hear what I said?" Maria's voice rose in anger.

"I'm sorry, dear, what did you say?"

"I asked what you thought of Caleb Elia."

"I don't know if he's right for her." Seth absentmindedly twirled a pencil between his fingers. "You know he's an Arab."

"Seth Jacobs, you sound like your mother back when you first brought me to meet her!" Maria turned to look out the window again at the two frolicking teenagers. Her voice softened. "We used to be like that, remember? There was a time when all I had to do was touch you and it would drive you crazy." Maria turned around with a gleam in her eyes. But Seth's attention was already diverted again, his head bent, his focus on the papers on his desk.

He rubbed his eyes with his thumb and forefinger, not listening. "I'm sorry, honey, what did you say again?"

"I'm saying I'm in the mood, darling." Maria strode over to Seth and began massaging his neck and shoulders with her adept hands.

"I'm sorry, Maria, but I've got the worst headache," Seth apologized. "Can I take a rain check?"

"I've been giving you rain checks for the past several months," Maria crossed her arms, her voice reflecting a mix of anger and contempt.

She walked out of the room, not turning back to see Seth wearily bury his head in his hands.

Caleb broke the news to Angelica that night as they lay back in each other's arms in a lounge chair on the pool deck, watching the sun's last rays dip below the horizon.

They had spent that lazy Memorial Day afternoon together swimming and sunning, then eating a picnic dinner poolside, and now just lingering, watching fireflies light up the night sky.

"I can't believe it's almost graduation." Angelica contentedly rested her head on Caleb's bare chest, a terry robe wrapped around her bikini to ward off the night air. "One more summer before we go off to college. At least we're not going to be very far apart."

Caleb had been admitted to Boston University while Angelica would be attending Boston College.

Caleb sat up, pushing Angelica forward into a sitting position. "Hey, what the..."

"We've got to talk." Caleb interrupted Angelica's protests with his serious tone. She drew her robe tighter around her and turned to face him, sitting cross-legged on the end of the chair.

"What's wrong, Caleb?"

"I didn't want to spoil our day together so I held off until now, but it can't wait any longer. There's been a change of plans. I can't go to BU. It's my parents..."

Now Angelica interrupted. "Your parents? I thought they wanted to you to go to Boston!"

"They do. They did. It's just that...well, now we have to move."

"Move? Move where?"

"We're moving back to Syria, Angelica." The sun had vanished and the rising moon backlit Caleb's dark frame so that Angelica couldn't see that his features were contorted in pain.

Caleb could see Angelica's face, which crumpled in shock, confusion and fear. He hurried to explain. "My father has been offered a position by our country to go back and help the new President build a better government. It's a chance of a lifetime. His people...my people...want to bring him home to Syria where he can be of more help to them at a time when they really need his expertise."

"But why do you have to go?" Angelica remained still, her voice soft and small.

"My father wouldn't take the position unless my mother

and I agreed to go back with him. I want to help him. I want to help our people."

"What about college?"

"I can attend the university there and major in political science just like I was going to do here. But this gives me a real chance to put it to use." Caleb knelt before Angelica on the rough patio stones and gently brushed away the tears that started to fall down her cheeks. "I'm sorry, Angelica."

"You can't go, Caleb!" Angelica's voice started rising, coming out between fractured sobs. You can't leave me! You can't leave our baby!"

Caleb looked at her in bewilderment. "Our…baby?"

Angelica covered Caleb's mouth with her hand to silence him and lowered her voice, remembering her parents were still in the house and the windows might be open. "Caleb, I was going to tell you tonight. I'm pregnant."

"Oh my God." Caleb's words came out in little more than a whisper. "That changes everything." He stood up and began pacing the pool deck, then came back to where Angelica still sat frozen in place.

"You can come with us." The look of shock shifted from Caleb back to Angelica. "You would love our country, and we would come back to visit your family as often as you'd like since my father gets free air travel. You could go to the same university and…we could get married."

Caleb blushed as Angelica stared at him with a dumbfounded expression. He reached out his arms, took her hands in his and knelt again on one knee before her on the rough stones.

"Angelica, I love you. Will you marry me?" Caleb asked softly. "I know I don't have a ring and this wasn't exactly the way I wanted to propose, but I don't want to leave you either, and…"

"Yes!" Angelica said, cutting him off, wrapping her arms around his neck.

Suddenly the automatically timed floodlights washed the pool and deck in a bright white light, nearly blinding the two teenagers wrapped in each others' arms.

"I'll call you tomorrow and we'll start making plans," Caleb whispered in her ear excitedly, giving her one last quick hug before heading for the bath house to change and go.

"Goodbye for now, Romeo." Angelica blew Caleb a kiss, as she had done in the high school theater production in which she and Caleb had played the leads.

"Parting is such sweet sorrow." Caleb bowed and dramatically flung his towel behind him, then turned to go.

Angelica's eighteenth birthday was two days after graduation, so Seth and Maria had planned a surprise party to celebrate both events the following Saturday.

They'd invited dozens of friends, several of Angelica's fellow graduates, her grandparents and her aunts and uncles, and of course, Caleb.

Seth had to try his best to get motivated to entertain anyone given his circumstances. *But it really doesn't matter*, he thought. *Maria has enough energy for both of us.*

Maria had always loved to entertain, and before the accidents that had befallen their family, she had executed the many dinner parties she and Seth threw for local and national business associates, government officials, employees and friends.

Then the recent pall upon their home and family, and budgetary constraints with Seth's failing business, negated inviting anyone over at all.

But Angelica's planned surprise party gave Maria the perfect outlet from the gloom and despair that had recently enveloped the Jacobs' household. She delved into the preparations, single-handedly coordinating the caterer, the music, the decorations, the housecleaning and landscaping that needed to be done.

Her pride and joy had always been her gardens. She and her employees had made the grounds of the Jacobs' estate into a gardener's paradise worthy of the home and garden magazine covers it had adorned.

"So should I make arrangements from the yellow roses, or the pink?" Maria fluttered through the house, stopping a moment to ask Seth's opinion before she flitted away to make the next phone call on her list.

Seth sat at his desk in the library, buried again in paperwork.

His wife stood still and put her hands on her hips in exasperation. "Seth Jacobs, this is the day before our daughter's eighteenth birthday and graduation party and here you are hiding in your little library doing the same thing you do day in and day out, whatever that is, leaving me to do all the work as usual!" The social butterfly slammed its wing onto the desk for effect.

"I'm sorry, dear, but I thought you liked doing all the work." Seth removed the reading glasses he had grown accustomed to wearing of late, and raised his tired, blue eyes to meet his wife's, which were almost black with anger.

"No I don't *like* doing all the work, but I *have* to do all the work if it's going to get done, especially since you're no help at all."

"I have to go out for a late lunch with Michael Powers and his partner Jerry Rogers. They're going to help me sort out what course of action to take with this whole business mess. I know you've been busy with this party, Maria, but you need to know we're facing serious financial trouble. The Perfect Place may have to declare bankruptcy."

Maria, who had been headed out the library door, stopped and turned to face her husband with an icy glare. "I guess the Perfect Place isn't so perfect after all."

"Where is this coming from?" Seth couldn't believe the venom that was now spewing from his wife's lovely, red-lipped mouth. "I'm just suggesting we cut back a bit on our spending until we find a way to supplement the losses we've incurred."

"You mean the losses you've incurred."

"I'll take full blame for what's happened with my restaurants, even if I still don't know how or why, but that doesn't change the fact that our bank accounts are soon going to be empty if we don't change our ways."

"So I guess you don't think we should be having this party for Angelica, then?" Maria's tone was acidic and challenging. "Because it's too late to cancel since it's happening in less than a week."

"No, I'm not saying that, I'm just saying perhaps you don't need to be so elaborate." Seth was afraid to ask Maria how much she had spent on the party, knowing he'd find out soon enough when he received the bills. *Still, I need to warn her, try to gradually help her cut back so she won't be in total shock once she realizes how bad things are,* he thought.

"Well none of this is my fault, so I don't see why I have to pay the price." Maria's full lips turned into a pout, which Seth used to find extremely sexy but now just saw as a signal of the biting words that were to follow. "A part of me always doubted whether or not you should start your own business. But I always supported you, even when it meant giving up my own dreams and desires and taking care of three kids. And now look where it got me. You better fix this, Seth, or so help me, I'm..."

Her threat was left hanging like a cold, damp breath of air.

Seth had been the target lately for so many darts of pain

that he wondered if he must have become calloused or numb, because Maria's words seemed to fall off and around him like bullets hitting a bullet-proof vest. *She is so beautiful, even when she's angry and hateful,* was all he could think, looking with detachment at the creature before him in the lime green linen suit, her freshly-cut, dark chocolate hair falling on her shoulders, her dark eyes smoldering.

"Well, aren't you going to say something for yourself?" Maria's shrill tone snapped Seth out of his reverie.

"I will try my best, Maria. You know I love you and the children and will do anything to make you happy."

"We'll see." Maria turned and left the room.

People began arriving at five p.m. and the guest of honor, who had been staying at a friend's house, was due at six.

Maria, who had ignored her husband's dour warning and treated herself earlier that day to a full spa treatment of a facial, manicure, pedicure, massage and hairdo, looked like a model, albeit one who had matured into womanhood. She acted the part of the perfect hostess, personally greeting each guest with a smile as they entered the Jacobs' home.

The staff of three Maria had hired, including an event coordinator, a caterer and a decorator, had turned the Jacobs' huge living room into a party room replete with color coordinated linens and balloons and flowers arranged by the hostess herself.

Waiters circled the expansive room with trays of crab balls, shrimp tempura, and skewered lobster. Punch fountains, huge trays of fruit, vegetable and cheese arrangements and assorted petite dessert displays were in strategic locations throughout the room. A bar was set up with non-alcoholic beverages, as most of the guests were still underage, and a two-tiered cake lavishly frosted with butter cream roses was the centerpiece.

Seth had lost track of time in his meeting with the two attorneys and walked in at five fifteen. Maria hissed at him through clenched teeth to help her greet guests and make them feel at home.

A few minutes before six, the event coordinator, a thin, prim, energetic woman in her fifties who matched Maria if not in looks than in verve, started bustling about, herding the guests away from adjoining rooms and hallways into the middle of the party room to surprise Angelica as she walked in from the foyer.

Voices were kept to a low buzz and the anticipation in the air was palpable. As minutes turned into a half hour, then close to an hour, excited whispers became anxious grumbling. A panicked Maria grabbed Seth by the arm and veered him away from the young girl he was politely trying to listen to into the kitchen, away from the crowd. "Where is Angelica?" Maria kept her voice down, but just barely.

"I have no idea." Seth put his hands on Maria's shoulders, but she pulled away. "Calm down, I'm sure there's an explanation. Call her girlfriend's house and see if they've left yet."

Maria dialed and spoke into the receiver, then hung up, slack-jawed. "Kayla's mother said Angelica never came over today. She said Kayla has been out all day and said she's sorry she couldn't make the party, but she knows Angelica would understand. How would she understand? They're best friends! This doesn't make any sense!"

"Okay, Maria, calm down. Let's focus here. Angelica took the car, right? Let's think where she could have gone."

"Well Caleb's not here either. Maybe she's with him." Maria dialed again and got Caleb's voicemail on the other end. She slammed down the receiver in frustration. "Go tell 'wonder woman' out there to make an announcement to the guests that Angelica's been delayed so they can relax a little until we find out where she is. I'll go upstairs and look in her room for her friends' phone numbers. Maybe one of them will know where she is." Maria strode out of the kitchen, putting on a plaster smile as she walked past a few guests lingering in the hallway, then went up the staircase.

Seth pulled the party planner aside, gave her Maria's instructions, then followed his wife's lead upstairs and into Angelica's room. He found his wife sitting on their daughter's bed, holding Snuffy, the ragged old brown bear Angelica had received for her second birthday and had often slept with ever since.

Maria rocked back and forth, holding the stuffed animal in her arms, quietly crying. Sensing Seth had entered the room, she held out an unopened letter to him as he quietly approached her from behind. "Her clothes are gone," Maria said, her voice muffled into the little brown bear's fur, then looked up at Seth, her eyes filled with tears.

Seth wordlessly ripped open the envelope, pulled out the single sheet of paper and read it aloud.

"Dear Mom and Dad,

I'm sorry to have to tell you this way, but I'm afraid it's the only way to tell you. By the time you read this I'll be on a plane to Syria with Caleb and his parents, so please just sit and read this letter before you do anything else, because there's no way to stop me now. Caleb and I got married at the courthouse downtown by a Justice of the Peace on Thursday, my birthday.

I know you didn't forget my birthday because Kayla told me about the party you planned, and I'm really sorry about that. But please don't blame her. She knew this was something I had to do and I swore her to secrecy. For a long time I have felt that I just don't belong here anymore. I know you have more than you can handle with Aaron in jail and Adam in a coma, and I don't blame you for not having time for me.

Caleb has been wonderful and I love him with all my heart, which is why I hope you'll understand when I tell you this, but I gave myself to him in love and now I'm pregnant with his baby. Please, please don't worry and don't be angry, especially with Caleb. It was me who talked him into making love, and he who talked me into getting married. We wanted you to be there, but I knew you wouldn't have allowed it to happen, much less allowed me to go to Syria. Caleb's father has been offered a really great position with his country to help build a better government for his people, and they (we) had to leave now bcause his country needs him to take the position and start immediately. Caleb wants to help him, and of course, once he found out I was pregnant, he wanted to do the honorable thing. We both plan to go to college, and Caleb's parents have said they will support us until we can support ourselves, and that there will be plenty of room in their home for us to live until we can afford a place of our own. Caleb and I haven't told them about the baby yet, because we're not sure how they'll feel; but we know, just like you, once they get over the initial shock, they'll grow to love their grandchild too.

Please don't blame them either, they are good people—they thought I had your permission to go (sorry, I didn't want to lie but it was the only way). Since I was turning eighteen, I knew I could get a visa and go without it, but they believe you were both going to meet us at the airport and just didn't make it in time. I hope one day you'll forgive me for all of this and find it in your hearts to understand. I know you need to be with Aaron and Adam now, and I know you have always loved me and always will. I promise I will come back home once the baby is born so you can see your new grandchild.

Until then, please don't worry, I'm in good hands. Caleb says Syria is beautiful and I'm looking forward to a fresh start for our new family. Caleb and I really love each other and he will be a good husband and father. I know because I have been raised by the best parents a girl could ever ask for.

I'm sorry. I miss you already, and I love you. — Angelica"

Seth fell to his knees, doubled over against his daughter's bed, tears falling onto the letter he clutched in his fingers, as Maria continued to rock back and forth, weeping, holding the stuffed bear.

My children. Seth felt his heart break while his mind just kept replaying the same words over and over like a broken record. *My children. I've lost all three. I've lost all three children.*

Chapter 12

Since Angelica had left, weeks and months had dragged on with no letters, no phone calls.

Seth managed to track down Mister Elia's work address at the Syrian Consulate, and had sent two letters there but had not received any in return.

For his many contacts, Seth still had no luck.

Something is wrong. He knew it, but with all that was falling apart around him with his business, his sons, and, most likely, his marriage, he couldn't devote all his time to tracking down his daughter or trying to rescue her. His phone calls to government officials only made the situation seem more dire and impossible. They told him that it was highly dangerous for Americans to travel to or from Syria given the still volatile situation in the Middle East. Seth was told he needed to wait a while until things calmed down a bit more. His daughter was there to stay, at least for the time being. He just hoped she was safe and happy.

Seth had little choice but to accept the fact that Angelica was overseas and hold onto his hope that she would keep her word and return in several months with his grandchild. But he just felt like she was gone, that he had lost her.

Once the fact that Angelica was no longer living with them settled in like a bad toothache, painfully reminding him each day that this was his reality, Seth had to face the complicated web of problems that plagued his livelihood.

Time had become surreal, fragmented, between visits to prison, visits to the hospital, talking with doctors, employees, police and lawyers.

It had been almost ten months since the food poisoning debacle, which was still under investigation. Since nothing had turned up, Seth had been allowed to open the Perfect Place restaurants back up for business, but only a handful remained under his ownership. He had been forced to let go of the rest. Those that he hadn't managed to sell to buyers who bought them for less than half of what they were worth, he lost to foreclosures. Seth reopened the three original Perfect Place strongholds in Boston, New York and Los Angeles and a few more that were successful, such as the one in New Orleans thanks to Miss Carla's entertainment. But they struggled under the weight of the pall cast by the bad press that hovered like a constant storm cloud over Seth's life.

The media coverage, while it fed on many other sources, waited hungrily for tidbits to be thrown their way. When the news had gone from major headlines to inside blurbs in metropolitan papers, the tabloids had taken over for a while. Likewise, television news coverage gave way to talk show and comedy fodder.

Even though the original news blitz had died down, newspapers and radio and television stations across America kept constant vigil on Seth Jacobs. His reputation had turned almost overnight from one of the country's most successful, wealthy, favorite sons to one of its most ridiculed and pitied. It seemed most human beings loved to watch other human beings suffer.

Still, when Maria handed Seth the newspaper that summer morning at breakfast and he saw the bold *Boston Globe* front page headline, it was like being hit with ice water. It read, "Perfect Place Restaurant King to be Dethroned?" with a subhead that read, "Class Action Lawsuit Asks for Millions."

Seth blinked several times as if his eyes weren't focusing correctly on the words before him. He hadn't slept well the past several months and knew he was tired from getting just a few hours' rest, but his bleary eyes saw the same words staring back at him.

Just then the phone rang. Maria answered it then handed him the receiver. "It's Jerry, that attorney friend of Michael's. Seth tiredly nodded and took the phone. Maria quietly left the room, shaking her head.

"Have you seen the paper?" Jerry sounded like he was already at work with a few cups of coffee in him.

"Unfortunately, yes."

"I'll be right over. We need to talk."

Jerry Rogers was sitting across from Seth's desk in his library a half hour later, dressed in his customary starched white shirt, tie and pinstriped suit, with his short, salt and pepper hair combed just so.

Seth, in contrast, had not bothered to shower or shave and was sitting at his desk in a rumpled gray sweat suit. His tan had faded, his face was wan and stubbly, and his eyes were murky with gray circles underneath. If Jerry didn't know better he would have surmised Seth was either drunk or completely out of it.

"Seth, as I explained when we met at lunch, unlike Michael, I'm a civil attorney and can represent you in a lawsuit as well as help you deal with any financial matters that need to be handled."

"I know all of that, Jerry," Seth edgily snapped. "I'm not a child." He saw the attorney's offended reaction and changed

119

his attitude. "I'm sorry, I trust you both implicitly."

"I'll do my best to help you sort all this out. But we've got a lot to sort out, Seth."

"Give me the worst case scenario, because I highly doubt anything can get much worse in my life right now."

Jerry cleared his throat and shifted in his chair, suddenly looking uncomfortable, while Seth just looked weary.

"Well, I'm afraid this lawsuit, spearheaded by Senator Caine's family and their attorneys, needs to be dealt with, and fast. Otherwise, it will drag on, more names will accumulate on the list of plaintiffs, the numbers will climb, the press will continue having a field day and the whole thing will snowball." Receiving no response from Seth, Jerry continued. "We'll have to come up with some type of settlement offer. So, as a first course of action I recommend we sell the remaining restaurants immediately. They've been putting a huge strain on your finances, which are already wearing thin, and you'll need whatever's left to…well, to live on once this is all over."

"I don't agree." Seth sat up in his chair. "I've been in business probably as long as you've been practicing law, Jerry. If I get rid of the rest of the Perfect Place restaurants, I'll be admitting complete defeat. The investigators haven't found who is behind all of this yet. All I know is that it's not my fault, and not my employees' fault, and I don't see why we have to keep suffering. Let's just fight this thing."

"Seth, the Senator died. His family wants retribution. And the Democratic Party wants it too. This guy was selected to become the next president of the United States, for God's sake."

"But the police told me after reading the hospital report that they believe it was highly unusual for just one person to die from food poisoning and not the rest. There had to be something else, some other complication that made Robert

Caine die. Surely a thorough investigation of the autopsy will clear this up."

"The hospital records and autopsy are in question and I'm sure they would be brought out in court. But even if we could miraculously prove how Caine died, which would take hundreds of man hours, not to mention a lot of money, you've still got all of the other plaintiffs who were sick, claiming lost time from work and home, lost wages, loss of consortium, pain and suffering...the list goes on, and will keep running on and on if we don't take action fast. These people want you to pay, and if they feel you drag your feet, they'll get angrier and want more blood. On top of that, if you keep the restaurants open under your name, the same restaurants that made them sick, it's a constant reminder to other people that their health may be threatened, and we're just setting ourselves up for more lawsuits, unfounded as they may be."

Seth was so tired that he rubbed his eyes and didn't even realize he had tears in them. "I've done so much damage to my employees already...I've had to fire hundreds of people. These people have families that are suffering too. To repay them after all these years of service to me by letting the rest go...I don't think I can do that."

"I'm sorry, Seth, but I'm afraid we have no choice. Unless...well, how much do you have left in your bank accounts? Maybe if you sell the house and all that's in it... maybe if you liquidate all your assets...that's the only possible way I can think of to keep the three restaurants open and buy some time to fight this class action suit. It's a huge risk, but..." Jerry stood up from his chair and started walking around the room, fingering the leather bindings of some of the oldest and most valuable books on the shelves that lined the walls of the library. "It's possible."

"No, actually it's not." Seth took out a tiny key and opened one of his desk drawers, pulled out a document and handed it to Jerry, who sat back down and put on his reading glasses to review it.

Jerry let out a soft whistle. "Seth, this is a bank foreclosure on your house!"

"I know what it is, Jerry."

"Seth, what have you done?" Jerry's tone was accusatory, reprimanding. "Why haven't you been making your mortgage payments?"

"It's called paying the doctors' bills for one son, and a defense attorney for the other. It's called paying the only employees that have stuck around and remained loyal enough to accept pay cuts and what little I could afford to give them before paying myself to try to keep my family name and reputation above water. It's called pride. I have nothing in the bank accounts, Jerry. If I did, I would have made the mortgage payments now, wouldn't I?"

Jerry sat silent.

"I'm sorry, Jerry, I don't mean to take this all out on you. I just haven't been able to talk to anyone else about it."

"You haven't told your wife?"

"Are you kidding? She's had enough to deal with. I didn't want to send her over the edge."

"But you have to tell her, Seth. The house is hers too."

"I know. I've been waiting for the right time and something else bad just keeps rearing its ugly head demanding my attention. It's almost as if fate is conspiring against me. If I didn't believe in God...well, I don't know what I'd do."

"I admire your faith, and your strength. Most people in your shoes would have gone off the deep end by now. But you have to stay strong, Seth. Think with your head, not your heart. I guess the only resort is for you to declare bankruptcy."

"I can't even afford to keep you as my attorney, can I?"

"I'm afraid not, Seth. I can at least draw up the necessary paperwork for the bankruptcy, and file a settlement offer from any proceeds once your company is closed. And I'm sure Michael can probably stay on as Aaron's attorney as a favor to you. I'll have him call you." Jerry stood slowly, and extended his hand. "I'm really sorry, Seth. You didn't deserve any of this. If there is a God, I'm not sure he's a very just one. It makes me question what little faith I have, that's for sure."

"Thanks for all you've done, Jerry. I guess I better go have that talk with Maria."

"Good luck, Seth."

I'm going to need it, Seth thought. *God help me, I'm going to need all I can get.*

Michele Chynoweth

Chapter 13

Seth didn't know how long he had been sitting in his desk chair after Jerry left before Maria walked in with a cup of coffee for him. The heavy drapes across the floor to ceiling windows were closed, so he couldn't tell that the sun had started to drag across the white summer sky.

He couldn't get warm, no matter what time of day, or time of year it was. And it wasn't the automatically regulated central air conditioning that made him feel a perpetual chill. It was fear.

Lately, Seth had started feeling like he had a constant hangover, even though he didn't drink. Each morning he was met with fatigue, nausea and depression, all of which grew as the days waned one into another.

"It's past lunchtime, but I wasn't sure if you were hungry or just wanted a cup of coffee." Maria sat the steaming cup carefully on his desk.

"No, I'm not hungry at all. This is perfect, thanks." Seth took the cup and sipped the coffee, made just the way he liked it with just the right amount of cream and sugar.

Maria turned to go. "No, don't go just yet. Can we talk?" Seth motioned for her to sit in the chair Jerry had just left.

"That sounds serious." Maria sat, crossing her long, tanned legs. She was dressed in flower-printed Capri pants and a soft pink blouse and Seth marveled for the millionth time how his wife grew more beautiful with each passing day. Her long, dark hair was swept back off her face and tied up in a pink ribbon, revealing her slender neck and high cheekbones, which she had brushed with a little pink blush.

She should have been a model. Seth had thought this from time to time, but dismissed it, realizing their lives were full and would have been too chaotic if his wife would have taken on a career. *Besides, we didn't need the money. Or didn't use to.*

"So what did you want to talk to me about?" Maria's impatience snapped Seth out of one of the many daydreams that frequently claimed him of late and seemed to increasingly annoy her. "I don't have all day, you know. The gardener is here and waiting for me to give him some direction."

"He'll just have to wait. This is important."

Maria crossed her arms and stared back at him with steel gray eyes.

Here goes, Seth thought. "Things aren't going well for us financially, Maria. I'm sure you're aware of that to some extent with all the bills that have come through the mail from the hospital and from Rogers and Powers. But I don't think you know how bad it is, and I wanted to try to explain it to you."

"I'm not stupid, Seth. Just give me the bottom line."

Seth rubbed his hands together, beads of perspiration forming on his brow. "I have to close down the remaining six restaurants."

"Well, that's fine. I mean, I know it's hard, but the people who work for you have got to understand we've got bills to pay, a house to keep up. I've heard businessmen say on television that you should always pay yourself first, before you pay anyone else."

Seth sighed. "That's not it, I'm afraid. We're going to lose the house too. We're going to have to move."

Maria's eyes turned black and her tone was menacing.

"I'm not selling this house, Seth Jacobs. You can move if you want. I've worked too hard to make this house our home. Maybe you've forgotten who bought all the furniture, all the decorations, who selected the paint, who planted the garden, who hired all the contractors, and cleaning people...me, me, me."

"I know that, but you don't understand. I've been meaning to show this to you, but I knew what it would do to you, so I held off. But now I can't wait any longer." Seth pushed the same foreclosure notice across the desk that he had showed Jerry. "It's actually a third and final notice. I threw away the others, hoping it would go away somehow or that we could find the money to pay the mortgage. But the bills just kept piling up."

"What about our savings?" Maria's voice was becoming high-pitched now with panic.

"Gone. School bills, doctors' bills, lawyers' bills... everything just got out of control. It makes me sick to even have to tell you. In fact, I think I really have been sick to my stomach for quite some time, but I know now we don't have the money for me to go to the doctor's, so I'm hoping it's just stress and will soon pass. I'm sorry..."

"You better believe you are." Maria's anxiety turned to rage and she cut him off mid-sentence, uncrossing her arms and legs. She stood up and started pacing like a caged lioness. "How dare you keep all this from me, Seth?"

"I was trying to protect you from it. Now I know that was wrong."

"You, the big restaurant owner, the big businessman! You're nothing but a weak, sorry little man. Look at you, all thin and pale and depressed." Maria spat out each word as if it were venom on her tongue. "You make me sick."

And with that, she knocked over what was left of the

coffee in Seth's cup onto the foreclosure notice and strode out of the room, slamming the door shut behind her.

A cold war ensued in the days to come between Seth and Maria. They slept in separate rooms. They ate meals alone, Seth usually at his desk when he remembered and tried to force something down, and Maria either out with friends or if it was sunny but not too hot, at one of the patio tables under an umbrella around the pool.

She had just finished a sandwich one gloriously sunny July day when she heard the front door close and the small used car they shared drive off. She knew Seth had to go to court before the judge on the bankruptcy and class action settlement hearings. While they rarely spoke to one another, they did keep a calendar on the kitchen wall filled with appointments so they could know where and when the other would have time available to take turns visiting Adam and Aaron.

Seth had marked off the rest of the afternoon, so Maria was left with several hours to herself, since she had just visited Adam that morning and it wasn't her turn to see Aaron until that weekend when he was allowed to have a visitor again.

Maria finished her lemonade and decided to go for a swim.

She had worn her bathing suit under her oversized tee-shirt, which she pulled off over her head before diving into the sparkling blue water.

They would only be able to take advantage of the pool a few more days. Then the bank would be kicking them out the door and putting the house on the auction block.

Maria had been busy the past few weeks packing their things. She and Seth had talked little, so it had still not been decided where they would live. But Maria chose not to give Seth the satisfaction of knowing that she even cared, so she avoided the subject.

Instead, she took great care packing her clothes and belongings. Many of the expensive paintings, sculptures, vases, lamps and other accessories in the house she had sold to interested buyers.

She had kept her jewelry to pawn if needed for cash, and had packed most of her clothes and shoes, knowing she wouldn't be shopping for anything new in the near future.

One by one, Maria had let the staff go until no one was left to work on the Jacobs' estate except the gardener, who occasionally came to mow the lawn and cut back the hedges and flowers so they didn't become wildly overgrown. Maria told Seth she had to keep up their image, even though the house was going to foreclosure.

"Even though you don't, I still have my pride," she'd said sardonically one night when they chanced to speak to one another. "You never know when I may be rich and famous again. Besides, let's fool those bloodthirsty reporters for as long as we possibly can."

After her swim, Maria climbed out of the pool and eased into the adjoining hot tub, closing her eyes and letting the jets of water massage her arms, legs and back.

After about ten minutes, she opened her eyes and stood up, her body dripping.

Her eyes met the piercing gaze of Raphael, the gardener, who had timidly approached her to ask her if any more work needed to be done and stood unsure whether to interrupt her soak.

They were both startled at first, then the young Mexican quickly averted his eyes, but not before Maria saw the unabashed lust within them. She sat back down in the churning hot water and called him. "Raphael. Please come here."

The gardener, sweaty from work, had stripped off his shirt and his brown muscles, hard from outdoor labor, glistened in the sun.

His brown eyes met hers again and the lust was still there, even though he tried to hide it. He approached her, avoiding looking directly at her voluptuous body, which curved in all the right places around her silvery blue string bikini that shimmered when teased by the sun rays.

"You've been working so hard today, you look like you need a break. Why don't you join me?"

"I...I'm afraid I must go, Señora," Raphael replied, stuttering.

"But why? Your time's not up yet, and I'd like some company." Maria pouted, then gave him a tempting smile.

"But, but...I don't have a suit." Raphael stammered.

"Go in the bathhouse and get one of my husband's." When Raphael tried to protest once more, she interrupted. "That's an order."

Two minutes later he was back. Seth's suit fit him perfectly.

He eased into the warm, pulsating water as far away from Maria as he could get. But all of a sudden she crossed the few feet between them and before he could move away, she sat on his lap, straddling her legs around him, her arms around his neck, arching her back so he was looking directly at her bikini top.

He couldn't take his eyes away, and his whole body was frozen still, despite the hot water enveloping him. Maria bent her face to his and started kissing him, her tongue exploring his mouth.

Deftly, she untied her bikini strings one by one. Raphael moaned, clutching her to him, unable to resist this gorgeous wildcat.

When they had finished, their sweat mingled with the foamy water dripping from both of them.

Maria languidly smiled. "Thank you Raphael," she whispered, kissing his salty neck. "That will be all for today."

She was sitting in the living room on the oversized couch, her legs tucked under her, reading a book by the end table lamp, when Seth got home from court that evening.

Seth stood in the arched entranceway from the foyer for a moment studying his wife, who had not yet bothered to look up from her book. A small smile played upon her lips and he noticed something different about her.

She looks content, he mused. *She hasn't looked that way in a long time.*

Maria looked up at him, her dark eyes dancing. "How was court?"

Seth, surprised she even bothered to ask, took a moment to reply, gingerly seating himself in the armchair next to the sofa.

"It was alright, I guess. We officially now have nothing to our name. But at least we don't owe anything either. I guess it's just the end of another chapter in our lives. Now we need to get busy with moving." Seth paused to make sure he still had his wife's attention. She closed her book and continued to listen. "I found an apartment the other day in the city. Nothing fancy, but plenty of room, and I think we can afford at least the first year's rent. It will give me a chance to get back on my feet. Maybe we both could look for a job…"

"I had sex with the gardener today."

The statement came out hard and cold and hit Seth in the stomach like a ball of ice.

Maria stretched her legs out in front of her, stretched her arms out wide, hugged herself, then yawned.

"You what?" Seth wasn't sure he had heard correctly. *Here's my wife, stretching and yawning like she just woke from a nap, telling him she just had sex with the gardener!*

"You heard me. It was great. He was so...such a man. More man than you'll ever be. I wanted to keep doing it again and again but he had to go. Too bad he won't be back. But there are others out there, I'm sure, who will stand in line to do the same." Maria stood, gave Seth a tight, closed-lipped smile, and tried to walk past him and out of the room. But he stood and grabbed her by the wrist and spun her around to face him.

"How could you do this?" Seth's voice came out choked. He felt like his whole chest had been caught in a vise that was clamping his lungs and heart together so he couldn't breathe, couldn't feel, could barely speak or move.

"Oh, it was easy, in fact." Maria stared back at him, contempt gleaming in her eyes.

I should smack that smug look right off her face. Seth raised his other free hand to do it, then realized how wrong that would be.

Seth lowered his hand, then he dropped her wrist and limply fell back down into the easy chair.

Maria put her hands on her hips and stood before him. "You actually thought I was going to go along with your stupid little plan of moving into some stupid little apartment? What kind of idiot do you think I am? But that's been the problem all along, hasn't it? Good little Maria, always going along with whatever Seth Jacobs plans. Well not any longer. I'm getting off this train before it runs off the track and crashes."

Seth stared at this woman that was his wife, not recognizing her. *What happened to the sweet, loving woman I married? When had she become so unhappy, so bitter, so hateful? What have I done to turn her against me and make her despise me so?*

After a few moments, he managed to choke out one word past the bewilderment, anger and sorrow that entangled him. "Why?"

Maria let out a shrill little laugh and flung out her arms. "Why what? Why did I have sex with the gardener? Why did I waste all these years with you? Why do I continue to waste one minute more? Why is your supposed 'God' so mean and nasty that he takes away my three children?"

Seth gasped at this last statement, his skin going white, starkly contrasting against the dark burgundy upholstery of the chair in which he sat. He gripped the chair arms with his hands as if to steady the room which spun around him.

His wife's face contorted in a mask of anger and loathing. Seth wasn't sure if it was completely directed at him, or that perhaps a little bit was aimed within. Maria fought back tears as she shouted, barely keeping her hysteria at bay. "Why am I still married to this pitiful man with nothing? Why am I left with nothing after all the years I sacrificed? Why am I completely humiliated to the point that I have no friends? That every person who sees me feels sorry for me? That I'm the laughingstock of Boston...no, make that the whole United States of America? Why am I a victim here when none of this is my fault?"

She picked up the book she had been peacefully reading just a few minutes earlier and flung it across the room, where it hit the wall with a loud crack. "I don't know why, but I do know that I'm sick and tired of being the innocent victim and I refuse to be one any longer. If you would stop playing holier than thou and say forget God, maybe I'd have a little more respect for you. But I'm not letting you drag me down with all of your humble 'just have faith' crap any longer. It's gotten me absolutely nowhere and I can't stay in this pit of a marriage, this poor excuse of a life with you one minute more. I'm getting out of here."

"But what about us?" Seth stood and nearly doubled over from the pain that clutched his insides and fought the urge to cry out, not wanting to show any signs of weakness. "We still have each other. We can get through this. We've been blessed with so much, had so much for so long, that it's not right to give up now when things aren't going our way. I know we're going through some really tough times, but I'm sure God will see us through this. You're just not thinking clearly right now. I can forgive you for what you've done if you can forgive me for not paying attention to your needs."

Maria's features softened a bit, her voice lowered with a hint of sadness. "It's too late for forgiveness, Seth. What's done is done. It's over."

And with that, Maria Jacobs turned and left the room. The sun was just setting outside the long bay windows and cast an orange glow on Seth as he sat alone in his chair, staring at the oncoming night.

Seth didn't hear the taxi cab pull up early the next morning, didn't hear Maria walk out the door and load her suitcases into it, didn't hear it drive off down the long, winding entrance.

He was finally sleeping after hours of tormented, failed attempts to do so.

The sound of the doorbell woke him, vaguely cutting through the fog of slumber that shrouded him. And even though he hadn't heard her leave, he knew deep down inside his wife was gone and wouldn't be coming back.

Seth sat up in bed and listened for the doorbell again, but it didn't ring. *Maybe I'm hearing things,* he thought, contemplating lying back down again and giving in to the blessed relief of sleep. *No, I'm sure I heard it.*

He ambled down the staircase into the foyer and opened the door. The sun was high in the sky and nearly blinded him when he opened the door. He looked both ways to see if anyone was on his property, and saw a FedEx truck pulling out of the drive onto the access road. *Thank God no one saw me.* Seth realized he would probably scare someone who chanced to see him right now. *I probably look like Lazarus risen from the dead or something.* He hadn't showered, shaved or combed his hair in two days, and was still dressed in the grungy gray sweat suit he had worn the day before.

After his eyesight adjusted to the bright sun, he noticed an envelope at his feet, stooped over to retrieve it, and went back inside to open it. He stopped for a few moments in the dark foyer blinking to regain focus again and looked around. The vast size of the house made him keenly feel the impact of his solitude. *It's still home*, he reminded himself. *Just not for long.*

He opened the envelope and pulled out a single sheet of paper. It was an eviction notice that said he had twenty-four hours from noon that day to leave the premises or he would be removed by police authorities.

Suddenly, Seth's stomach cramped with nausea and he felt a sickening bile rise from his throat into his mouth. He ran to the powder room off the front hall and got there just in time to throw up the remains of his last meal into the toilet. *When and what was that last meal?* Seth wondered with a strange sense of surreal detachment. Then he noticed a spot of red in the brown mass of his insides. *Odd. It looks like blood.*

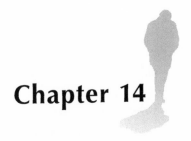

Chapter 14

Seth lay in bed and slept, for how long he wasn't sure. He didn't have the strength to open the shutters to look outside, or he would have seen it was dark out. When he tried to prop himself up to look at the alarm clock on the nightstand, a sudden wave of nausea washed over him again.

Maybe I'm dying, he thought, easing his head back down on the pillow. *No, that would be too easy.* He looked over at the empty space where his wife used to lie. *Maybe I'm just sick to death of how my life is turning out; sick with loneliness now that Maria is gone.*

Sleep overtook him again and this time, instead of a light, fitful sleep, Seth was unconscious. He woke suddenly, sitting up in a panic, drenched in sweat, his heart racing. He had dreamed his wife had left him and someone was tearing down his house.

Sun streamed in tiny bands through the slits of the blinds and he heard a pounding sound. *Or is it the blood pounding in my head?* He sat there and wondered, then heard the pounding again, this time louder. And the awful imagining that his dream might be coming true brought fresh bile to his throat. He stumbled to the master bathroom and vomited again.

When the dry heaves finally subsided, Seth wiped his mouth on his sleeve and stood up, feeling shaky but relieved.

At least the nausea is out of my system and I can focus on something else besides throwing up, he thought, steadying himself with his hand along the wall as he walked back to his bedroom. He heard the pounding once more, and realized it was coming from the foyer. Someone was knocking at the door. Seth remembered he was being evicted.

He stumbled down the steps and flung open the door.

A Sheriff's deputy, armed with a nightstick and holster, stood at the front entrance and was clearly taken by surprise when Seth appeared. "Mister Jacobs?"

Seth looked down at his dirty gray sweat pants, the same he'd apparently worn for three days now. He was barefoot, still un-showered and unshaven and smelled bad, even to himself. *No wonder he's looking at me like that.*

"Yes, I'm Seth Jacobs."

"I'm here to make sure this house is vacated by noon and it is now eleven forty-five. Are you aware that you are being evicted and if you are not out of this house in fifteen minutes, I will have to remove you by force and you will be arrested for obstructing justice and violating a court order?"

Seth's face suddenly turned white, not because of the deputy's words, but what he saw over the deputy's shoulder. It was a photographer with a huge zoom lens on his camera pointed straight at him. The photographer and another man dressed in a suit, probably a reporter, had positioned themselves at the bottom of the sloping front lawn, waiting for Seth to open the door.

Seth felt the same, uncontrollable, queasy faintness flood through him that he'd been feeling for the past couple of days. Standing there, faced with the officer and reporters and a sun that overwhelmed him with its brightness because he'd been in darkness for so long, he felt lightheaded. He didn't even remember that he hadn't had anything to eat or drink for the past forty hours. "I...I think I need to see a doctor." Seth exhaled the words before crumpling in pain and exhaustion to the foyer floor.

Minutes later he was being rushed by ambulance to Massachusetts General Hospital.

En route, he had enough presence of mind, despite the nausea that threatened to consume him, to ask one of the paramedics in the ambulance to phone ahead and ask that Doctor Benjamin Grason meet him in the ER.

Seth was relieved to see Ben's friendly face looking down on him as he was brought in on a stretcher. Ben walked with the gurney as the paramedics quickly rolled it into the ER, keeping his hand on Seth's shoulder while hurling questions right and left at the emergency personnel.

It was the last thing he remembered before passing out again.

Seth came to in a hospital bed in his own private room at Mass General. He briefly wondered how he was going to afford all of this when Doctor Grason came in to see him.

Now that the nurses and interns had regulated his fluids and his vital signs were stable, Seth felt better, although still weak. He sat up in the hospital bed, watching his gross, sickly image appear across the television monitor that was perched in a corner of the room. Behind the still photo, caught by that photographer that had been waiting for him to answer the door, there was footage of the ambulance whisking him away. He pushed the button on the nearby remote, turning up the volume despite his misgivings.

"...speculating that the former restaurant baron is suffering from food poisoning, the very same illness that caused the death of Presidential hopeful, U.S. Senator Robert Caine, who along with hundreds of others, was poisoned by tainted caviar at Boston's Perfect Place restaurant. The Senator's family recently settled a multi-million dollar lawsuit against Seth Jacobs, who has since filed for bankruptcy. This is Rebecca Williams. Back to you Chad."

That reporter must be building her career off me, Seth ruminated, punchy from the painkillers that were shooting through his veins.

The camera went from the reporter back to the anchor desk, where a young man with perfect hair and teeth adlibbed, "Well, you know what they say. What goes around, comes around."

They're actually making fun of me, Seth thought, his high from the drugs waning. *They just don't know when to quit. I can't believe these people get such a kick from another human being's pain.*

He clicked off the television just as Benjamin Grason walked into his room, chart in hand.

"Well, you look much better than you did when they brought you in here. How do you feel?" The doctor shook Seth's free hand and smiled.

"Better. I couldn't look or feel much worse than yesterday. So what did I have, a stomach bug or something? Please don't tell me I had food poisoning."

Ben pulled up a chair and sat down by Seth's bed, cupping his face in his hands for a moment, then clearing his throat.

"Seth, I know the last thing you want or need is more bad news, but I've always told you I'd be straight with you. I'm really sorry, but the X-rays, preliminary tests and symptoms all seem to be pointing to one thing. We hope we're wrong, and we're going to do a lot more tests and probably exploratory surgery to make sure, but it appears that you may have stomach cancer."

Seth turned his face away from his friend so he wouldn't

see the tears that sprung to his eyes.

"We detected a tumor the size of a medium-sized orange in your stomach, so we need to do surgery right away to remove it. We'll find out at that point whether or not it is malignant, but the fact that it is causing the symptoms you've been suffering isn't a good sign. Have you noticed anything else besides nausea, weight loss, lack of hunger or fatigue lately?"

Seth tried to focus on the past few days, willing himself not to think about Maria's betrayal or her leaving him. "I noticed a spot of blood when I threw up yesterday...or was it the day before? I've kind of lost track of time."

"That may be due to a tear in your stomach lining from the tumor. There is a chance that the tumor is benign. I need you to stay positive and hopeful, Seth. And I will too." Seth noticed tears in Ben's eyes and was grateful and glad his doctor was his friend.

"Well, Doc, I'm glad I have friends in high places." Seth managed a weak smile, his hand still holding onto the doctor's. "They always said it pays to know the right people."

"By the way, Seth, where is Maria? I need her to sign some papers before you go into surgery."

The smile vanished from Seth's face and tears again filled his eyes. "Maria left me, Ben. Right before I got sick. I thought my feeling so tired and sick might be a reaction to her leaving. God, I don't even have anyone to sign my papers." His lower lip trembled and the tears spilled down his face. *How pathetic my life has become,* Seth thought, and tried hard not to break down. *I really am all alone.*

Ben was quick to try to help Seth regain his composure, knowing his patient would need all his strength and hope to pull through the surgery he was about to undergo. "Alright, Seth, don't go feeling all sorry for yourself. You've still got two sons and a daughter that need you. You've got to stay strong.

Think of them. They're going to need their father to pull through for them."

Only they're not here either. Seth couldn't help feeling sorry for himself. *But they are still alive, and right now they're all I've got...and maybe I'm all they've got.* He prayed for God to replace his self-pity with acceptance and hope.

"Okay, Doc, I'm ready."

Doctor Grason pulled out his clipboard and a pen and put it in front of Seth. "If you sign your consent, I'll do the rest."

Seth woke groggily to the smell of antiseptic, the sounds of someone snoring and the vague glare of white light above him.

Where am I? he wondered, then realized he was lying in a hospital bed. As he regained the full strength of his senses, he felt a sharp pain in his abdomen, then a slight nausea creep over him. *Oh great, they haven't done the surgery yet,* he thought.

But then he gently lifted up the bed covers, moved aside the hospital gown and noticed huge gauze bandages crisscrossing his midsection.

He looked up and saw the person snoring was Rabbi Jonathan Mosha, whose stout form was crumpled into a plastic-covered chair in the corner of his room.

Wow. How nice that old Rabbi Mosha could be here for me, Seth thought. Then, in a rapid series of flashbacks, Seth remembered Maria leaving, Angelica leaving, Aaron and Adam gone. No family. Just the Rabbi from the synagogue where he worshipped here by his side. *Well, at least someone's here.*

Doctor Grason entered his room just then, as if he had read Seth's thoughts. *Make that two people who care about me.*

Ben's entrance startled Rabbi Jon awake. The older man sat up straight and, after refocusing his rheumatic blue-gray eyes, stood and took Seth's hand in his own.

Seth introduced the two men. The Rabbi, an old friend of the Jacobs family who had officiated at his bris as a baby, his Bar Mitzvah as a teen and had concelebrated his wedding, hadn't changed much in Seth's forty-nine years on earth. He looked a little heavier and a lot older, his hair had receded and his beard had grown longer, both becoming white with age, and his skin had wrinkled with time. But he still was quite agile at, Seth guessed, an age that must now be in the eighties.

"Jon." In his adult years, Seth referred to him by his first name as the two had become friends. His voice came out as a groggy whisper, the anesthesia just beginning to wear off from the surgery. "Thank you for coming. How did you know…?"

"What, are you kidding me? You are still a celebrity in this country. Everyone knows what you're up to already. You have always managed to appear, how do they say? On the radar screen." Seth winced as he smiled, trying not to laugh and cause a major disruption down below.

Ben Grason cleared his throat impatiently and the Rabbi resumed his seat. The doctor sat at the edge of the hospital bed to deliver his news. He looked from the rabbi to his patient, silently questioning if it was okay to proceed. Seth nodded.

"How do you feel?" Ben's kind brown eyes were sympathetic under his gray eyebrows, which were knitted together in concern.

"Like a sledgehammer just hit me in the stomach. Other than that, just fine."

"Okay, wise guy, tell me how you really feel."

Seth took a deep breath and halfway through inhaling, groaned in pain. "A little sensitive where you cut me open."

"Seth, why didn't you come see me sooner?"

"This all just came on in the past week. Plus, I'm sure you've read the headlines, Ben. It hasn't been exactly…well…

boring around my house lately. Not to mention I'm flat broke and can't afford your rates." Seth exhaled slowly, carefully, and forced a smile.

"Come on Seth, we're old friends. You know we can work around that. I have been seeing you on the news. Things are pretty bad, huh?"

"If you consider losing your business, your kids, your wife, your house and your health bad, yeah, I'd say they're pretty bad."

"No need to get testy with me. I'm here to help."

"I'm sorry, Ben."

"Me too, Seth." The doctor suddenly looked weary, and he covered his patient's hand with his own.

"So what's the news, Doc? Do I have cancer?"

"I'm afraid so, Seth."

"Well, did you get it all out?"

"Only time will tell. We did remove the tumor, but since the cancer ate away at your stomach, we had to remove part of it. That means we had to insert an apparatus for a feeding tube. "

Seth clamped his jaws together, his eyes sparking with anger. "God, when does it end?" His cry was no more than a whisper but was filled with the grief and rage of months of pent-up emotions that, if he had let them out full force, might have split him in two.

Rabbi Jon got up out of his chair and came over to the bed to comfort him.

"How long…?" The words escaped out of the elderly man's mouth as he gazed up at the doctor, echoing Seth's own unasked question.

"We don't like to give people amounts of time they have left anymore because we're usually wrong." Ben stroked his goatee with his hand, hedging his words.

Seth's eyes suddenly had a feverish gleam in them. "Ben, I want to know how long I have to live."

"It's hard to say. Stomach cancer is probably one of the fastest spreading, most vicious kinds of cancer. We can try to slow it down with radiation and chemotherapy and stop it from spreading to other parts of your body. Of course, there's no cure, but we can always hope for remission. So my best guess is that it could be anywhere from a few months to several years."

Seth pulled away from both friends and curled up as best he could on his side and refused to look at either of them.

"Seth, my boy, it's not good to be alone with this." The Rabbi touched Seth gently on the shoulder, trying to get his attention.

"I'm sorry, Jon, but I need to be alone right now." Seth curled up tighter, trying to shut everyone out and isolate in his misery.

"The Rabbi is right, Seth. You don't want to withdraw at a time like this." Ben tried to help, but Seth turned around angrily, the feverish gleam still in his eyes.

"Well thank you both for being here, but you just tell me who else I've got to turn to. It isn't my children and it isn't my wife. And it sure doesn't seem to be God lately."

The Rabbi and doctor exchanged worried glances. "Okay, Seth, we'll leave you alone for a little while, but we'll be back." Jon reached out his hand, but when Seth didn't take it, he put it in his pants pocket, shifted uncomfortably from foot to foot, and cleared his throat. "Alright, already, I'll be going. You'll call me if you need anything?" His question unanswered, he quietly left the room.

"Just leave me alone." Seth mumbled to Ben, turning away from him again.

"I'll prescribe a sedative and some painkillers which should help you get some rest. I'll be back in the morning to check on you."

Ben was almost out the door when he stopped to hear the one word that faintly came from the hospital bed in a scraggly whisper choked with tears.

"Thanks."

After several weeks of hospital rest, liquid nourishment and physical therapy during which he slowly regained most of his strength, Seth was ready to be discharged so he could begin a scheduled treatment plan Ben had drawn up involving radiation, chemotherapy, tests and checkups.

But even though Seth had physically begun to feel better, his mental and emotional states had sunk to all-time lows. He knew he was about to undergo pain and sickness like he had never felt before, having had Ben warn him of all the gory details of radiation and chemotherapy. And his anxiety over that was surpassed by a deep depression that he would undergo it alone, with no home to go to and no one to love him and support him through it all.

Adding to his despair was the reality that he, a man who had been in his prime and was not even fifty years old yet, would be leaving the hospital to stay at a nursing home.

The arrangements had all been made by Michael Powers, who was now Seth's power of attorney. Michael told Seth he would be able to stay in the nursing home for as long as he could afford it and that it would be the best possible solution since it was close to the hospital and would provide transportation for Seth to come in for his radiation and chemotherapy treatments, as well as all his medical needs, at a reasonable cost.

Michael had calculated from the small amount still left of his client's assets that it would only be for about two months. After that, he told Seth he would confer with Doctor Grason and figure out what to do based on the progress of his health and the legal proceedings of his business.

The young attorney agreed to keep Seth on as a pro bono client until he could get back on his feet, both literally and financially. After all, the law firm of Rogers and Powers had made a great deal of money handling the Jacobs' family matters over the years, especially lately with Aaron Jacob's murder trial and Seth's civil litigation.

And now, added to the pile was a contentious divorce just filed by Maria Jacobs.

When the two months contracted at the nursing home were about to expire and Seth's funds were all but gone, Michael took a break from his myriad legal duties and called to see Doctor Grason.

He asked to meet him one day at the hospital when the doctor was scheduled to see Seth following his chemotherapy treatment.

Michael needed to see Seth too. Unfortunately, he had to deal with the unpleasant task of delivering the divorce papers.

The two talked in the hallway outside the chemotherapy room, where a nurse was just finishing injecting the toxic mix of chemicals that would hopefully kill the cancer cells in Seth's abdomen. Unfortunately, they and the radiation rays had killed a lot of other cells too, and Seth looked like he had aged by twenty years in just the past two months.

Seth lay back in the chemo chair with his eyes closed, trying to clear his mind of the self pity that had gathered there like a storm cloud of late. His back to them, Seth didn't see the two men talking but could tell it was his attorney and his doctor. *They must think I'm asleep,* he surmised. He kept his eyes closed and strained to listen to what they were saying.

"...just as well he not know about the notice from Maria's attorney," he heard Ben say.

"Okay, but you've got to tell him soon," he heard Michael respond.

The two talked back and forth in the distance and Seth focused harder on what they were saying.

"How is he?" Michael asked.

"Not too great. We removed the tumor but couldn't get all of the cancer, which has spread from his stomach into his esophagus and other parts of his body. The poor guy's been really sick. He can't keep anything down, he's losing weight, and he's really weak. He's in a lot of pain and I'm afraid he's getting really depressed. We can't add to that right now."

"Well I need to talk to you both about something else too, Doc. I'm afraid it's more bad news, but this can't wait."

"Shoot."

"The nursing home is going to have to release him soon. The Jacobs' well has finally run dry. But I'm afraid our friend here has nowhere to go. There's no way he can afford to continue to live at the home, much less in an apartment or motel room even. As you know his kids are all gone and he has no one else to turn to. I'm at a loss here and wondered if you, as his doctor, would have any suggestions."

Ben Grason stroked his goatee thoughtfully. "The only other person who has come in to see him at the hospital besides you is his Rabbi, Jonathan Mosha, but he's in his seventies or eighties and couldn't possibly take care of someone else. I've got three kids myself so my house is packed, not to mention my wife and I both work and aren't home during the day." He frowned, and then his brow un-furrowed and he gazed at Michael with a look of hope in his eyes. "There's only one other person I can think of whom he could possibly turn to."

"Who?"

"You."

"Whoa. Wait a minute." Michael protested loud enough for Seth to hear very clearly. "I can't possibly keep a bedridden invalid in my apartment. I'm single, got a girlfriend, et cetera, et cetera."

"I know you work a lot of hours, and I'm sure we could get a visiting nurse to stop in each day. You're the only one… the only other thing I can think of is a homeless shelter, but I'm afraid he wouldn't make it very long…"

They're talking about me like I'm halfway in the grave, Seth thought. *My life has been reduced to this. Maybe I'd be better off dead.* And a tear trickled down his face.

Chapter 15

It was finally arranged that Seth would be moved in temporarily to live with Michael Powers in his townhouse, where he would be tended to by a visiting nurse.

Ben Grason would be on call at the hospital and Jonathan Mosha agreed to visit him as often as possible.

The day before Seth was to leave the nursing home, all three of his friends came to help him prepare for his move.

Seth had spent the morning in his room, dwelling on the past sixty days he had spent at Bayside Senior Care.

Why they called this place Bayside was beyond him. It was a brown brick building wedged between two brick and cement office buildings three city blocks from the behemoth Mass General. No bay or water at all in site. Perhaps it was a chain of nursing homes in which at least one was near a bay somewhere.

Why do I even care, Seth wondered. *At least I'm getting the hell out of here. Or getting out of the hell that is here.*

He rose from sitting on his bed to look into the mirror above the sink that, together with the tiny shower and toilet, served as his bathroom. Other than the bed, a desk and nightstand served as furniture except for a little table around which three wooden chairs sat. Seth hadn't decorated his room with knick knacks like some of his neighbors. Nor had he received any flowers or cards. So he spent each day between these bare four walls, breathing in the same air that smelled constantly of staleness and sickness with a hint of urine. Smelled like old people.

Like I have become, Seth thought dismally. *They say you feel young when you are surrounded by young people. I used to feel that way around my kids. Well the converse must be true then.* Seth felt like a hundred and fifty.

He looked at his reflection in the mirror. *And I look like it too.*

A scary, skeletal man stared back at him with red-rimmed eyes sunken into hollows of gray. He had lost about fifteen pounds, all of his hair, and his skin, dry and brittle, was the color of oatmeal. *This isn't a living man standing here,* Seth realized. *It's the look of a man who is dying, one day at a time.* It dawned on him that he looked like one of the Holocaust Jews at Dachau, awaiting his death in the gas chamber, slowly dying along the way.

He couldn't bring himself to watch TV for fear he would see his sick face, or that of his imprisoned son, or perhaps a beautiful woman who would just remind him of his treacherous wife who was now divorcing him. He tried to read but couldn't concentrate on the words, which just blurred and jumbled on the pages.

And so each day stretched endlessly, the stillness only broken by the occasional cackling or howling cries of a resident who had lost his way, or teeth, or bowels, or mind.

He looked at the calendar that hung nearby on the wall. He had crossed off each day after it mercilessly droned by. Today was Saturday, September twenty-ninth. *Why does that ring a bell?* he wondered. And then it hit him. It was exactly a year ago today that he had taken the T to the Perfect Place and it had derailed en route, starting a chain of catastrophic events that would bring an end to life as he knew it and leave him with nothing except a vile illness that promised to slowly torture and probably kill him.

A year filled with tragedies too large and numerous to comprehend.

His body, mind and spirit had all been crushed under the horrific weight of those tragedies.

My life has become reduced to this: being dependent on uncaring nursing home attendants, eating crap for food and feeling like I have to vomit all the time, having absolutely nothing to do, no one to love, nothing to call my own, nothing to look forward to day after day except deteriorating.

How sad is that.

Why live? Seth thought to himself dismally. *Only to die from this cancer that's eating me up from the inside out.*

And now his burden of a life would be passed along to someone else. He almost couldn't bear the thought of that.

A knock on the door to his room broke his reverie.

It was a staff member informing him it was time for lunch, and he had visitors in the lobby asking to see him.

Lunch. Probably canned peas, and some tasteless, unknown piece of processed meat, and instant potatoes, instant pudding, instant coffee. And Seth started to laugh to himself, a small, bitter, soundless laugh that made him hurt inside. *How ironic. Me the most renowned chef of the world, who could whip up a sinfully rich chocolate soufflé or a silky lobster bisque using only the freshest ingredients. To die for, not from, like this bland fare that they call food.* If he had a choice, he would have skipped mealtimes, preferring not to waste the little energy he had forcing down something that would most likely come back up anyway, but the staff came for him and made him go.

And to top it all off, he had visitors.

This is what insanity must be, Seth thought, and laughed aloud.

The orderly frowned at him and reminded him of the visitors.

"By all means, send them up," Seth said, forcing a modicum of civility.

Despite the poison that coursed through his veins and the pain that robbed him of what little energy he could muster each day, Seth did have occasional moments of clarity, which he would usually wish away, preferring to dwell in his depression or try to sleep, anything to escape from the nightmarish reality his life had become.

The clarity this day now brought with it bitterness, which made him feel alert and hyper, as if he had just downed a few cups of espresso.

When the three men arrived, he choked down the anger for a moment and politely welcomed them into his room. He couldn't tell if they noticed the hint of sarcasm in his tone. He motioned for them to sit in the three spindly chairs around the table, which they settled into, looking awkward and uncomfortable. Seth sat on his bed facing them, a wicked smile plastered on his face. Only the delirious gleam in his eyes somewhat betrayed his true feelings.

Lucky for them I don't have a baseball bat in my hands. He savored the thought and almost laughed aloud again, holding himself in check. *I'd smash each one of their smug, smiling, self-righteous faces and wipe that look of pity off.*

"Good morning, Seth, how are you feeling?" Ben checked the chart he brought with him from the hospital, mercifully not looking up to see the look in his patient's eyes.

"Not good, Doctor." Seth forced his words past teeth clenched in a bitter rage he was unable to hold back any longer and spit them toward the three men seated – the doctor in his white lab coat, the lawyer in his pinstriped suit and the Rabbi in his tallit, or prayer shawl and yarmulke.

Ben stood and pulled a vial out of his lab coat pocket, explained he had something that would ease Seth's pain a bit, filled a glass with water from the bathroom sink in Seth's room, and approached him with two pills in hand.

But Seth stood and knocked the pills out of Ben's hands, his glare stopping the doctor from picking them back up. Ben set the glass of water back down on the table, and slowly sat back in his chair.

"No. I want to make sure I'm clear when I talk to all of you." Seth's words came out in an icy monotone as he stood in a defensive stance, his arms crossed on his chest, before them. Jon and Michael looked at Seth with worried expressions in their eyes.

Seth's appearance wasn't a surprise to the doctor, who had been seeing his patient along the way as he gradually changed, but Jon and Michael were both shocked to see how thin, frail and sallow Seth had become over just the past several weeks he had been here. His face that just weeks before had been tan, healthy and handsome, now looked gaunt, gray and old. And of course, the baldness only added to the aging effect.

Seth realized they were trying to hide their looks of disgust and pity but he saw them all the same, and their attempts made him even angrier.

"I want you to know that I'm not on board with this plan of yours to move me into Michael's house where I can lie and rot. I know I can't stay here either, and I know I've got nowhere else to go and no one else to take care of me. So I propose that we just get this whole mess over with. Ben, I'm sure you can prescribe something I could take to um…well, to end my misery."

"Seth!" His three friends shouted out his name simultaneously.

"No, I mean it. What's the point in going on living? It's

not like I have anyone who really cares or any place to go. I heard you talking, and I know I can't stay here and I'll be a burden on Michael."

Michael shifted uncomfortably in his chair, lowering his eyes to look at the thinly-carpeted floor.

"No, Michael, that's okay, I can't blame you for feeling the way you do. I wouldn't want to take care of somebody like me either. I've done a lot of thinking lying in the hospital bed, then here in this nursing home, in between throwing up and sleeping. I realize I've lost everything. My entire family… my parents, children and wife…are gone. My livelihood is finished. My health has deteriorated. My reason for being, my purpose has vanished. What do I have to look forward to? Agony, misery, pain, uselessness, depression? Death? Since I'm dying, why not end it now instead of prolonging the inevitable? I wish God would just strike me dead right now."

The three men listening intently all raised their eyes to the ceiling for a moment, as if expecting a bolt of lightning to hit them. When that didn't happen they looked back at Seth, who took a deep breath and continued to vent as vehemently as he possibly could given his evaporating strength.

"I don't see why I was born in the first place, come to think of it, only to end up like this, with nothing. It took a long time for my mother to get pregnant with me. She took a great risk bearing me, and she never came out and said it, but I think it damaged her health, put a strain on her heart, so she died earlier than she should have. I probably caused the death of my own mother. I wish I had never been born."

Seth sat back down on his bed, his strength now gone, and covered his face with his hands and began to sob. The three men watched, helpless.

After several long minutes, the rabbi spoke.

"Gentlemen, could I have a few words in private with Seth? We have a little while before he has to go, right? I think I might be able to help."

Without a word, the doctor and lawyer nodded and left the room.

Jon took a deep breath and moved his chair closer to Seth's bed.

"Seth, can I talk to you?" Jon gingerly laid a hand on Seth's shoulder, which had stopped shaking.

When Seth didn't answer, his face still covered by his hands, the rabbi took no answer as an affirmative one.

"I'm sorry you're feeling so badly, Seth. I can see that you're very sick, physically and emotionally. From hearing you speak, I can also see that you are spiritually sick as well. And who can blame you with all you've been through? But suicide is not an option, Seth. Self-pity won't get you anywhere either." Jonathan Mosha reached out his thick, weathered hand again to comfort his friend. Seth sat up and looked at Jon with a vague, confused stare, as if he wasn't hearing him.

The rabbi continued. "I know you have helped many people in your life, Seth. You've employed them, turned some of their lives around by helping them make an honest living. You raised three children and were a source of strength to your friends and your family. You helped a lot of people overcome a lot of problems." The Rabbi smoothed his beard and the deep crags of his face with his thumb and fingers in thought, then toyed with the tzitzit, or long, knotted pieces of fringe that hung from his prayer shawl, in concentration before continuing his monologue.

"Now when you are having problems, it's as if you can't deal with it. You can't even fathom that you should have any problems at all. But I tell you, Seth, no man leads a perfect life. Challenges are put before us all."

Rabbi Mosha stood and started pacing back and forth at the foot of the bed.

"I had a dream last night, Seth. A nightmare it was. I woke up from it trembling in a cold sweat, my heart racing. A ghost came to me, a dead, decaying man with hollowed sockets where there should have been eyes. Maggots were crawling on him and his flesh was falling off his bones. He told me he had seen God, and that no men, not even the priests nor prophets, are ever pure in the brilliant light that shines from God. He warned me to tell you that you will die, just like the rest of us, and your body will rot away like those of all men, but your soul, like everyone else's, will wander the earth until each and every sin you committed is atoned for."

Jonathan didn't notice when Seth rolled his eyes. Once he was done recanting his dream, the rabbi stopped pacing and stood at the foot of Seth's bed. He delivered the rest of his speech addressing Seth as though he were part of the masses in the synagogue, speaking loudly and waving his hands.

"You need to be reminded that no man is perfect. Only God is perfect. Have you not heard of divine justice? I believe in divine justice, Seth. I believe, as those of our faith believe, that if a man is good and does good, he will receive good things from God. So it only makes sense that if a man sins, bad things will befall him. We are all sinners, Seth. Somewhere in your past, you must have sinned enough to bring on God's wrath. Perhaps because you didn't marry a Jewish woman, but instead a woman who didn't believe in the power of God and defiled you and God with her adultery; perhaps because you chose not to follow the faith you were taught in your Jewish upbringing and religion and did not raise your children as Orthodox Jews to the full extent of that faith; perhaps because you did not pray enough or in the right way, or did not attend temple services enough, or did not make enough amends or were not devout enough. It's not easy being a Jew, being a member of the chosen people.

"But as you should know, in our religion you can admit your faults and atone for your sins at any time with your Maker. Your life has been spared so far, Seth. I think that's what the ghost was trying to tell me in my dream. God has given you time to repent. I believe God is forgiving so there is hope for you. Yes, you are sick, but God can do anything and I believe He can make you well again. I believe He can make you whole again somehow. I love you like a son and it pains me to see you like this, hating yourself and hating God. Since I am your rabbi and friend, you can talk to me if you like, Seth. Perhaps I can read from the Torah and together we can pray and ask God for mercy on your soul."

A few silent minutes passed when all that filled the musky, sterile room was the loud ticking of the black and white clock on the gray wall.

Finally, Seth stood to face the rabbi. "Jonathan, don't you think I've wracked my brain asking myself what I did to deserve all of this?" He let out a long sigh of despair. "I truly cannot think of anything I've done to bring down God's wrath on me this way."

Jonathan's face was full of pity and he shook his head back and forth. He started to respond but didn't get a word out before Seth interrupted, gesticulating to get his point across.

"If you had suffered all that I have, lost your entire family, your job, your home, your health, your future and your reason for living, you wouldn't say the things you do about atonement and hope. You'd want to die too. You say you're my friend and yet all you do is lecture me about the sins I must have committed. I say, prove it!" With this last statement, Seth poked his finger right into the rabbi's old, robe-clad chest.

The rabbi sat back in his chair, as if Seth's finger and forceful words had pushed him backward. His gray, bushy eyebrows were raised in astonishment, and he opened his mouth to protest, but Seth ranted on.

"The sins I've committed are between God and me and I don't need your help to repent, Jonathan. I know I'm not perfect, but I will tell you that I have always strived to be the best man I could be, to be giving and loving and kind, to serve others. When I was wrong, I admitted it and made up for it whenever I could. I've done the best I can and if God wants to smite me for that, I don't want to live anymore. Abraham asked that his son be spared and Moses asked that his people be spared. I know enough from reading the Bible of my wife and her family to know that even Jesus asked that his cup of anguish be spared. Why can't God spare me and just strike me dead right here, right now?"

A sharp pain in his abdomen caused Seth to spasmodically curl forward and clench his face in agony. After a minute the pain subsided and Seth sat back on his bed, sweat trickling from his forehead.

Jonathan didn't say a word, but the message that emanated from his face and body language was unmistakably one of "I told you so."

Seth saw it and his anger rose again. "If you were truly my friend, Jon, then instead of trying to scare me with ghost stories, you'd talk to the doctor out there and come up with a way to let me die in peace and with some dignity." He received no answer from the rabbi, who still looked stunned by Seth's tirade, so he continued. "I don't know why you look so shocked at that. Why not put me out of my misery? It's not like I haven't already suffered enough. But you're not my friend, Jon, none of you are. I give up. Just send them in and do what you obviously think must be done."

The rabbi painstakingly rose up out of his chair, looking up to the ceiling again as if he was afraid lightning may hit them both, and walked out of the room.

Two minutes later he returned with Ben and Michael and one of the nurses on duty, who pushed a wheelchair to the bedside. Suddenly the room was filled with chatter and activity, as they all helped Seth from the bed into the wheelchair. Ben and the nurse gave Michael last-minute directions for the patient's care and a myriad of prescriptions to be filled while Jonathan carried out the nurse's request to gather Seth's belongings.

Resigned to his fate for the moment, Seth remained quiet throughout the hectic proceedings, his thin body like that of a rag doll, so that he was easy enough to maneuver. He had dutifully acquiesced to taking the pain pills Ben had offered earlier, which made him feel listless.

Why fight them? He limply let them put a hat on his head and a blanket around him. The late September air had taken on a chill, they said. *They're all a bunch of fools anyway, thinking that I'm worth all of this,* Seth thought, mutely watching them. *They could have saved themselves a lot of grief if they would have just ended it here and took care of my affairs by phone. So I'll just let them go through all of this fuss, since it will obviously make them feel better about themselves.*

Minutes later Seth was in the back of Michael's BMW, comfortably stretched across the plush leather seat, headed for the townhouse that would be his new home.

Michele Chynoweth

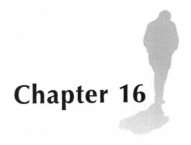

Chapter 16

The shiny BMW pulled up to the three-story brownstone where Michael resided.

It was in the middle of a tree-lined street just off the Commons in a high-rent part of Boston, inhabited by upscale yuppies and some wealthy holdout families who didn't want to give up their love of city life to move to the suburbs.

The late fall sun blazed golden on a group of children playing hopscotch after school. Restless and bored of their game, the dozen or so neighborhood kids welcomed the sight of the car as it pulled up and watched with fascination as a wheelchair and suitcase were lifted out of the trunk by the driver, and an unfamiliar, ghostlike man slowly exited from the passenger's side.

"Hey, who's that?" One outspoken twelve-year-old boy, apparently the leader of the group, ventured boldly to approach Michael, whom he had seen before.

Michael ignored him, which spurred him to wave the rest of his gang closer to check out the welcome disturbance on their street. The boy got close enough to see Seth's weary face. "It's some old bald dude who looks like he's half dead," the boy shouted to his rapt followers.

"Probably some old drunk who couldn't make it home last night," said a gangly, ten year-old boy, bravely trying to keep pace with his fearless leader.

"Yeah, some old wino," a preteen girl chipped in.

"Ewww, and he stinks!" the first boy added, trying to keep his audience enthralled. He had gotten close enough to catch a whiff of the mild yet disturbing aroma of nursing home mixed with the colostomy bag that now accompanied Seth wherever he went.

"Stinky, bald old wino!"

"Stinky, bald old wino!" the younger children picked up the phrase and gleefully chanted it in chorus.

"Shut up and leave him alone!" Michael Powers bellowed loudly, hushing the group long enough for him to guide Seth up the steps and through the front door of the rowhouse where he lived. The attorney shut the door behind them, but not before hearing a last parting shot from the gang leader. "Crazy Mister Powers and one of his drunk old friends."

Often keeping oddly late hours during heavy caseloads and living the life of a bachelor who worked hard and played hard, Michael wasn't a favorite of the local children, nor a fan. His introverted lifestyle both piqued their curiosity and disdain, which in turn increased his confidence with each passing day that he would never have children.

"I'm sorry, Seth." Blinded by his transition from sunlight into the darkness of his foyer, Michael groped for the light switch. "Those urchins don't know what they're saying."

Michael led his new roommate down the hall into a spacious den that adjoined a small kitchen. It would have to do for a patient room, since there was no way he could lug Seth upstairs where the bedrooms were if the need ever arose.

Exhausted, Seth asked Michael to let him take a nap. Michael happily motioned for his sick friend to lie on the leather couch and covered him gently with a blanket.

Michael turned on the television and sat in a recliner in front of a tray table to finish a dinner of leftovers.

"It's hot in here," Seth complained. Michael had cautiously wrapped his friend in a second blanket as the evening waned.

"Sorry," Michael mumbled in between bites. The young attorney got up and removed the heavier of the two blankets, then propped a pillow behind Seth's back so he could sit up better. "Can I do anything to make you more comfortable? Do you want something to eat or drink?"

"How about a little cyanide?" Seth's sarcastic dart, intended to evoke humor, only drew scorn.

"You know, I do feel bad for you, Seth, but really, talking about killing yourself? Isn't that a bit extreme?"

"I don't know, Michael, don't you think the pit of hell I've fallen into is a bit extreme?"

"Well, the drugs Ben made you take finally must have worn off, huh? You want to talk?" Michael pushed away the tray and remnants of his dinner and sat up to face his friend.

"Yeah, why don't you lecture me some more like Rabbi Jon?"

"Such sarcasm." Michael stood up and started rifling through a stack of mail on the nearby credenza. "Actually, while you're feeling spunky like this, I have some mail for you. But I want to warn you, it's not all good and if you start feeling upset, please let me know and I'll save it for later."

"How kind of you, but my eyes are really tired and my head hurts if I try to focus on anything for too long, so can you just read it to me and get it over with?"

"Sure." Michael sat back down in the recliner and took the tie off from around his neck. He was still dressed in his suit slacks and customary pressed white dress shirt, although he had rolled up the sleeves before eating. He was a handsome attorney that people usually liked or disliked instantly upon meeting him. His intense demeanor could either come off as charming or ingratiating. Women, especially those sitting on juries, often were captivated by his charm, which, when coupled with his dark, wavy hair, big brown eyes and boyish good looks, could prove irresistible.

Seth had liked him from the start because Michael had always been candid with him, although sometimes Michael's frankness could hit him like a blunt-force object to the head.

"Let's start with the bad news." Michael pulled papers from an open manila envelope.

"Hey, you already opened my mail?"

"Actually, it was addressed to you in care of my firm, and I knew it was a legal document, so I figured you wouldn't mind. It's from the law offices of Smiegel & Leatch. I'm really sorry, Seth, but it's a set of divorce papers from Maria." Michael started to hand them to Seth, but he motioned them away.

"That's alright, Michael. I already knew they were coming. I overheard you and Ben talking about it when I was in chemo, pretending to sleep. I figured they'd come one day. Just not this soon. Has she no ounce of compassion? I really don't know the woman she's become. It's like she walked away from everything in her life, her family, even God. Oh well, please just cut to the chase."

Michael looked sternly down at the papers and thumbed through them until he found what he was looking for. "It says here she's claiming marital negligence, emotional abandonment, loss of consortium, et cetera, et cetera. Basically, she's divorcing you on the grounds that you left the marriage first. She also asks for alimony from any future proceeds that may come in from the business, the estate, any savings, et cetera. Of course, we can fight this thing, claim she committed adultery and abandoned you and the kids. You know I can fight with the best of them. Arrange it so you win, you get everything, she gets nothing."

"Since there's nothing to win, I'd just as soon not bother fighting, Michael."

"But Seth, you're the victim here. You should at least claim for the record it's her fault. You never know if, financially, things will turn around. I bet you're just feeling weak right now. You need to work with me here. I'm acting in your best interest you know."

He just doesn't understand. Seth sighed. *I really have no energy left to feel angry or resentful toward her. Just empty.* "Just give it up, Michael. I surrender on this one to God's will."

Michael stared at Seth with incredulity. "You still believe all that's happened to you is God's will?"

Seth felt himself starting to simmer. All he wanted to do was switch the subject. "Look, I'm the client and what I say goes. Let me just sign the papers. You said you have something else for me?"

Michael handed him an unopened, letter-sized envelope. It was addressed to Seth and Maria and it was in Angelica's handwriting and postmarked from Syria.

Angelica! Seth felt a rush of joy for the first time in a very long time. *My baby girl sent me a letter.* His hands trembled with emotion, so Seth asked Michael to read the letter inside.

"Dear Mom and Dad," Michael began, pausing and looking up to make sure Seth was listening. Seth actually sat forward, his hands folded tightly on his lap, straining to hear each word. *"I'm sorry you haven't heard from me before this. It's not that I haven't tried. I have written to you, but I found out my letters weren't being sent out by Caleb's family like I thought."*

Michael sucked in a sharp breath and took a moment to clear his throat, hesitating. "I'm not sure you want to hear the rest."

"Michael, it's a letter from my daughter who I haven't seen in almost four months! Read it!"

Michael continued. *"Things aren't going well. Syria is so much different than I expected…than Caleb made it out to be. Women don't really have much of a say in the part of the country where Caleb's family lives. They say they've made progress, like we don't have to wear the scarf coverings over our heads and faces all the time, just for services in the mosque. But it's still so foreign and backwards. Caleb and his family would never forgive me for saying that out loud though. Caleb has been kind to me, but he's gone a lot helping his father and I have little to do except go to the market, help his mother prepare meals and clean house. We're living with his parents since Caleb doesn't get paid nearly enough for us to get our own place.*

His parents were way more upset than I thought they would be when I started to show and they found out I was pregnant before we got married. In fact, they are still angry with me and treat me like I'm filthy or something. They said since I'm with child there is no way I can study at the university, that I have to prepare for the baby and that my husband and children will be my life now. At first Caleb argued with them but the more they and his aunts, uncles, cousins and friends influence him, the more he is starting to look at me differently, like I tricked him or something and I'm the enemy. And if I even talk about coming back to America, he gets really angry, saying I should feel lucky he married me and his family took me in.

I hate it here. It's hot and dry and I feel sweaty and dirty all the time. I'm going out of my mind with boredom and loneliness. I don't like the food at all, but I'm trying to force it down for the baby, even though I feel sick almost all the time.

And Daddy, Caleb told me he heard you were sick too, with cancer. I'm so sorry. I tell myself that if you can go through all you're going through, then I'll make it too. I just miss you both so much I feel like crying all the time, but the more I cry, the more I think they hate me.

It seems I'm always being watched by my mother-in-law, but the one time I tried to call you, Caleb came home early and found me on the phone. He yelled at me not to try to come back to the U.S. because I was carrying his baby and said we weren't going anywhere, that his baby would be raised a Syrian and a Muslim and there was nothing I could do about it except get used to it. The phone disappeared after that.

I have no money to go anywhere and since I don't know the language, I can't ask for help. Caleb says it's useless anyway, that the U.S. embassy in Syria is closed now because too many Americans were trying to sneak over the border from Iraq and Iran and this country has had enough of America's intrusions.

I don't know what to do except beg for your help. Caleb promised me he'd send this letter, but no more, so please try to find me. I'm so scared, but I'll try to be brave for the baby. I love you and miss you so much it hurts. I pray every night that your grandchild and I will see you soon. Love, Angelica."

Michael finished softly and looked up to find Seth quietly weeping.

"My baby is having a baby and she's all alone and there's nothing I can do." Seth felt his broken heart shattering still further into jagged little pieces. "God, what if she doesn't make it back to me?"

Suddenly, he could feel his pulse quickening, his head thumping, a strange heat rising in his chest cavity and his breaths coming in short, quick gasps. "Michael, I've got to get her out of there. You've got to help me." Seth started coughing, then gagging, gasping for breath.

Michael saw Seth's face turning red and sweating and realized his friend was probably having a panic attack.

"Seth, calm down. Don't talk. Just breathe. That's it, in and out, in and out."

Michael rushed into the kitchen and came back with a

glass of water and two more of the pills Ben had prescribed and handed them to Seth. "Here, take these."

But by the time Michael had returned, Seth had stopped coughing, his breathing had already slowed and he had willed himself to calm down.

"No, I need to think." Seth waved his hand and accidentally hit Michael's, sending the pills scattering onto the floor. "Sorry, I'm calm now. What can we do?"

"I don't know. I'll start making more phone calls and try to find a way to get her a flight out of there somehow. It's a long shot, but between your old contacts and mine maybe I can find someone in the CIA or FBI to help. Don't worry. You just have to get better so you can see her when she gets home."

"Hey, Michael, tell me about Adam and Aaron."

"Seth, I think you've had enough excitement for one day."

"You know Ben said I'm not well enough to visit them now and I know he's keeping tabs on Adam, as you are on Aaron. So please Michael, just tell me the latest."

"Only if you promise not to get upset." Michael settled in his chair again to tell Seth what he knew.

"I promise." Seth willed himself to be peacefully receptive and gave Michael a small smile of agreement, folding his hands on his lap and relaxing his posture.

"Okay. Aaron is doing fine, although honestly, I think people just have it out for him because he's your son. First Judge Henry, and now the warden."

"I thought Warden Johnson was a decent guy."

"I thought so too. Unfortunately, he's showing his true colors. Turns out he doesn't like rich boys either. He's got Aaron doing hard time, working the old chain gang kind of back-breaking jobs outside and it's been really hot. Luckily, being the athlete he is, Aaron will survive. But I don't think he's getting any breaks. Unfortunately, his appeal hearing is coming up and I don't think the warden's going to give him a great report. Not to mention, if we get Henry, we're done. At least he can't increase a life sentence. I'm sorry, Seth, I wish I had better news."

"I'm afraid to ask, but have you heard anything about Adam?"

"Ben told me he's stabilized, still not responding to any stimuli. Adam is a strong young man so there's still a slight chance he can come out of the coma, but…well, a whole year has passed, Seth, and they're just not sure that if he comes out of it he'll even survive. You know your insurance isn't covering all the bills and to be honest, you have no money left. It may be time to, well, think about…"

Seth cut him off. "I am not pulling the plug on my son!" he yelled hoarsely.

"But Seth, he is probably already brain dead."

"I just can't. Not when there's a chance. Besides, you know if I did that might make matters much worse for Aaron. That would mean both of my sons could die."

"It's a possibility, but you can't avoid or control the inevitable."

"I look at it as staying faithful that God will save us. Although I have to admit it's getting harder each day to keep believing God is even paying attention anymore."

Michael sighed. "Then I guess we'll just keep praying for a miracle."

"And here I thought you were an atheist."

Michael shot him a self-deprecating grin. "Agnostic. Big difference. I just was never much for obeying the rules of any one religion. But that doesn't mean I don't believe that God is a possibility. In fact, I've been giving it more thought lately, especially watching you go through all you have. I'm starting to believe that there has to be a Higher Power that's testing you for some reason."

"Why me? I keep asking myself that question and coming up blank."

"Whoa....you're asking the wrong guy. Didn't your rabbi friend give you any clues?"

"No, in fact he annoyed the heck out of me, preaching to me about repentance and atonement, telling me a scary ghost story about sinners and other stuff. I'm fed up with him. I thought Jonathan was my mentor, my friend, but he just turned on his preacher schtick. What I really need is some empathy. I need help understanding all of this. Any of it, for that matter." Seth suddenly felt exhausted. *I don't know what's worse, the cancer eating up my body or the feelings of forsakenness, frustration, hopelessness, self-pity and doom ravaging my soul.*

"Are you sure you want to hear what I have to say?"

"Why not?" Seth sighed, slumping back on the couch. "You're going to tell me anyway, Mister Attorney."

"Even though I claim to be an agnostic, I do believe there's a force that guides the universe," Michael began, standing up for effect and pacing out of habit like he would before a judge and jury. "Yet I believe we have free will and that we determine our own fates by our actions. I've been a defense attorney for twenty years now. I've represented drug lords, robbers, rapists, murderers and everything in between and I can honestly say that I believe that ninety-nine percent of the time, justice has prevailed. That doesn't mean I've always won of course. Sometimes, as good as I am, my clients have been found guilty."

"Humility was never one of your strong suits, Michael." Seth's weariness began to subside again and he listened in earnest.

"Many times, I've managed to strike a plea bargain where they possibly got less time than they should have, but they still got time, and in most instances, somehow got what they deserved." Michael stopped in front of Seth, as if making his closing argument. "Occasionally, albeit, very occasionally, but it has happened, a guilty man has gone free or vice versa. But I can assure you, truth usually has a way of shining through."

"What's your point?" Seth felt his patience ebbing.

"Sorry for the lofty discourse, but what I'm trying to say is that it's been my experience that most people do get what's coming to them. I believe Aaron, although the judge was a complete jerk, did deserve jail time for his offense. I mean, the kid got behind the wheel with drugs and too much alcohol in his system. Then he uses his black belt karate and kills someone. I know Dominguez was a total scumbag, but still, he died at Aaron's hands just for picking a fight.

"I know Adam was an innocent victim in this whole mess, but he did make a poor choice getting in that car with his drunk, drugged up brother. And forgive me for saying this, but it seems Angelica, in sleeping with Caleb, made the bed in which she's lying, no pun intended.

"You've heard of paying for the 'sins of the father.' Perhaps in your case justice has happened in reverse. Maybe you are paying for the sins of your children."

"Enough!" Seth had become red-faced and his high-pitched bark knifed through the room. "How dare you?" He stood up, the blankets falling around him to the floor, anger sending newfound energy through him. "Even if you're right – and I'm not saying you are, but just for argument's sake, let's say my kids are paying the price for their mistakes – why would God take it out on me?"

"I'm just saying that if there is justice, for the most part, in our human world, why would you think that God is not just?" Michael put his hands on his hips in an exasperated manner. "I would think that, in your condition, your only position is to, as we say in the business, make a guilty plea of some sort and ask for the mercy of the court – with a capital C." Michael sat back down in his chair, signaling he was finished, and pleased he had argued his case successfully.

"Do I get a rebuttal?"

"Of course."

"You seem to imply that God is sitting up there like Judge Henry, dishing out justice for good and evil. Well how do you explain criminals that *do* get off the hook? You just said it happens. And how do you explain innocent victims getting hurt or killed by these criminals? Judges and juries are human and make mistakes just like the rest of us. I'm not saying God is imperfect like we are, or wrong in his justice. I'm saying God must not be handing out justice like we human beings do. Because if He did, then I wouldn't be guilty, as you, and my other so-called friend Jonathan seem to think. So your argument that God is always just so I must be guilty is wrong, and your advice that I need to admit my guilt and plead for mercy is false."

Michael just sat shaking his head back and forth. *In his irritating, self-righteous, lawyer-like way,* Seth thought, suddenly feeling sick to his stomach, his anger and his energy rapidly fading as he felt the after-effects of his last batch of chemo catching up with him. He sat back down wearily on the couch. "We all end up suffering and dying, Michael. I just don't see why my family and I are suffering so much. There's no reason, and it seems there's no way to fight it, no way to fight the all-powerful, almighty God."

Seth summoned the last bit of strength he had left to shout at the ceiling. "God, I can't fight you! Just end it all now, why don't you? No, you're not fair or just! I'm just like a little ant to you! An ant that's struggling up his little hill of sand with a crumb in his mouth, with his leg amputated so that he can barely climb, and you're sitting up on top probably plotting a way to handicap me a little more. Here, take my crumb away and let me starve! Take another leg from me! No better yet, just stomp on me!" Seth let out a maniacal laugh.

Michael got up while Seth was ranting, took two more pills from the prescription bottle he had set on the end table, reached out and pressed the pills into Seth's hand, and once again handed him the glass of water.

Seth obediently took and swallowed the pills and water. He was done arguing and just stared at the television set, not really seeing the program on the screen. Blessed relief finally started coursing through his veins, and he lay back down on the couch and gave in to slumber.

Maybe, if there is a God, I won't wake up tomorrow, he thought before sleep overcame him.

Michael quietly covered Seth again with a blanket. Dusk was settling in on the neat little brownstone, so the tired attorney rose, turned off the lamps in the room, and ascended the stairs to his room.

Chapter 17

A week later, and a few more pounds lighter despite Michael harping on him like a mother hen about getting his nutrition, it was time for another round of chemo.

Sometimes I feel like a boxer entering the ring, but I'm fighting an enemy I can't see, hear or feel, Seth thought, getting dressed to go to the hospital. He looked down at his sagging skin and protruding belly where the cancer seemed to stick out even though the tumor had been removed, and felt the depression waft over him again. *And my opponent is definitely winning.*

The pain had gradually become worse and right now needled through him, pooling in his abdomen like a constant abscess.

He was never hungry anymore, but Michael had forced him to eat some tomato soup for lunch before his appointment. Now he felt it rising in his throat, and stumbled to the bathroom just in time to retch it up.

I just wish I could numb my feelings, he thought, fighting back the threat of tears. *Forget that I feel sick and tired and that my body literally hurts like a cramp all over that won't go away. I can take the physical pain. It's the anxiety, anger and depression – the mental, spiritual, emotional agony that's far crueler.*

With excruciating effort, he changed into a fresh shirt and pants. As he changed he looked down at his bony, white legs and wanted to vomit again in disgust.

Dressed, with his mouth rinsed out with a mild mouthwash – he didn't have the strength or desire to brush his teeth and knew his gums would probably bleed anyway – he called Michael.

Seth had lost track of time but knew with the leaves falling from the trees that it was sometime in late autumn.

The sky was slate gray and it was raining as Michael maneuvered the BMW by rote through Boston's afternoon traffic to the hospital's front entrance. The attorney helped Seth walk through the huge sliding doors past the cascading, plant-ensconced fountains and sculptures that framed the vaulted atrium, welcoming incoming patients and visitors with its airy, attractive entranceway.

But Seth knew what lay behind the hospital's happy mask. He was reminded when a young couple with red-rimmed eyes, hanging onto each other for support, limped past, not looking at the pretty scenery, not seeing anything through their grief.

It dawned on Seth that hospitals were a lot like purgatory. He remembered Maria once imparting the old Catholic teachings of her youth on the afterlife. If one committed a mortal sin – an intentional bad deed grave enough, like robbery, rape or murder – one went to the fiery pit of hell. *At least if you weren't sorry and repentant enough,* Seth figured. If one's sins were venial, or not so bad, like lying or petty theft, and that person was really sorry and made up for them through attending mass and confession, he or she would probably get to heaven. And everyone in between had a pretty good shot at ending up in purgatory, a kind of waiting room, or stuck elevator, before going up.

Probably a place with antiseptic smells and bad food and colorless walls and emotionless workers that couldn't tell you when you were leaving or where you were going until the last minute, just like the real hospital that lies beyond this phony entrance, Seth thought. *The place where I'm going now to be subjected to various trials and tribulations again. To my body and my soul.* Seth had figured at the time he would probably end up in purgatory, if there was such a place. He smiled grimly to himself now as he and Michael stepped into the elevator. *Well here I am.*

Doctor Grason was in this particular day and greeted them after they got off the elevator and entered the chemotherapy department.

"Seth, nice to see you. Saw that you had an appointment today so I figured I'd check up on you since I'm making rounds today. How are you?"

"Oh, just peachy, Ben, and you?" Seth couldn't hide the caustic drip in his voice any more than he could hide his scrawny body.

"I'm fine."

They both glanced at Michael, whom they caught checking his watch, looking impatient.

"I'm sorry, guys, but I have a case in court in a few hours that I am totally unprepared for. Usually I don't mind staying with you, Seth, you know that, but since Ben is here, would you mind if I take off and come back for you in a few hours when you're done?"

Seth looked at Ben, who answered for both of them. "I can sit with Seth for a while today, Michael. I've got a light schedule and actually have an early dinner break coming up. You go to court and we'll call you when Seth is done."

"Thanks." Michael shook hands with Ben, then Seth. "Hang in there, roomy."

Seth rolled his eyes and gestured for Michael to go.

Seth was a little early for his treatment, so Ben took a seat with him in the waiting area of the large chemo room, where two other patients were sitting in recliners receiving their injections.

"You don't have to wait with me, Ben." Seth wasn't feeling too great but didn't let on. He felt the old self-pity mixed with resentment creeping in and didn't want anyone to be around when his grouchiness took over. Usually Michael just sat quietly with him, and Seth was grateful for that, preferring not to make pleasant conversation during the four or five hours he sat in the chemo chair. Sometimes they played cards, and sometimes they both just read magazines. Occasionally Michael talked about an interesting case just to take Seth's mind off his illness.

"That's okay, Seth, I've been wanting to talk to you and see how you're doing."

"Same old, same old. Really Ben, I'm feeling okay." Suddenly he winced from a pain crossing his midsection.

"You don't look it. Maybe it's time for some more tests. I'll schedule them as soon as possible."

Seth's foul mood kicked into gear. "The pain has been growing worse each day. So has the nausea. And so has the depression, which is the worst of all. I'm so sick and tired of being sick and tired that I think I'm starting to lose it. And I'm just so angry and frustrated all the time. I just don't get it. I want you to tell me how a man with my health record ends up with stomach cancer. It doesn't make any sense. It's not like I smoke or drink or do drugs. I exercised, ate right..."

"Seth, I'm afraid I don't have the answer." Ben stroked his goatee, trying to find the right words to say. "People get cancer every day. Young or old, healthy or not."

"You believe in God, Ben, right?" Seth knew Ben was a

relatively devout Catholic.

"Of course."

"And that God has a plan for all of us?"

"Yeah, I guess that fits with what I believe."

"Well then, none of this makes sense. I've been good all my life. I've looked out for others. I've been the best husband, father, friend and employer I could be. Why would God hit me when I'm down?"

"Cancer doesn't choose between good people and bad. Why would you be exempt? Maybe you're being knocked down a peg because you think you've been so good and giving. Hey, I have an idea. Since you have a little extra time, there's something I'd like to show you."

I've got all the time in the world, or maybe no time at all, Seth thought glibly. Lately, everything seemed like a double-edged sword. He felt like his disease made him feel hypocritical, like he should be trying to make the most of his life each day when he didn't even have a life worth living. *God is definitely ironic,* he thought.

"What the heck? You're the boss. I got nothing better to do."

"Good. It won't take long." After informing the nurse stationed at the desk that he would bring his patient back for treatment in about twenty minutes, Ben gently took Seth by the arm and led him out into the hallway.

"Where are we going?"

"You'll see."

"Ooooh, a surprise, I love surprises. Or at least I used to. I'm not so sure I do anymore."

Ben sighed. He led Seth down the hallway of the cancer ward and stopped before Room Twenty-Four. The door was partially open, but Ben still knocked. "There's a patient in here I want you to meet," he whispered into Seth's ear.

Before Seth had a chance to protest, Ben opened the door into the room and pulled Seth by the arm up to the hospital bed, where a very small, frail boy lay sleeping. He must have been having a good dream, as a small smile played across his thin, grayish-pink lips. His face was pale and he had no hair at all. But there was an unmistakable look of peace about him.

"This is Joey." Ben continued to whisper so as not to wake the boy. "He's ten and he has terminal cancer of the lymph nodes. They said he had two weeks to live if he's lucky. That was five weeks ago."

The boy opened his eyes, large and round and blue, and when he saw his visitors, he smiled. "Hi, Doc. Who'd you bring with you?" His voice was small but clear.

"This is Seth Jacobs."

"You've got cancer like me, huh?" Seth met those blue, unblinking eyes for a moment, then looked away. *Children can be so direct. Guess the bald head gave me away.*

Ben came to the rescue. "Yes, Joey, Seth has cancer too, only his is stomach cancer. How are you doing?"

"Great. I always like having visitors, even ones I don't know, 'cause my mom has to work a lot to pay all the bills and doesn't get to come in to see me that much. Can you stay a while?"

Seth felt a pain, but not in his stomach. This one was in his heart.

"Actually, Joey, we can't because Seth here has to get to chemo, but I'll tell you what, next time one of us stops in, we'll bring some cards and stay a while. You like playing cards?"

"Sure. Bring some change and I'll beat ya at Texas Hold 'em."

"That's a deal." Ben reached out and shook the boy's hand.

"I have something for you." Joey reached over to his

bedside table and grabbed a sheet of paper and handed it to Seth, who looked down at it and saw a drawing of a hillside in fall, with multi-colored trees under a blue, cloud laden sky. It was very good, especially for a ten-year-old. Seth looked up and noticed the walls in the room were covered with a variety of such drawings, most done in colored pencil, featuring animals and landscapes, flowers and fruit.

"Wow." Seth swallowed hard. "Thanks. You're a very good artist."

"Yes, he is." Ben beamed proudly at the boy. "He brightens up a lot of people's lives around here with his artwork."

"I don't know how good I am, I just like doing it, it keeps me busy," Joey said. "Nice to meet you, Mister Jacobs."

"Call me Seth. And it was nice to meet you, Joey. I hope I can be half as brave as you are in the future." He turned to follow Ben out the door when the small boy's voice stopped him.

"I'll pray for you to be brave, Mister Jacobs."

Seth turned around, fighting back tears. "Thanks, Joey."

Once out the door, Seth turned to Ben in the hallway.

"Why are we…"

"Shhhh, you can ask questions later. For now just listen. We don't have much time."

Seth told himself to be patient.

"The woman I want you to meet next has ovarian cancer. She just had her second surgery to remove what they could after finding it spread into her uterus. She's only twenty-one and we tried to save her womb with her first surgery so she could have children one day, but it didn't work out. Now we're just trying to save her life, but I'm not so sure we're going to win that battle either."

The doctor turned and began walking brusquely down

the hall to a room four doors down, not giving Seth a chance to ask more questions, or any choice but to follow.

Ben knocked on the door to Room Twenty Eight and a young woman's voice politely said, "Come in."

"Hi, Jennifer, it's just me and a friend of mine, Seth Jacobs, stopping in to say hello."

"Well hi, Doctor Grason, it's nice of you to visit."

The ghostly white, emaciated young woman who was lying in the hospital bed seemed too weak to extend her hand but turned her head slowly in their direction and offered them a small smile. She looked like she had been pretty once but now seemed to be about fifty instead of twenty-one. Her head was wrapped in a bright pink scarf that made her face seem paler than it was, but her green eyes shone bright despite the pain that dwelled in them.

"Your surgery went well, Jen." Ben checked the chart while Seth nervously shifted from one foot to another, not knowing what to say.

Jennifer gazed at him and smiled.

How can these people smile like that? Seth wondered.

"Nice to meet you, Seth Jacobs. Forgive me if I'm a bit out of it, but I think I'm still a little loopy from the anesthesia. So are you a fellow cancer patient?"

How could you guess? Seth was finding it difficult to breathe, but forced a response because he felt Ben's stare. "Yes, I have stomach cancer."

"Do you have kids?"

Seth hesitated. *These people are so darned honest,* he realized. "Yes, three."

"You're lucky then. It was a real blow to my husband and me, finding out we couldn't have kids 'cause of my cancer, but I told him we should adopt. He's not too thrilled with that option right now, but I'm going to keep working on him. I've always wanted kids."

What a jerk, Seth fumed, thinking of the husband's selfishness in the face of this woman, his poor wife, suffering here, still with hope left in her heart.

"Adoption would be a lovely thing," Ben said, breaking the silence. "But right now, you just focus on getting stronger and better so that you can get out of here and get home."

"Good luck." Seth found the words to say, suppressing his anger. "I'm sure you would make a great mother."

That brought a small smile to the young woman's face and she closed her eyes. "I'm really tired still, so I hope you don't mind if I doze off."

"Not at all, Jennifer, get some rest and I'll be back later." Ben patted the young woman's shoulder.

"Thanks, Doc."

Ben gently closed the door behind him and both men wordlessly walked back to the chemo department.

Seth took his seat as instructed and quietly waited as a nurse hooked the IV line into the port in his neck that would enable the chemicals to enter his carotid artery, a process invented to save the other veins in the body from collapsing from the destructive toxins injected and the patient from being poked all over.

Ben pulled up a chair to talk, but Seth was not so sure he wanted to listen anymore. He watched as another patient, a man who looked to be about his age, got up from his chair and limped first to the nurses' station and then out the door. While he was busy being hooked up, Ben had stopped by and spoken briefly with the man before coming over to his chair.

"That's Rusty, a man a lot like you, who has cancer in his hip. But he's got a complication you don't have. He's limited to the pain medication he can safely take because he's a recovering drug addict. Be glad you don't know his pain."

Seth had heard and seen enough. "Why are you showing and telling me about all these other patients, Ben? As if I don't have my own misery to deal with, you've got to unload all of their stuff on me. Let me tell 'ya, it ain't helping."

"Can you just shut up for a minute so I can talk?"

Seth pursed his lips and nodded his head.

"If you could look beyond yourself and forget your self-pity for just a little while, you would know. I have shown you cancer patients who are in just as bad, if not worse, straits than you. Why would God bring such an awful disease on a sweet, innocent, ten-year-old boy? Why would he take a healthy twenty-one-year-old woman whose only goal in life is to have children and destroy her reproductive parts so she can't have any? Why would he torment a man with a drug addiction with cancer so that he can take virtually nothing for the pain?"

"You're asking me?"

"If you could stop being sarcastic and bitter for just a few moments, I'd appreciate it. They're rhetorical questions because neither you nor I have the answers, and that's my point. All I know is that these people are making the best of it, and you should too. What makes you think you're special anyway, Seth? Maybe your lack of humility and your arrogance are the problems."

Seth could feel his temperature rising and his cheeks grew red with anger. "So you're suggesting God is working on my pride with cancer? That sounds ludicrous!"

"Really? By the way, let me remind you that you need to lower your voice or I'll have to leave."

Seth took a deep breath and nodded silently again. "I *have* been humbled by all of the catastrophes that have made up my life of late. I just don't know how much more I can bear."

"Humiliation and humility are two very different things,

Seth. For a good example of the latter, look at Joey or Jennifer or Rusty."

"But don't look in the mirror just yet, right? Am I supposed to feel grateful or something that I'm not in their shoes, because let me tell you something, I don't. I feel bad for them, I can sympathize with them, but it doesn't make me feel any better, if that's what you were after."

"Yes, I think you should feel grateful after seeing them."

Seth barked out a laugh, then spoke in a hushed tone after getting the evil eye from the nurse at the desk. "Easy for you to say, Ben. You don't have cancer. You don't have any sickness or disease that I know of. And you haven't lost your entire family, your kids, your wife, your house, your practice... all that you live for. Talk about a lack of humility. Who do you think you are to play God and tell people not only how long they have to live, but what to do or not do with the life they have left, how to think and feel?"

"I try to heal people with my God-given talents, that's all."

"Well, bravo!" Seth clapped softly.

"It is my humble opinion that God is bringing you down a peg, Seth, and that you should be glad. Perhaps you can use your experiences to help others. Joey looks outside himself to give others the gift of his artwork. Jennifer wants to adopt a baby, which, God willing, she one day will be able to do."

"But you know the odds of either one of them living very long aren't so great. I think you shoot down your own argument that God inflicts misery, like justice, on those who aren't grateful, humble or hopeful, because what have these other patients done to bring God's wrath upon them? I have always been grateful for everything in my life. I have always had faith. Who are you anyway to give me advice, other than medical? You are as bad as Jon and Michael giving me their opinions on why I've suffered all these calamities. But not one of you has so much as walked an inch in my shoes."

"I'm just trying to tell you that a little humility and hope will go a long way…they may even help you forget your misery. But you won't find hope wallowing in pride and self-pity."

Seth decided to switch tactics, since he was getting nowhere. "Ben, you're a Catholic. You believe in ashes to ashes and dust to dust and that we all must die and will one day rise up when God comes to all of us again. And although I'm Jewish, I can even buy into the resurrection. So I say, bring it on." Seth looked at the ceiling of the chemo room and shouted, "God, if you hear me, bring it on!"

Ben sat in shock as he watched Seth try to take the IV tube hook out of the port in his neck to make his point. The doctor grabbed his patient by the forearm and stopped him.

"Seth! Now that would be the worst thing you could do."

Seth slumped into his chair in defeat. He didn't want to argue with his doctor, or with anyone else anymore. *This isn't over, God*, he said wordlessly. *I don't give up this easily.* "Okay Ben, you win," he said aloud. "I'll take your advice into consideration if you'll just leave me alone for awhile."

Ben patted him on the back and went over to the desk to talk to the nurse. *Probably telling her to keep an extra eye on me*, Seth realized. "That's okay. I'm done. I give up," he shouted over to the nurse and Ben.

Michael came a few minutes later to pick him up and take him home.

Chapter 18

Weeks passed and Seth sunk into a morose depression. To him, living with Michael was almost worse than living in the nursing home. At least in the nursing home he had people around him, many as bad off as he to commiserate with, and he had staffers checking on him, even though most of the time it was intrusive and annoying. Now he missed the interruption of endless, empty time that now faced him, stretching before him like a long, dark tunnel with no light at the end.

Michael tried to interact with Seth as much as he could, but was often gone each day working on a demanding caseload that just increased over time. He was always gone in the morning before Seth woke up, and tried to be home for dinner each night, but often called like an overworked husband to say he'd be late, usually with instructions for Seth to pop something in the microwave.

The early winter weather in Boston was especially dismal, which didn't help. Most days were cloudy and cold and often rainy. Not conducive for Seth to go outside, even if he managed to have the energy.

He would fill his day somewhat with reading and when Michael was gone in the evening, he would watch television. But the shows were so ridiculous, in his opinion, that he often was irritated instead of entertained watching them, especially the reality shows which seemed to dominate the airwaves. *Forget "Survivor". At least those people have their health and their families and homes to return to once the show is over. They should do a reality show about contestants who lose everything and are stuck in that reality forever, and see how long they survive,* Seth thought one night. *It could be called "How Much Can You Take?"*

Michael would occasionally give him progress reports on his children, but nothing changed. Adam was still in a coma, Aaron was still in a maximum security prison for life and Angelica was still missing in Syria. The FBI and CIA had their priorities and the Jacobs family wasn't one of them.

Apart from his weekly visits to the hospital for chemo treatments, nurse visits and a phone call every now and then from Jon, Seth was alone. And extremely lonely.

One day when Jon called, Seth realized he needed to get out of the house, so he asked the rabbi for a favor.

"Jon, I'm going stir crazy and I've got to get out of here before I do something drastic. Can you please come pick me up and take me to the synagogue with you? I haven't been in a long time and would really like to go."

"Well, we have Shabbat service as usual on Friday evening at seven, would you like to come to that?"

"I don't think I'm up for a big group setting yet Jon. I'd like to talk to you, but I'd also like to pray a little. Besides, I don't think I can wait that long." Seth glanced at the kitchen calendar. He had lost all track of time, so he had to concentrate for a minute, but if he figured correctly, it was Tuesday. "How about this afternoon?" Seth could hear the desperation in his own voice and hoped the rabbi could hear it too.

Jonathan Mosha said yes and an hour later, after informing Michael of his plans, Seth climbed into his old friend's Buick and rode to Temple Sinai.

It had been a long time since Seth had worshipped at the temple near his home where Jonathan was rabbi. He was glad the yarmulkes and prayer shawls were at the entrance. Otherwise, he may have forgotten to put them on, it had been so long.

Seth entered the sanctuary and gasped. He wasn't sure if he was suddenly winded because of the overpowering awe he felt when he saw the beautiful interior, or by the fact that he felt God's presence nearly strike him in the heart, or because he was so sick that his lungs had started to suffer and any emotional stirring took his breath away. Perhaps it was a combination of all three.

"Why don't you sit here a while and pray, and I'll be back in a little bit." Jonathan helped him into the pew. "I've got some work in my office down the hall to do."

"Thanks, Jon." Seth sat in the back row and bowed his head. Words didn't come to him. Only feelings. Feelings of self pity, self righteousness and anger floated freely into his thoughts.

Despite the overcast sky, a tiny beam of sunlight shone through one of the temple windows and refracted into a prism of light that seemed to dance before him.

And suddenly, he felt humbled and frightened and the words came. "God, please help me understand your will and your ways," Seth whispered at the dancing beams of soft-colored light. "I feel so frustrated and hopeless. You are the great Creator of all. Why did You create me only to bring me to this bottomless pit of despair? All that's left for me is to die a sick, lonely, miserable death. If this is it, if this is Your will, I cannot understand it. I have been faithful and tried to do Your will my whole life. If this is punishment, for the life of me I don't know what sins I committed to bring it on. If You are testing me, that would be cruel, and that would mean You are not the God I've known. I still believe in You, God. And so I ask that You bring me some relief, either by taking away this cancer eating me alive, or bringing back just one of my children, or just taking my life once and for all and ending my misery…"

"Don't you think you're asking a bit much?" The rabbi's voice came to him from behind.

"How long were you listening?" Seth felt a twinge of annoyance that the rabbi had overheard his prayer.

"Long enough to realize that you don't sound very humble in God's presence, young man. What makes you think God is just going to give you a miracle right here and now?" The rabbi fingered his prayer shawl tallit, sighed and took a seat next to Seth. "You're feeling sorry for yourself, I know. But you need to find your purpose in life, Seth, and know the world does not revolve around you. Only God can give you the answer."

"Well that's why I'm here and I get no answers."

"Perhaps you're not asking the right questions. Or perhaps not listening hard enough?"

"That's easy for you to say, Jonathan. Just try to put yourself in my place, just for a moment."

"Ah, ye of little faith." The rabbi crossed his arms. *Here comes the sermon*, Seth thought. "You cannot know God's will in a day, in a year, perhaps not even in a lifetime. And yet, I am convinced that everything that happens here on earth happens according to God's plan."

"Like my losing everything and getting cancer? I just can't believe that's God's plan."

"Yes, even these things. I am much older than you, old as your father would have been, and I have seen a lot of triumphs and tragedies in my lifetime. I have been blessed to survive the Holocaust, escape to Israel and again to this country, preside over hundreds of Jewish celebrations for many family members and friends, lead many a Seder and Shabbat, see much sickness and death including the passing of my parents and sisters, and even witness a few miracles. I too have been tempted by Satan and managed to live to the ripe old age of eighty-two. And yet I have not experienced half of what some of the prophets of old have been through: Abraham, who was put to the test to kill his only son; Moses, who was orphaned at birth; Joseph who was abandoned by his brothers and left to die; Daniel who was thrown to the lions…the list goes on. Do you claim to be more knowledgeable or wiser than these men?"

When he received no answer, Jonathan walked up the step at the front of the sanctuary onto the bema and stood at the lectern. He reverently unrolled the Torah and read a few lines in Hebrew. Then he closed the scrolls. "It has been written here that wicked men will suffer. And here you are, a young man who had everything for much of his life, challenging God just because you have lived for several months with cancer? Just because you have lost the very things God gave you in the first place? Who are you to even have been so blessed with riches in the first place?"

"I have been truly grateful for all God has given me, I've tried to put all of my talents to use, be the best husband, father and employer I could be. I just don't understand why God would give all of these blessings to me only to snatch them away, and then some. Look at me, Jonathan. I am weary, in pain, sick, can't eat or sleep, alone, depressed and suicidal. Is this what God wants? Is this what God has planned for me? How can He have a reason for all of this? I just can't believe that it is God's will for me to suffer like this."

"Then perhaps you do not believe in God at all."

"You may be older than me, Jon, but I can't see that you're any wiser. I'm sorry to say that, but I feel it's the truth."

The rabbi dramatically laid his hands over his chest, as if clutching his heart.

"Go ahead, Jon, mock me. I am dying – I have nothing to lose in saying what I do. But it seems I need more than your advice or wisdom right now. I guess this is between God and me."

The rabbi watched, quietly shaking his head back and forth, as Seth slowly removed his yarmulke and prayer shawl and exited the sanctuary.

"So how did it go at the temple?" Michael had managed to get home early and fix dinner for the two of them. Seth sat across from him, absentmindedly poking his fork around in the mashed potatoes on his plate.

"Not good."

"Care to elaborate? And by the way, I worked hard on this dinner, the least you could do is try to eat some of it." Michael, sitting across from Seth at the little dinette, helped himself to seconds.

Seth looked at the roast beef, mashed potatoes and corn on his plate and suddenly wanted to vomit. Not from the food itself. Michael was a pretty decent cook when he made an effort. It was the turmoil inside churning its way through the hole in his stomach and curling its fingers around the cancer cells growing through his insides. *Sometimes I swear I can feel it spreading*, Seth thought. He swallowed down the nausea, trying to be pleasant company and a good houseguest. "I'm sorry, Michael. The dinner looks great. It's just that I'm kind of upset about today and it's hard for me to concentrate, much less eat. I went to talk to God and ended up getting lectured once more by my dear old rabbi. I swear I think he's losing it in his old age."

"I know I've only met him a few times, but I thought Jonathan seemed pretty smart."

"Oh, he's smart, alright. More like a pompous know-it-all. Here I am confessing my darkest secret to him, that I see no purpose left in my life and I don't want to go on living, and he accuses me of being self-righteous and of questioning God. He thinks that just because he's older, that he's wiser than me."

"Well, he has been a rabbi for quite a while, and he is old enough to be your father. I'm sure some amount of wisdom comes with age. Maybe the truth hurts. Maybe it's just that you're feeling sorry for yourself again. You know, you should be glad you got out of the house, if nothing else. Stop focusing on yourself and your woes."

Seth threw his fork down on his plate with a clang. "I'm not asking for another lecture here! You are no better than Jonathan! Listening to you both, you would think I'm going crazy. Well I'm beginning to think I'm the only sane one around here."

Michael stood wordlessly and cleared the dishes, laying them in the sink, then turned around and faced Seth, hurt and pity mixed in his expression. "You know, Seth, I have done my best to be a gracious host and a good friend to you, but now I'm wondering why I bothered. I'm not sure what you're expecting, but it sure sounds like you want everyone to stop what they're doing and give you the answers you're searching for, to stop their own lives to save yours somehow. But the world doesn't work that way. If you could be a little more grateful, a little more unselfish, a little more humble…"

"Blah, blah, blah, Michael, I'm sick of your babble!" Seth stood and nearly toppled his chair over. "Look at me!"

The well-built, handsome young attorney looked at Seth for a moment, then averted his gaze to the table, which he started to wipe with a damp cloth.

"You can't even look at me for more than a few seconds without being disgusted. I know the feeling; I can't look at myself in the mirror anymore either. My skin is peeling off, I have no hair, I've got sores all over, my clothes are hanging off me, my gums bleed when I brush my teeth and my eyes are red and swollen from a lack of sleep. And the worst part is that I feel worse than I look. Not one person has put themselves in my place. Jonathan lectures me, but who is he to know if I've sinned? Maybe I have somehow brought at least some of this onto myself, but that's between God and me. And now you... but how can you possibly relate to me now? My employees and friends have all forgotten about me. My children are gone. My wife is repulsed by me and is divorcing me. Even the kids in the street thought I was a creepy old man. I appreciate all you've done, providing me with a home and food. I just thought you could also offer a little understanding, a little compassion. I guess that was just too much to ask."

The next morning, Seth was awakened by the telephone incessantly ringing. He looked at the little clock on his nightstand. Seven a.m. He listened after the phone finally stopped ringing, and was greeted by silence. Michael had left for work early. *Probably wanting to avoid me altogether after last night's dinner.* Then the phone jangled again. He reached out and picked up the receiver.

It was Ben Grason asking him to come into the hospital as soon as possible. He needed to give Seth an update in person. *Could be good, could be not so good.* Seth pushed any hope or heartache from his mind. *What will be will be.*

He called Michael at work to ask for a ride. About an hour later Seth sat waiting for the doctor in his office. It wasn't his regularly scheduled chemo day.

Ben came in, shook Seth's hand and sat down across from him at his desk.

"So am I getting good news or bad news, Doc?" Seth thought he was prepared.

He was wrong.

"Seth, I don't know how to tell you this, so forgive my bluntness, but there's no easy way to say it. The cancer has metastasized. That means it has spread from your stomach and intestines into your lungs, the marrow in some of your bones, and part of your brain. When that happens, there really is nothing more we can do to try to eradicate it. It means there really is no more reason for you to keep undergoing radiation or chemotherapy."

"Well, that part's good news, right?"

"I guess you could look at it that way."

"But what...I'm going to die faster?"

"Well, that's my prognosis, yes, but miracles do happen, Seth."

"What's the down side? Am I going to be in more pain? I don't know if I can take feeling any more sick or hurting more than I do, Ben."

"I'm not going to lie to you, Seth. You will feel sick more often, and weaker, and the pain, when it comes, will be greater. But we can give you stronger stuff for the pain. I will prescribe a morphine pump which you can hit anytime you feel the pain coming on."

"So that's good news, too. Wow, here I thought you had bad news, Doc." Seth refused to give in to the despair that skirted along the edge of his mind and heart, threatening to engulf him, paralyze him and render him catatonic. Instead he chose to be funny, but like a bad comedian, his humor fell flat, not disguising his true feelings of anger, self-pity and fear.

"Seth, I know you're being sarcastic to hide your true feelings, but you can be honest with me. I know this is hard to take, and I'll make things as comfortable for you as I possibly can. I want you to know I'll be right by your side as your doctor and your friend."

"Lately I could use one. Jonathan and Michael are both thorns in my side."

"We are all trying to help you, Seth, but you have to let us. You'd be stubborn to think that God will take this cancer from you somehow. You saw the other patients I showed you, how they are dying too, despite their apparent innocence, and there is nothing they can do about it."

"What a hypocrite you are, Ben! First you say I should have hope, and then you smash my hopes, telling me I'm going to die. Certainly I could not have sinned enough recently to make my cancer worse."

"I'm just saying you can't fight this anymore, Seth. You'd be a fool to think you can. Maybe it's time that you set your house in order, so to speak, knowing your days are numbered."

"And what is that number, Ben? You, the wise doctor, along with my wise attorney and wise rabbi, seem to have all the answers that I don't. You all think I've done something to deserve all of this, that I need to atone, repent, be humble and beg for mercy. Well I think you're all wrong. You're going to die just like I am, just like Hitler and Stalin and Judas, and it doesn't matter how much any of us sinned, some of us will go easily and peacefully and some of us will go miserably and wretchedly, tortured all the way to the grave. So tell me, oh wise one, how much time do I have left so that I may be prepared?"

Ben furrowed his brows and rubbed his chin. "I would say it's a matter of a few weeks, perhaps days."

As soon as Ben was finished speaking, without warning, Seth doubled over in his chair and threw up the small amount of dinner he had eaten from the night before on the shiny, clean floor of his doctor's office. And once again, Seth saw spots of blood there.

Chapter 19

"…I went skydiving, I went Rocky Mountain Climbing, I went…" Seth angrily stood to turn off the radio before the song could finish. *It figures I'm here dying of cancer and the most popular song on the radio is "Live Like You Were Dying." Like I'm supposed to run out and go skydiving. I can barely move from this couch without needing morphine.*

The pain had spread into his hips and it hurt to stand, much less walk most of the time. Seth had just given his morphine pump a squeeze and was standing to turn off the radio when the phone rang. *Oh well, I'm up so I might as well see who wants to bother me now.*

Jonathan Mosha's voice was on the other end. "I've heard about your cancer spreading, Seth, and I wanted you to know I've been praying for you."

"Well gee, thanks, Jon." Seth could not help keeping the sarcasm from seeping into his tone.

"I know you're afraid of what's happening to you, and I know you have a right to feel that way. I guess maybe you felt a little afraid confronting God in the temple. And perhaps you should have. You see, God doesn't need you, Seth. You need God."

Here we go again, Seth thought wearily. He pressed the speaker button on the phone and sat down, trying to make himself a little more comfortable before listening to the lecture he knew he was going to receive. "I tried to find Him, Jon, but he doesn't answer my prayers."

"While you were in the temple talking to God, did you repent of your sins?"

"I truly couldn't think of any while I was sitting there."

"Well that's the problem, I'm sure. I have always believed the saying, 'Pride goeth before the fall.' You were the rich owner of many restaurants, Seth. Surely you could have given more to the church? You employed thousands of people. Surely you could have given more to the poor? If I can make you see the light, Seth, if you can agree with what I'm saying, than maybe you'll be right with God and find some sort of peace. Would you like me to come over there and help you find God, and find the peace you're looking for, Seth?"

Several seconds of silence ticked by. Seth closed his eyes in thought. "No, Jon. I need to talk to God myself. I just don't know where to find Him. And if I do, I will tell Him where it's at. He may be the Almighty Creator, but He created me, so why can't I argue with Him? I have gone to the temple and can't feel Him there. I have spoken to these walls in this dark, little house and I can't find Him there. I have looked into the faces of other cancer victims and I don't see Him there. And I have sought Him through you and Michael and Ben, the only three friends who have listened, and I don't hear Him there.

"I am scared, Jon, scared to death. There are evil people in the world that go unpunished; people who rape, rob and murder and carry on doing what they want to do, unscathed by God's wrath. And for some reason, according to you, God thinks what I have done or not done is somehow far worse. I just fail to believe this. I know I don't have the answers, Jon, but neither do you. I just need to find God Himself to get them. I guess it might take dying to do it." Seth heard a key turn in the lock on the front door. "Look, Jon, I have to go, Michael's home. Thanks anyway for your help." Seth painfully stood and clicked off the speaker phone button and turned to face Michael, who set down his briefcase and loosened his tie.

"Who was that?"

"Jonathan. It seems the rabbi thinks I need more help."

Michael looked hard at the gaunt, graying man before him. "Perhaps you do. Seth, I'm sorry, Ben called me with the news. Is there anything I can do?"

"I'm afraid not."

Seth sat down again on the couch. Night was fast approaching and the house was getting dark, so Michael switched on a lamp. "Seth, I know I've advised you several times and I just can't help but do it again as your attorney; we have got to write a new will for you. The one now in place that was written up for you and Maria of course will not be any good since you're getting divorced. And even though there isn't much to the estate right now, you do still have some assets and I'm sure you don't want the current one to stay in place. Seth, we need to get on this."

"I just don't have it in me right now, Michael."

"Alright, I guess it can wait until tomorrow. When you have a little energy, just jot down a few notes for me and I'll draw something up. You hungry?"

"No."

"Mind if I fix something to eat?"

"No.

"Sure you don't want to talk about anything?"

"Yep."

"Okay, I'll be in the kitchen if you need me." And Michael left to fix dinner.

Seth lay down on the couch and blinked, but he had no tears left to cry. He squeezed the morphine pump and closed his eyes, trying to escape into sleep.

He awoke with the dawn, alone. Michael had already gone to work. Seth wrapped his blanket a little tighter around himself. It must be frigid outside, he surmised, since Michael usually tried to keep the heat high enough to keep him comfortable.

Probably so, since it's December. Seth had lost all track of time but figured it must be getting close to Christmas, since the radio and television stations were peppered with holiday songs and commercials. *Ebenezer Scrooge has nothing on me this year,* Seth thought bitterly, feeling every bit as "Bah, humbug" as Dickens' fictional character.

Then Seth remembered Michael's suggestion about drawing up a new will. He found a legal notepad on the coffee table in front of him and grabbed it, along with a pen lying next to it. *Michael must have left them for me just in case. Well, no time like the present.*

And Seth wrote, not an outline for a will, but a letter from the heart:

Dear Adam, Aaron and Angelica,
Somehow I hope this finds you all, and somehow finds you well. I am being taken care of by my three friends; my attorney, Michael Powers, my doctor, Ben Grason, and my rabbi, Jonathan Mosha. All three try to take care of me spiritually as well as physically, because I am ailing in both ways, but I'm afraid I'm too stubborn, or they are not capable of helping me. I just can't come to terms with why God has chosen to torment me. They insist I deserve it somehow, that my sins have brought this all about, but I am writing this to tell you that I have searched my soul and can't find any truth in that. I know all of you used to believe that I was a wise father, but I am writing to tell you that none of us is really

that wise; I guess God put wisdom at the far reaches of the earth for only a few to discover, and only after they spent their lives searching for it, many in vain.

I miss you all terribly but there's nothing I can do to be with you except draw on fond memories of days past that we spent together. Remember when Adam built that robot when he was just ten years old? How he got it to bring me a piece of cake and then how Adam projected his voice through the robot to say "That will be fifty cents, please." Or remember when Aaron got his first karate trophy? I think it was bigger than he was. I was so proud that I stood up and cheered so loudly that the lady in front of me on the bleachers hollered at me to sit down and shut up. I told her, "No way, that's my son" and started cheering even louder. And I'll never forget the time when Angelica brought home that lost kitten and nursed it to the point that it was one big walking bunch of bandages. We laughed together a lot, didn't we? Today, my heart aches for those days.

I really did have it all and so the losses I've suffered are almost too painful to bear. On that fateful night of the train wreck, I remember reminiscing on my life; it was a beautiful autumn day – warm, sunny, and bright. That day I was the beloved son, husband, father, friend; I was the respected, even adored employer of thousands. The whole world knew me and thought of me as blessed.

But not so anymore. Today it is winter – cold, overcast. I am in the headlines now as a villain, a sick and dying man to be loathed or pitied. Children see me and laugh at me or run the other way. Even my so-called friends see me as an outcast who has brought this on himself, only making me feel worse than I already do.

I have tried to keep my faith that God will look out for me and guide me in His will despite all of the recent catastrophes and the misery my life has become. But it's so very hard to keep going. I can't see what I have done or not done to deserve all of this. I only wish there were a court I could appear before to answer to God. But there isn't, and so I am writing this letter to you as a testimony of sorts to my reputation and faith, flawed as they both may be.

I have been told my cancer has spread from my stomach and intestines into my bones, lungs and brain and I might only have days to live. How many days isn't certain; all I know is that I am sick, nauseous, in constant pain, dazed, confused, angry, bitter and depressed. I really don't know how much faith I have left to withstand much more. Each morning I try to pray for faith, for God's will, but honestly, there are many days I contemplate killing myself, thinking death would be a relief.

And then I think of you: Adam lost in a coma, Aaron suffering in a jail cell, Angelica trapped in a foreign land, and a tiny light of hope flickers in me, even if just for a few moments. I hold onto it like a candle stub in a dark tunnel, but sometimes, it feels like it is in danger of burning out. I just feel so alone without you. I get no answers and it just doesn't seem fair.

I want you to know that I have been completely faithful to your mother during our entire marriage. I don't know why she turned against me. I guess she just had no faith left, or maybe not enough to begin with. I feel like I never really knew her at all. I have looked back on my life and find that I have always tried to help the less fortunate, giving a good percentage of my profits to youth programs, synagogues, missions and much more; but you wouldn't have known about those, as I tried to be humble and not let it be known. I gave jobs and a future to those in need like Miss Carla and Bill Brown and was always fair in my business dealings. I tried to look out for other people like the lady on the train that broke down, giving her a friendly ear and my good coat to ease her discomfort. I was careful not to get in trouble with the law. I forgave all of the people who somehow persecuted me or you, including police officers, judges, reporters, government officials, tax *collectors, insurance agents, lawyers and doctors. My home and my offices have always been open to anyone who needed shelter or a temporary haven. I have fed the rich and the poor, giving food away to the needy. I always prayed and tried to be grateful for the all the riches God gave me, never taking them for granted. I tried to be a good son and be obedient to my parents. And I hope you found that I was a good father.*

I'm not saying all of this to boast, or to say that I was perfect, because I believe no man or woman is. But I tried to lead the best life I could and be a good example, and I hope you are proud of me. When I die you will know that I am leaving you with a clean, although heavy, heart.

Consider this my "will" (although please always follow God's will, not mine or your own): I am hereby leaving everything I own to all three of you, to be distributed equally between you and your heirs. Michael Powers will be my power of attorney to handle everything that needs to be handled.

Just know that I love you always.

- Your father, Seth Jacobs

After Seth was finished writing and had read the letter back to himself and was satisfied with it, he sat back and thought, *Now how to get this to all three of my children?*

And then he thought of the good old U.S. Postal Service and decided to mail the letters himself. *Maybe the cancer is really eating at my brain and I'm losing my mind. Oh well.*

Having made his decision, Seth disengaged the morphine pump, holding onto the furniture in the room and wincing with pain, and made his way into Michael's office down the hall. He looked around for a few minutes, albeit with some difficulty, and then found what he was searching for: Michael's copying machine. He made three copies and put them in envelopes, slowly and with concentration, writing their names on each.

Now what were their addresses? Seth looked at the envelopes, confused. *Darn those chemicals.* They were messing with his brain, he was sure of it. Seth was so determined to handle the mater himself that he didn't stop to think that Michael could take care of it. *Oh well, they'll help me at the post office.*

Now to mail them. After leaving the original letter on Michael's desk in an envelope with the attorney's name on it, Seth summoned every last bit of strength he had to go to the kitchen and find the bottle of morphine tablets in the back of a cabinet. He read the label. Normally Michael gave him one tablet when his morphine pump was exhausted and he moaned in pain. There were only three very large pills left in the small container. He filled a glass of water and took all three.

I will need these for what I am about to do, he justified to himself. Then he walked back into the living room, put on his shoes, saw one of Michael's jackets nearby and put it on, grabbed the cane he used for walking, and headed out the front door of the townhome.

The bitter, mid-December wind hit him like an electric shock and somehow energized him. It was overcast, a gray, colorless day, yet there was enough light on the horizon that Seth realized it was late afternoon.

He zipped his jacket, gathered his strength and, using his cane, walked down the three front porch steps and turned left, toward downtown Boston where he knew he could find a post office to mail his precious letters.

Three blocks down and he was on Summer Street. He walked past attractive brownstones outlined with twinkling lights, shop windows merrily decorated with holly wreaths, Santas, elves and angels. *It's Christmas*, Seth realized. A time for love, joy and family. And his heart felt a new, heavy ache like never before.

But I've got a job to do, he thought, fingering the envelopes in his pocket. He knew if he walked a few blocks more he would reach the nearest post office. Seth felt lightheaded with the cold air and the morphine starting to kick in, but at least his walk was bearable.

It seemed like he had been walking for hours when the streets of upscale townhomes and storefronts began giving way to rundown rowhouses, warehouses, cinderblock buildings and seedy corner bars. *This isn't near the post office*, Seth realized. *I don't think I've been here before.* Seth blinked, trying to refocus. *I must have taken a wrong turn.*

He was nearly knocked over when he bumped into a stranger passing by, who mumbled something at him. He asked the man for directions to the post office. The man, hunch-backed, elderly and smelling faintly of booze, didn't say anything but motioned in the direction Seth was headed.

Confused, Seth decided to walk a little further. Now he started to smell saltwater. *I must be close to the harbor and Rowe's Wharf. Maybe I can get to the Perfect Place and ask for directions*, he thought, proud of himself. *But wait a minute. There's a problem with that. I just can't put my finger on it.* His thoughts were getting tangled in the morphine web that was spinning in his head. *Oh right, it's closed.*

Unsure what to do, Seth was finding it increasingly hard to see with the oncoming dark, so he decided to press on and walked forward two more blocks until he came to the end of the paved street. A wave of nausea struck him and he shut his eyes and doubled over with dry heaves. He had nothing to throw up because he hadn't eaten all day. When the nausea released him of its grip, he stood up and nearly lost his balance from the dizziness that ensued.

Seth fought not to black out and tried to regain his composure and eyesight. He squinted into the hazy, dusky street ahead. It was no more than an alley, really, walled in on one side by a huge, slate gray concrete building with no sign and on the other by a metal gate and fence that enclosed an empty parking lot. He stared ahead and could make out the inky black water of the harbor. He also saw some sort of glowing light ahead, around which a few people seemed to be gathered. Freezing cold and with nowhere else to turn, he decided to approach the people and light for further direction.

Then he heard a roaring noise above him that deafened him. It was the commuter train straight above his head. He looked up and realized he was directly under one of the many bridges that headed out from the city and across the water to neighboring communities and towns, taking passengers from work to home. *Home.* It seemed like such a foreign word to Seth now.

Don't lose it, man, he told himself. *You've at least got to make it back to Michael's house in one piece.* Putting one foot in front of the other, Seth walked toward the glow, which he saw now was a fire. *So this is how the other half lives.* He saw a dozen people gathered around the fire. People he would call skid row bums, bag ladies, the homeless.

Seth stuffed down the fear that rose in his throat like the countless amounts of bile that had risen there and walked forward, approaching them. A few glared at him menacingly, while the others ignored him, warming themselves by the fire which rose out of a big metal trash barrel. *They must be really bad off,* he thought. *They're looking at me as if I'm the pariah.* If he had had a mirror, he would have known why, with his bald head, discolored, sickly, gaunt face with its protruding cheekbones, Michael's expensive jacket paired with the dirty, baggy pajama bottoms he had forgotten to change in his morphine-induced state, and of course, his cane.

The rancid odor that met his nostrils nearly made him have the dry heaves again, but he fought it down. It was the stench of stale alcohol, old, burning ashes, urine, grime and decay. Seth managed to speak.

"Excuse me, sorry to interrupt, but I'm lost and was wondering where the nearest post office is?"

A lady and man howled with laughter, apparently at his expense.

"Ye ain't gonna find it here, buddy." The man that had laughed spoke in a heavy Irish brogue after his guffaws subsided. "Yer as lost as ye can be. And I wouldn't go anywhere till mornin' if I was you. Bound to be attacked by thugs or dogs or cops. You can hang here if ye like. Looks like ye don't have a home nohow."

"I do but I'm not sure how to get back there. Mind if I stand here by the fire? I'm sick, and I'm afraid I didn't wear the appropriate jacket for this weather. You see, I have..." Seth was cut off from telling them of his illness. A few of them looked pretty sick themselves and probably wouldn't care anyway, he realized.

"Come." An old black man with half his teeth missing, a dark wool cap on his head and graying whiskers, interrupted him with the order. The others seemed to back off, like he was their leader. Wearing a ripped, plaid hunting jacket and pants that were too dirty to tell what kind they were, the scraggly old man thrust his bony hand toward Seth and pulled him by the sleeve closer to the fire. "Here." The man handed Seth a plastic cup after pouring some type of liquid in it from his Thermos. "Ain't gonna kill ya."

Seth took the cup warily. *Oh well, I can't get any disease that's going to make my life any worse than it is already.* He was so thirsty he felt dehydrated. Besides it looked like water so he gulped it down. The liquid nearly burned his insides, but he swallowed it before he could spit it out. It was vodka.

"It'll warm ya up some."

"Thanks." The word came out in a choked whisper.

"What's your name?"

"Seth Jacobs."

"Why ya here?"

"Like I said I got lost and…"

"Ya look bad."

"Well, I'm sick and…"

"Shut him up!" A woman's screech came from the far side of the fire. "I gotta headache!" A woman with wild wisps of stringy hair flying out in all directions from her head rose up from the fire like an apparition. *Like a devil woman.* Seth started to wonder if he was hallucinating. *Maybe I've died and gone to hell.*

"Don't mind her. She's an ol' hag that nobody minds."

Seth chose to be quiet. The stench and thick smoke from the fire started to suffocate him and Seth felt close to blacking out. He didn't realize the vodka and morphine were helping him along. A black fog began to whirl around him, carrying sparks from the fire, and the faces, streaked with black and glowing red from the embers, started swirling around him too, appearing close then far, like ghouls in a nightmare circling him, fading, then looming again. The thundering, grinding of the train and the ghostly howl of the wind enveloped him. He was suddenly burning hot, thirsty, choking and sick to his stomach.

I am in hell. Seth thought. *God, let me just die here. Or maybe I should ask you, Satan.*

The devil woman sidled up to him bearing a syringe in her hand. "You want some of this magic potion? It'll help ye out."

"Cut it out!" The leader pushed the woman away.

But Seth held up his arm toward her, ready for relief in any form. *I'm ready, God, just take me.* Then he vomited, and felt the ground coming up to meet him. That, and the cries of the screeching old woman were the last things he remembered.

Chapter 20

"Seth?"

At the sound of his name, Seth tried to slowly open his eyes into thin slits, but the light that pierced through hurt his head, so he shut them again. A female voice spoke his name once more. Keeping his eyes closed, he listened to the gentle, pleasant timbre of the voice. The white light hurt, but the voice did not.

"Where...?" Every word was like sandpaper rubbing his sore mouth and throat.

"I found you at the fire under the bridge."

Hell. Was he still in hell?

"You are very sick. You had a high fever which I brought down but you almost didn't make it. You were delirious and passed out. I'm sorry I didn't get your permission, but I couldn't leave you there to die, so I brought you home with me. You are in my apartment in Boston. And you're safe here."

He tried once again to see, opening his eyes a tiny fraction at a time until he could make out a face. It was the face of an angel. *So I must have made it to heaven after all.* He closed his eyes again and smiled.

"Seth, stay with me. Please keep listening to my voice. Try to open your eyes again."

For you I will. Seth opened his eyes into slits again,

tolerating the light to see her face once more. He squinted and focused as best as he could on her. *Definitely an angel.* It was how he had always pictured one to be. Long, silky blonde hair, an ivory complexion, large, translucent blue eyes framed by long lashes. She was wearing something of a gossamer white fabric. *No halo or wings, but that's okay.*

He reached up to touch the ethereal light that was her face and his hand was met with the softest, smoothest surface he had touched since holding his children when they were just born.

Seth concentrated for a moment and realized he was lying in a bed. He felt the cool sheets under him, a soft pillow under his head. *Maybe I'm still alive.*

"How…know…my name?"

"I know who you are because I saw your photo in the paper and on the television news. My mother described you a little over a year ago when she told me you came to her rescue on the subway. My name is Lucille."

Lucille. The name came to him from some distant place in his brain. He didn't know where or how or why.

He closed his eyes and withdrew his hand, covering his face with his arm, hoping she would disappear. *That this heavenly lady is even gazing at this hideous mask of a face, this ghost of a body, this travesty of a soul, this monster I've become is more than I can bear.*

"Seth, please stay with me." Lucille touched his arm with her fingers. "Open your eyes."

"No….ugly." *Even my voice is ugly,* he thought, keeping his eyes shut and face covered. The cancer had insipidly crept from stomach to esophagus to trachea and was rapidly branching into Seth's lungs, making speaking and breathing more difficult with each passing day.

"I know appearances can be deceiving." *Oh God, she's*

still there. Yet Seth strained to hear her melodious, clear voice despite his shame. "I remember the man my mother showed me in the picture. He was beautiful, both inside and out. She spoke of a man who was kind, caring, giving, patient, brave and strong."

"No more." Seth forced the words out in his raspy voice.

"Yes, I'm sure that man is you. My mother's name was Ruthie. Ruthie O'Hanlon. You helped fix her injured leg when the T crashed. No one else would help her. You gave her your overcoat. She still has it. More importantly, you showed her compassion even though she was a lonely, poor, old woman no one else seemed to care about. And even though she was unkind to you at first, you were still friendly to her.

"I've followed the stories about you since then." Lucille continued to speak softly, still holding her fingertips to his arm to maintain their connection. Seth put his other arm over his face, trying to shield it further from her eyes. But she didn't move, and in fact, reached out her other hand to touch him. It was as if she was determined to hold onto his attention despite his desperate attempt to shut her out. "Yes, Seth, I know all you've been through, all the crosses you've had to bear, that you continue to bear. And I believe fate…God brought us together in this place and that I am meant to help you like you helped my mother. If only you let me."

Seth slowly uncrossed his arms and lowered them to his sides, then painstakingly opened his eyes as far as he could until he was staring at this beautiful creature hovering above him.

"I'm a social worker and I was visiting the homeless people you were with around the fire under the bridge last night." A look of panic crossed Seth's face as he recalled the ghoulish faces, the awful sights, smells and sounds of the night before and the terror and confusion that had engulfed him. "Shhh, it's okay now." Lucille held his hand as she continued, trying to comfort him and hold his attention. "Those people are okay, they're just suffering like you. Most are alcoholics or drug addicts; some are just penniless and have nowhere else to go. It's my job to bring them clean syringes to prevent the spread of AIDS but sometimes I also bring blankets and food to help them make it another day. When I saw you, you were passed out on the ground and burning with fever but shivering with the cold, talking out of your head. You kept saying, 'Here I am, Satan, you win.' I was afraid you were going to have convulsions and I knew from the look of you that you were really ill, and that you didn't belong there but had to be lost. Even though the other folks wouldn't have killed you, they see people die all the time and are hardened enough that they would have left you for dead because they had no way of saving you themselves. So I brought you here, gave you cool compresses and some liquids I forced down, kept your temperature stable and let you sleep off whatever drugs were obviously in your system."

"Morphine...cancer." Seth wanted to make this wonderful person understand that even though he may be a loser, he wasn't a drug addict.

"Ah...that explains a lot." Lucille smiled at him, a beatific beam that radiated through him, spreading a warm glow.

It was the first real moment of serenity he had experienced since the nightmare that had become his life began and he closed his eyes to savor it. *Perhaps I truly am in heaven. If so, God, please let me stay.*

And Seth lost consciousness once more.

Seth woke up, still alone in a bed, but something felt different. He was able to open his eyes without pain now and looked around the room.

He was in a different bed in a different room. Seth had been here enough times to know he was in the hospital. He had IV lines hooked into his arms and he felt much better. *But where was Lucille?* Suddenly Seth felt his heart racing in a state of panic. *Had she been real, or was she just a figment of my imagination? Was she a messenger from heaven? But who am I to think I would be sent such a one?*

As if he had summoned her subconsciously, she walked through the door to his room, followed by Ben, Michael and Jonathan.

Seth wished the three men would turn and go, leaving him alone with Lucille. To bask in her light was all he really wanted right now. *There's just something about her*, he realized. *Something good.*

"So how did I get here?" Seth tested his voice and found it much easier to talk. It was still weak, but not nearly as hoarse or painful. *The pain meds must be working.*

"Hello to you too." Ben came up to his bedside to check his vital signs while the others watched from a short distance. "Lucille brought you in and, by the grace of God, found me and we hooked you up to the right stuff. You gave us all a scare, Seth."

"I'm sorry. Why did I leave your apartment?" Seth glanced over at Lucille, who stood across the room, arms crossed, looking concerned. She had changed into slacks and a soft beige sweater that made her long hair shine golden against it. "Or was that just a nice dream?"

"No, you were at my apartment, but your fever spiked up and you started losing consciousness again so I thought I better get you in here as quickly as possible. A card with Doctor Grason's name and the hospital address was in your pocket, so I figured I'd call him first. While I do have a degree in psychology, I'm definitely not a nurse."

"You could have fooled me." He saw her blush a bit before regaining her look of stern composure. "Thank you.

You saved my life."

He heard Michael clear his throat in the corner of the room. "Michael, Jon, what are you doing here? Nice of you to visit. Am I dying or something?"

"Don't start, Seth." Ben spoke for the group. "Actually, we thought you might be, so I called Michael as your power of attorney and the rabbi here to be with you. Sort of a last rites thing."

"But you're way too stubborn." Michael chimed in. "So here we all are looking like a bunch of idiots."

"Speak for yourself." Jonathan had to put in his two cents too, which made them all laugh.

"Actually, I'm glad you're all here." Lucille's sweet but firm voice silenced the men in the room, bringing them all to attention. "I would like to speak to you all for a moment." All eyes were on her. "I know I'm the new kid in this situation here, so forgive me if I speak out of line."

"You say anything you want, Lucille. I owe you my life." Seth didn't care what she said, as long as she stayed here. *She is so beautiful.*

"I read one of the letters in your pocket, Seth. Besides Doctor Grason's card, you had no other means of identification and I thought I should find out as much as possible to take care of you.

Seth looked confused for a moment, then realized his wallet must have gotten stolen at the campfire.

"I'm sorry, I didn't mean to get into your personal life, but I did. I found out a lot reading that letter and listening to you talk as I kept watch over you all night. I'm sure a lot of what you said was a little crazy, but much of it sounded...well, sincere. In your letter you spoke of these three gentlemen, whom I've gotten to know a little over the past several hours. You sounded as though they were persecuting you, along with

God. You spoke of being unfairly punished, and defended yourself as having done nothing wrong."

The three friends exchanged glances but didn't say anything, so Lucille continued addressing them. "I don't pretend to be wiser than any of you; I know I'm younger, but like you, I am in a profession of helping people and I believe wisdom is not something we learn with age, but comes from working with others and with God."

She spoke directly to Seth. "I know you believe you haven't done anything to bring on the losses you've suffered. And I know you say you understand you're not perfect. But I still don't sense a lot of humility in you." Seth felt sheepish and he visibly blushed. "The thing is, we are all human beings and we make mistakes, big and small. Only God is perfect. So when you question Him and ask why He persecutes you, you are arguing with perfection, which is fruitless."

"But...I..." Seth sat taller in his bed and interjected, wanting to tell her he was working on his humility, and to please not be angry with him, he had just been telling the truth. One determined glance from her cool blue eyes quieted him, and he slumped back down again.

"You can never win that argument because you cannot know God's ways." Lucille's voice was even but firm and full of conviction. "Who are you to say God is punishing you unfairly, or failing to reward you for living a good life? Do you think God is focusing all his energies on testing or punishing you?"

Seth didn't answer, so Lucille continued. "Have you even tried to listen to God, or have you just argued with him?"

She knows the answer to that I bet, Seth thought. *It's true, all I've done is argue. Caught up in my own anger and self-pity, I don't think I truly listened.*

"God speaks to us in so many ways, if only we look and listen," Lucille said.

Seth thought back to Jonathan's dream, his visits with Ben and the patients on the cancer ward, the song about living like you were dying on the radio in Michael's apartment, the homeless around the fire, and finally, the appearance of this angel who somehow was still present in his life. *I have not been even trying to see or hear.*

Seth wanted to crawl under the sheets and not show his face again. The three friends started shifting on their feet, looking uncomfortable.

Lucille turned and spoke to them again. Her tone was even more firm. "I don't understand why you take it upon yourselves to tell Seth what he should or shouldn't do to win back God's favor or make his misery end with some type of repentance. What makes you any more knowledgeable or wiser than Seth? You also cannot know God's ways. How do you know God hasn't heard Seth? There is no way Seth can hide from God. He sees and knows all, so how can you tell Seth that if he repents more, or confesses something he hasn't already, that God will change his mind? You all are making God out to be a vengeful, punishing God. That's not the God of my understanding."

Seth felt his face on fire with humiliation and shame, not only for himself but for his friends, even though they had worn him down with their insistence on their belief that God was somehow punishing him or that he had brought this all on himself.

"I don't understand, Doctor Grason, why Seth has not been receiving counseling." Lucille addressed Ben. "It seems you were busy treating him yourself, not only physically, but emotionally. I believe he needs the help of a professional psychologist, and that I could help." Ben just nodded. "I believe Seth should vent his emotions instead of keeping them in; otherwise they'll only fester. But he needs to do it in a way that he isn't always fighting. To keep battling God will only make him more frustrated. He needs to realize God is on his side. And I'm sure the God I believe in is."

Lucille faced Michael. "And, Mister Powers, no offense, but how could Seth take such a high dosage of morphine? Yes, the medicine takes the edge off of pain that could become unbearable, but I believe it is not meant to block it off entirely so that the one suffering becomes completely numb. I believe God meant for us to learn from our experiences of pain. I know you've been kind enough to allow Seth to live with you, but I think he needs more attentive care than perhaps you can give." She paced for a moment, head down, then stopped and looked at all of them, apparently hatching an idea. "It seems as though Seth will need more supervision in days to come so that he doesn't hurt or endanger himself. I know you're an extremely busy man with your law firm, while I only work about twenty hours a week and have excellent security in my apartment building. What would you think if I provide in-house counseling and that Seth comes to live with me?"

Michael didn't hesitate to answer. "Well, that would probably work out better, so if you don't mind Seth, I'll…"

"Don't mind a bit, buddy." Seth grinned. "She's cuter than you anyhow." He bit his lip when he saw Lucille shoot him a perturbed frown.

Lucille next turned to Jonathan and just stared at him for a moment. He lowered his eyes in a bashful gesture. "Rabbi, I wouldn't begin to pretend I know more than you when it comes to religion or spirituality." She spoke more gently with the elderly man before her than she had with the other two, yet her tone was no less serious. "But I do believe there's a difference between the two, and while you are quite learned and speak well of the first, the second is really a matter that is between Seth and the God of his understanding…not yours, wouldn't you say? I'm sure you were just trying to help him as his spiritual advisor. But I think Seth needs to face God and come to terms with Him on his own now." Jonathan Mosha humbly nodded.

Lucille turned back toward Ben. "Okay then, perhaps we should give Seth here some rest while we discuss these arrangements in your office, Doctor Grason?"

"Of course."

It was settled then, and that afternoon, with a small bag of medications and instructions packed, Lucille told Seth they were headed to the Trinity Apartments in downtown Boston. It was a nice complex located in a middle-class neighborhood five blocks from Boston Harbor.

Lucille drove while Seth rested, reclined in the back seat of her small Toyota. He wasn't paying attention and must have drifted off for a little while because when he opened his eyes, he was staring at the water through the car window.

"You live on the waterfront?"

"No, I made a detour."

Seth blinked and looked at the panorama before him. He realized now they were on the banks of Cambridge. The entire Boston skyline lay across the Massachusetts Bay before him as the sun set, casting a glorious rainbow of fiery color across the sky.

"Why…"

"I needed to talk to you, away from the hospital, the city, the people. Come on."

Lucille got out of the car and came around to the passenger side and opened his door. To his dismay she helped him swing his weak, spindly legs to the side, handed him his cane, then supported him under his other shoulder so he would have less trouble walking down the cobblestone path to the water's edge.

With a little effort, they were soon standing overlooking the harbor. It was unusually warm for a December evening. The sun was just descending below the horizon and lit up the bay like someone had set off hundreds of red and gold fireworks, casting their sparks on the water. Clouds, streaked with various shades of magenta and coral, added more color and depth to the sky's palette. And millions of tiny white lights had come on in the buildings of the skyline with the dusk, adding to the spectacular view.

"This is God." Lucille whispered the three words softly, staring across the water. Strands of her golden hair, flung behind her with a gathering breeze, shimmered with the colors of the sky.

Awestruck, Seth did not speak, and the two stood for several minutes, watching the colors deepen to dark reds and purples. "How can we human beings possibly understand the ways of the Almighty?" Lucille turned to look at Seth, her eyes liquid pools of emotion reflecting both the beauty before them and her own beauty within. She then turned back out to gaze at the wondrous scenery before them.

The wind picked up and began to whistle. A storm was quickly mounting from the east, but its approach was beautiful to watch. The clouds started to darken, and whitecaps began to flicker on the water's surface.

Finally, thunder cracked and streaks of lightning danced across the sky.

Lucille didn't budge, and Seth started to worry they may be caught in it. "No offense, Lucille, but I don't like storms. I think we better get back in the car."

"No, wait. This too is God."

A clap of thunder boomed so loudly Seth was nearly knocked down by the force of it, and then a huge bolt of lightning seemed to rend the sky in two. Seth was frightened, and still Lucille stood calmly, her hair whipping about her. Seth drew his jacket around him, feeling the oncoming chill, but Lucille didn't seem to feel the cold, her arms calmly dangling at her sides.

"Lucille!" Seth had to shout over the thunder. The sky had turned black, the clouds becoming one giant charcoal canopy above them.

Unable to face God or the storm, Seth turned his back to the sky, to Lucille, and he leaned onto the hood of the car, shaking from the cold and a mounting fear within.

And a voice inside his head, or maybe deep in his soul, said: "Who are you, Seth Jacobs? Where were you when I created the earth? Were you there when I made the sky, the sun that put on the show you just saw, or the moon and stars in the galaxies? Did you make these clouds, this thunder and lightning? Do you feed the birds or many wild animals that roam the earth? Is it by your command that the horse runs so fast or the eagle soars so high? You can't argue with Me, Seth, and you can't hide."

Seth slowly stood up, turned and faced the sky. He whispered, "I have no answers for you."

And he heard God speak to him again in his head. "If you are so great, Seth, you decide who here on earth is wicked and should be struck down. Or test your powers by going out to sea and single-handedly catching the great blue whale that swims not far from here."

"I'm sorry, God." Seth started to cry and his tears mixed with the rain that began to softly fall. "I'm sorry for being so weak, for wanting to die, for wanting to give up, for losing faith in You. I had no right to question Your will or Your ways. I know You are all-powerful and beyond my limited understanding. I talked out of my head; I didn't know. I'm sorry. God, I'm sorry." Seth hunched over, put his head in his hands and began to sob.

"It's okay, Seth," he heard, again silently, in reply. "I accept your prayer. You are My child and I love you. Just like I love all I have created."

Seth felt a warm, comforting breeze envelope him and gentle hands touch his shoulders before he fell to his knees and passed out.

Chapter 21

Seth came to once again in a bed in Massachusetts General Hospital. This time, only Doctor Ben Grason was at his bedside. Instead of feeling despair, confusion or emptyness, Seth felt only an overwhelming surge of peace. When his blue eyes met the doctor's sympathetic brown ones, he smiled.

Ben smiled back. "You look like you've had a revelation." The doctor sat taller in the chair.

"I did." Seth looked out the small hospital window and saw the morning sun shining in a cloudless blue sky. "For a change, I'm glad I'm here, and grateful I'm alive instead of wishing God had just taken me away and not let me wake up to face another day."

Seth remembered being on his knees in the storm at the waterfront. *Was it last night? A week ago?* He wasn't sure but he didn't care. It had happened. It was real. He had heard God, talked to him, said he was sorry. And he had been forgiven. *Maybe God didn't answer my question on whether or not I deserved all the bad things that happened to me, but I guess He didn't have to. All I know is that He still loves me and will see me through as long as I still have faith, as long as I still believe. And that is enough.*

It was all too much to explain to Ben right now, so Seth chose to keep his thoughts to himself for the moment, until he had a chance to sort it all out. *There will be time for talking about it later.* Somehow, that thought came to him and he felt comforted by it.

"You look tired." Seth noticed gray circles under Ben's eyes, wrinkles on his face where there had been none just a year ago, and his beard looked grayer than it had before.

"That's because I am. When Lucille brought you in here, we weren't sure you were going to make it again. That's my fault. I shouldn't have sent you out of here in the first place, and I'm really sorry."

Seth gave Ben a weak smile. "That's okay. I never thought doctors were perfect."

"After my rounds the night you came in, I went into the chapel here to pray. I realized it's been a long time since I've gotten down on my knees to talk to God, but all of a sudden, I was afraid I was going to lose you, that I had failed somehow, and I couldn't bear it. I have no idea how long I prayed for you to pull through so that I wouldn't have failed, but I must have dozed off right there in the pew between midnight and the early hours of the next morning.

"Anyway, I'm not sure if it was while I was awake or sleeping, but I heard God speak to me, Seth. He told me to stop being so selfish, that this was not all about me and whether or not I had failed. I think God was telling me I needed to focus on the physical part of your disease, not the emotional or spiritual. That these were out of my hands.

"I guess He 'suggested' that instead of lecturing you on trying to find ways to accept your illness, or feeling sorry for myself that I was going to lose you, I needed to stick to using the skills He gave me in the first place, and to concentrate on how I could best serve you, my friend. And after a long time thinking and praying, it came to me. I had to work on trying to find a cure.

"A nurse found me about three in the morning and woke me. I asked her to find another doctor to cover my rounds that day and told her I had urgent business to attend to. And after a quick shower and coffee, I went to see my friend in the hospital's research lab. I knew that he had been working with a team of researchers on various drug combinations that will arrest the spread of cancer and actually work to eliminate it. I guess you could call it a cure, but the scientists are hesitant at this point to make any claims to that effect. It's all been hush-hush. They've done a series of animal trials over the years, and were getting close to being ready to conduct human trials, but hadn't gotten that far yet.

"I begged them to allow me to try it on you, if you'd be willing. I've been working all through the past day and night to cut through a lot of red tape and get approvals from the hospital administration, the U.S. Institutional Review Board and the FDA. This morning I received the good news. I finally got it okayed." Ben took a deep breath, his eyes now sparkling in his haggard face. "But now it's up to you."

Seth was stunned into silence, so Ben continued. "I do have to warn you, there could be some serious side effects." He stroked his goatee. "Unlike chemo, which kills the good cells and bad cells, the new drug cocktail they've created identifies only the cancer cells and attacks them little by little so that they're gone. That's the good news. The bad news is that the dose has to be exactly right for the amount of cancer in the body. If too much is given, the drug goes overboard, causing the cancer cells to react and spread faster than before. In other words, it moves too fast, and doesn't thoroughly do the job, giving the cancer cells a chance to fight back."

"So they either kill my cancer, or it kills me?"

"I guess that's a good way of putting it, but yes, Seth, those are the alternatives, and we're just not sure what the chances are of one happening versus the other. It could be fifty-fifty."

Seth pondered his friend's offer. Both men could hear the tick of the clock on the wall. "Yes, let's give it a try."

Ben smiled, but then frowned with worry. "Are you sure? I hope I'm not talking you into this, Seth, because if I am…"

"Ben, remember this is not about you." Seth winked, trying to ease his friend's burden. "Besides, I really have nothing more to lose, and, God willing, a lot to gain."

Ben jumped out of his chair. "Well let's not waste any time then. I'll get the ball rolling. I'll be back in an hour with a few more docs to set you up. God, I hope…"

"Go!" Seth didn't want to give either one of them a way out. Ben was almost out the door when Seth stopped him. "Ben, where is Lucille?"

"She's out in the waiting room. I'll send her in."

She came in wearing jeans and a white tunic, her long blonde hair flung behind her shoulders, carrying a bouquet of daisies. To Seth, she looked like a messenger from heaven.

"Thank you for saving my life…again." Seth beamed at her.

"What does that mean, again?"

"The first time I thanked you, I really wasn't that grateful. I kind of wished you had just let me die there by the fire. Now I see that my life is really worth living. You helped me to see it for myself."

"Men can be hard-headed sometimes," she laughed, and Seth loved the sound. There was no other sound like it really, but he would have used it to describe the way pure joy sounds, rich yet warm, sweet and mellow, like music mixed with chimes and a stream flowing in the background, all perfectly mixed and muted to just the right tone. And he laughed too.

"I know." He watched as she went over to the windowsill,

where she found an empty vase and began arranging the daisies in it, her back to him. "Lucille, please come here."

She turned to him and he reached out his arms to her. "I need you to hold me."

She gently embraced him and he drank in her intoxicating perfume, breathed in the honey smell of her hair, closed his eyes and felt the soft strength of her. He held her at arms' length, gazing into her light blue eyes. "You are beautiful."

"You are too." She smiled at him again.

Mesmerized, he just looked at her perfect face, grateful beyond words. "Did you hear that Ben said he may have a cure for me?"

"I did."

"So what do you think? Should I go for it?"

"Only if you feel in your heart that you want to. It doesn't matter what I think."

"Oh, but it does." He reached for her hand, which she put in his own. He kissed it before she quickly withdrew it, looking a little uncomfortable.

"What's wrong?" Seth wanted badly to kiss her on the lips as well. *She may be an angel, yes, but she is also a woman. A woman with whom I think I'm falling in love.* As much as he would have liked to stay in the moment forever, he felt an urgent question rise within, so he broke his hold on her and searched her eyes.

"If I make it...will you wait...will you be here for me?"

"Yes, Seth, I will always be here for you. But we can't have a relationship right now. You're not emotionally ready, and even if I were interested in something more than friendship, it would not be professional of me to go there. Don't forget, there are others here for you too who will support you, but also need you in return. Others who are still tormented with all that's gone on and still need resolution. I think they're waiting to see you."

Seth was disappointed in her response. *Give her time*, he thought. And before he had a chance to ask who the "others" were, Lucille was out the door, then back with Michael and Jonathan in tow.

Lucille led the way into the room and sat back down next to Seth's bed. Michael and Jon hung in the doorway, looking hesitant.

"Come in, sit." Seth motioned for them to pull up a chair.

Jonathan spoke first. "Seth, when Ben called us and let us know you were back in the hospital and you might not make it, we were afraid." The elderly rabbi looked nervous, taking his black felt hat in his hands and turning it around and around by the brim. "I went to the temple and prayed until my knees were sore. And I heard God speak to me, Seth. He said to stop worrying about your spiritual state of affairs and start worrying about my own…that I could be of no use to others until I set my own house in order. And once that was done, I could help others, including you." The rabbi looked up with tears in his old, sunken eyes. "Can you forgive me, my boy? I promise I'll stop lecturing you and find a way to help you."

"There is nothing to forgive, Jonathan." Seth reached out, took his friend's worn, leathery hand in his and shook it.

Waiting his turn, Michael stood to speak, as if he could no longer sit still. "I think I was the most afraid I'd lose you, Seth." Michael's eyes filled with tears. "When I came home and you weren't there it was horrifying. Then to almost lose you a second time…" Michael's voice broke off.

Seth gave his friend a small smile, nodding for him to go on.

"I also found the nearest church and went to pray, and believe me, it's been so many years I can't remember when I had my last confession." This caused the others to laugh, knowing

Michael's current agnostic state. But his unusually solemn demeanor and hushed tone quickly brought them back. "God spoke to me too, I think. He told me that I needed to help you in the best way I knew how. And after giving that a little thought, I realized that instead of being your counselor-friend, I needed to be your counselor-*lawyer*.

"So, I thought, what to do to help Seth as his attorney? And the answer came to me. Restore his reputation and good name. No easy task, it's going to take some time, but I'm ready to start working on it, even though it is a holiday."

"Wait a minute, what is today?" Seth looked at them all, bewildered. He had totally lost all track of time and didn't realize he'd been in the hospital again for three days.

"You don't know? Seth, it's Christmas Eve!" Lucille and Michael spoke simultaneously, surprised he didn't know.

"Or, if you prefer, the last day of Hanukkah," Jonathan chimed in, causing them all to laugh again.

"Well, what are you all doing here?" Seth was incredulous that they were here in his hospital room on Christmas Eve. "What time is it?"

"Time for all of you to leave so Seth can rest." Ben motioned toward the door.

Michael, Jon and Lucille stood to leave. Seth thanked his attorney and rabbi for their prayers and wished them a happy holiday.

"No, thank you, Seth, for making me a better rabbi," Jonathan said, tears in his eyes once again.

"You can make it up to me." Seth smiled mischievously at the rabbi, who looked at him quizzically. "Can you say a prayer for me? I still think you've got that special connection."

"Of course, my friend." Jonathan placed his hand on Seth's forehead, and the rest of them quietly stood in the doorway, heads bowed and hands folded. The rabbi prayed in Yiddish, then gently removed his hand, waved to the others and left the room.

Faced with blank stares from the rest of his friends, Seth realized they hadn't comprehended Jonathan's words. "He asked God to watch over me, to grant me health and peace. He said that since, according to the miracle of Hanukkah, the lamps stayed lit for eight days, perhaps I could be cured in eight days. He asked that since Hanukkah is a time of miracles," Seth's voice choked with emotion and tears welled in his eyes, "could I please be included as one of them. And he thanked God for our friendship…for me." The tears spilled down Seth's cheeks.

Ben cleared his throat, reminding everyone it was time to go.

Michael approached Seth and shook his hand. "Happy Hanukkah."

Seth knew Michael was also filled with emotion and was finding it difficult to speak. "Merry Christmas, Michael."

"Bah, humbug." Michael and Seth smiled at each other. "I have to give my employees the day off tomorrow, but we'll be back to work on all your legal affairs bright and early the next day, and we'll set things right again somehow." Michael squeezed Seth's hand. "I know I might not have served you well as your lawyer recently, and I can only say I will try my best from here on out. But I can also promise you that I will always be your advocate…your friend."

"Get out of here before I really start bawling." Seth wiped away more tears and Michael and Jon hugged him, waved to Lucille and Ben, and turned to go.

Lucille stood by Seth's bedside, waiting her turn to say goodbye. "Don't go yet," he told her, holding her hand in both of his.

Ben cleared his throat loudly. "Seth, I'm afraid we have

to have this consultation now if we're going to move forward with this. Sorry."

Lucille squeezed his hands in hers. "I'll be back soon."

After the three of them left, Ben held the door open for the team of cancer researchers to enter the room and formulate their game plan.

Seth was asked a long series of questions about his history including his family, health, mental state, travels, medications, relationships and religion, until he was sure they knew his whole life story.

Then one of the doctors explained in length how the procedure would work. They would wait until the day after Christmas, giving Seth a chance to build his strength for a whole day so he could be in good enough shape for the surgery. Until then, he was told, he should have nothing to eat after six p.m. Christmas day, get as much rest as possible, and try to keep his mind on other things so he wouldn't worry too much.

At that, Seth laughed out loud. *But really, I'm okay with this*, he thought. *One thing…one person…would help though.*

"Ben, can Lucille stay with me tomorrow, if it's alright with her?"

"Sure." Ben noted the gleam in Seth's eye. "As long as you get your rest."

Christmas day dawned gray and cold with snow flurries and a harsh wind. Seth was just thankful he was warm and dry in the hospital and not out in the elements and said a prayer for the homeless people under the Summer Street Bridge.

Lucille arrived after lunch, explaining she had visited her mother, who was doing well and sent her love, prayers and a home-made fruitcake.

"One of these days I'm going to thank her in person… and not for the fruitcake." Seth thought fondly of Ruthie

O'Hanlon and his chance meeting with her on the train that memorable day it crashed. He remembered her touching her finger to his wedding ring, remarking how it was a shame he was married because she had a single daughter named Lucille who would make a fine catch. *Who knew what God had in store?*

The two of them spent the afternoon together, playing cards, talking and laughing. They even sang with the Christmas carolers who stopped by along their route down the halls of the hospital, filling the tiny room with warmth and joy while the world outside grew colder and darker with the passing hours.

When dinner was delivered by one of the hospital staff, Lucille stood to go. "Can't you just stay and have dinner with me? I know it's hospital food, and it's awful, but it's going to be even more awful if I have to eat alone. Please?" Seth gave her his saddest puppy-dog look and she acquiesced.

"Well, I do want you to keep up your spirits. So I'll stay while you eat and then until you start getting drowsy. I'll be out there waiting for you tomorrow, but I'll be in here with you in spirit."

"Lucille…I love you." *There, I said it. Because it may be the last and only time I can.* Seth's eyes started to droop with sleepiness, even though he had only eaten a few bites. He smiled as he drifted off.

"God bless you, Seth Jacobs. Everything will be alright." Lucille turned and quietly slipped out of the room.

Chapter 22

Miracles really do happen.

The drug concoction worked. Several days after the surgery, a series of follow up tests, including a CT scan, MRI and dye injection, showed no traces of cancer left in Seth's body. And in several more days, a healthy appetite, abundance of energy, hair growth, increased circulation and an overall glow in Seth's eyes and cheeks proved it.

I am cured. I'm a new man. Seth felt like running out of the hospital and shouting it from the rooftops, but he had to be present for all the tests, and for the doctors to make sure he was feeling better, back to normal.

Three weeks after the administration of the miracle drug, the team of doctors who performed the feat was willing to announce to the world they had arrested cancer in a human being and had made a huge stride in finding a possible cure.

A press conference at Massachusetts General was arranged, so Seth stayed at the hospital, getting stronger and healthier each day. They wanted to present their patient looking his best, and didn't want to take any chances that anything, even a common cold, would keep him from revealing their work to the world.

The day of the conference the hospital looked like the Capitol Building in Washington D.C on Inauguration Day. Swarms of reporters and cameras and video teams crowded on the steps outside the hospital's front entrance, jockeying for position and live feeds of what they were told would be a medical breakthrough.

Seth was extremely nervous as he studied himself in the mirror in his little hospital room, where he had been held prisoner for three weeks straight. The only thing that kept him from finding a back door and making a run for it was Lucille, who kept watch over him both for his sake and as part of an agreement with Ben Grason.

This is it, he thought, looking at his reflection. *Wow.* His hair had started to grow back, a darker and curlier version but still with a golden tint, now burnished and flecked with silver. His blue eyes had their sparkle back. *Thanks to Lucille.* He had gained ten pounds and his normal color had returned to his cheeks.

Seth had donned a navy suit and starched white shirt. He straightened the tie around his neck as he stared at himself anxiously.

"How do I look?" He turned and gave a worried smile to Lucille, who stood by in a conservative hunter green dress with long sleeves.

"You look marvelous. How do I look?"

"Hmmm…like Maid Marion…no wait, Lady Gwenevere."

Lucille stuck out her tongue at him.

"Hey, that's a compliment." Seth defended himself in mock self-righteousness. "They were great ladies…a lot like you, you know – outspoken activists always behind a good cause."

Lucille crossed her arms and frowned, still not satisfied.

"And beautiful besides."

She finally smiled and spoke in a British accent. "Thank you, kind sir."

"I know there have been times recently where I may

have told you that, or even that I was falling in love with you, and I realize you probably thought it was because I was doped up but...Lucille I am totally clear-headed now and I was wondering if...if you would do me the honor of allowing me to court you?"

The question took Lucille by surprise and she stared back at him, mouth partly open, not answering.

"I would love nothing more than to spend all the rest of my days with you, Miss O'Hanlon. Of course, I will wait until after all the hoopla is over with today to properly begin dating you, but just in case there is any doubt in your mind, I want to tell you that I am madly in love with you."

Lucille blushed and looked shyly away. "Seth, I...I don't know what to say. I don't think it's a good idea..." she stammered. Seth put a finger on her lips and silenced her.

"That's okay. You don't need to answer me now. We have a press conference to attend. But once that's over with, I plan to get on with my life...our life together. I don't want to waste one more day not making the most of it with you."

Seth leaned over and kissed Lucille on the cheek. Before she had a chance to object again, a knock on the door interrupted them.

"It's show time." Ben peeked around the doorway. "You ready?"

"As I'll ever be." Seth took a deep breath, took Lucille's hand in his, and followed Ben out the door. He looked back just for a moment. *I hope this is the last time I'll ever set foot in a hospital room again.*

An overcast sky and freezing temperatures met the small band of doctors, who shepherded Ben, Seth and Lucille to the podium. But the small group didn't even seem to notice the cold. Despite the fact that they could see their breath, and that they were bundled in wool overcoats, gloves and scarves, they were all beaming.

Ben took the microphone first as flashes popped and cameras clicked and whirred. As quietly as possible, the massive crowd awaited the news.

"Ladies and gentlemen, members of the press, we at Massachusetts General Hospital are elated to share some groundbreaking news. A group of our doctors and researchers, working diligently together for the past several years, have performed thousands of tests on animals to find a cure for cancer. Finally, we have tested a live human patient and we are proud to say we were successful in finding what we truly believe is that cure."

The reception was deafening as the media crowd reacted with gasps, shouts and applause. Even the most jaded of them appeared to be stunned. After a few minutes, the volume started to subside and questions were hurled at the podium.

"Before I answer any questions, I'd like to introduce you to our guinea pig, the man who made this possible by putting his life on the line to allow us to perform these tests. Now the drugs that we used can be further tested and eventually marketed to hopefully heal millions: Ladies and gentlemen, I present to you a man to whom we owe much gratitude, Seth Jacobs."

Ben moved aside and Seth, who had been standing hidden behind him, approached the microphone and looked out over the sea of reporters, camera crews and satellite trucks.

But this time, he wasn't sick or afraid. He was just Seth Jacobs, a man to whom God had given his life back. "Thank you Ben, and to all of the doctors, researchers and staff at Massachusetts General who made my recovery from stomach cancer possible and literally saved my life. I had been told I had only days to live, and I felt like it; I was dying, so my sacrifice was small. I am humbled and grateful and very glad to be alive and in your presence, and for that, ultimately, I have

God to thank." Seth bowed his head in reverence and then said thank you again into the microphone.

The crowd buzzed with questions, but Ben overtook the microphone again and held up his hand. "Mister Jacobs is still recovering from his near-fatal illness and needs to get his rest, so we will be issuing a statement and fielding all questions in our public relations office by phone and email throughout the next few days. Thank you for your coverage and support."

Seth felt like he was in a daze. He and Lucille, who had stood a few feet away from him during the press conference, were finally en route home.

Home. That word never sounded so good. Seth looked forward to moving into Lucille's apartment, even if it was only supposed to be temporary as they had discussed. The two left the hospital via a private basement entrance flanked by security guards. They were met by a valet with a non-descript rental car that couldn't be traced so they could make a clean getaway from the media, which had worked themselves into a frenzy over the cure for cancer story.

But the two were home only an hour, sitting in the living room unwinding and talking over a cup of tea, when the phone rang. Ben Grason told them they had to come back to the hospital; it was urgent.

"You're not going to believe this," Ben said breathlessly.

"What, the cure didn't work after all?" Seth was mildly perturbed that his moment of tranquility with Lucille had been interrupted. Hearing his words, Lucille's jaw dropped, but hearing Ben answer a quick no, Seth covered the receiver with his hand. "It's okay. Sorry," he mouthed to her, apologizing for his sarcasm.

"It's not about that. Everything is fine. You're still cured."

"Well, it's going to take something really big for me to

drag me all the way back to that hospital. No offense but we just got settled in here."

"Seth, it's not about you," Ben said with a hint of impatience. " It's about Adam."

Seth stared in shock at the phone in his hand, afraid to ask. *No. My son can't die now, now that things are looking up.*

"Seth, Adam is coming out of the coma."

"Oh my God!" Seth started to weep tears of joy. Lucille saw him smiling through his tears and knew the news was good. She came up to him as he hung up the phone and hugged him tight. "Adam is coming out of his coma."

"Let's go."

In less than an hour they were back at the hospital to meet with Ben and ride with him to the assisted care rehabilitation where Adam still resided.

Soon they were entering the facility, a sterile-looking, no-frills, three-story building where long-term, chronic patients were sent when it was determined it was too expensive to keep them in the hospital any longer.

The three slowly walked into Adam's room, where he had lain still and unconscious for one year, three months and twenty days. He had silently turned twenty-two-years-old and missed most of his senior year at Harvard and his graduation. Time had not stood still for Adam Jacobs, as life moved on around him, without him.

Adam lay on his back in bed, dressed in a standard hospital gown, covered to his chest with a sheet and light blanket. His body was still, save for his chest, which gently rose and fell with the help of the ventilation machine at his bedside. He was hooked up to feeding and breathing tubes, and aside from a loss of about fifteen pounds, he looked like he was merely sleeping. Except for the blip-blip of the heart and brain-wave monitors, the room was silent.

The three of them stood to one side of the bed, waiting.

Then, they watched in awe as Adam's right forearm rose slowly up, his fingers extending as if he were reaching for a glass of water. Seth quickly glanced at his son's face and saw his eyelids flutter.

"Oh my God!" Seth felt like he was screaming but his words came out in a choked whisper. "He's coming out of it!"

Ben radioed the nurse on duty and asked her to get the doctor on call in there, stat.

Minutes later, a doctor and two nurses burst through the door.

"I'll need both of you to stand over there, out of the way, while we examine him." Doctor Grason motioned for Seth and Lucille to stand against the back wall of the room. They quietly obeyed.

The series of actions that took place next were a blur to Seth. Tubes were checked, machines buttons were pushed, blood pressure cuffs and stethoscopes and all types of metal tools appeared, and somehow, it all transpired in an expeditious, yet orderly way.

Seth closed his eyes and prayed out loud like he had never prayed before, squeezing Lucille's hand in his own for strength. "God, Your will be done, but please, if You can find it in Your heart, let my son live."

When Seth slowly opened his eyes, he saw something he hadn't seen for a year, three months and twenty days. "Dad." Adam mouthed the word, his long disabled and still dysfunctional vocal cords unable to make the sound behind it.

"Adam!" This time Seth's voice came out strong and clear, a shout for joy.

Doctors determined Adam had to stay in the rehabilitation center for a minimum of twelve weeks to recover enough to be able to sit up in a wheelchair and begin learning to walk and talk again. Following that he would need constant physical therapy and intermittent tests to monitor brain and other organ functions, but an initial battery of tests had shown he had not suffered from a loss of brain activity.

Seth visited his eldest son every day, bringing him cookies and magazines and telling him as he grew stronger, little by little, of all that had gone on in the lives of the Jacobs family.

It was hard, telling him about Aaron still in prison and Angelica still overseas with no word about how she was doing or how the pregnancy was going. But when he got to the part about Maria leaving him, it was especially difficult. Still, Adam had to know. Seth tried to sound as objective as possible, sticking to the facts, leaving out the part about the affair with the gardener. *It still hurts, but thank God for Lucille*, he thought.

Seth had been living with Lucille in her apartment, and on her insistence they had kept their relationship platonic. Sometimes he thought his patience would wear out, but he believed she would be ready one day and he was willing to wait as long as it took.

Seth also reminded himself that he had decided it would be better to wait until the divorce was final before he dated anyone anyway. Not that Maria was spying on them, but on further reflection, Seth just felt it was the right thing to do. And Lucille of course genuinely cared that Seth fully recuperate and get his life – and his family – back together before anything else.

So Seth slept on the couch in the living room, which was spacious and comfortable for an apartment, and Lucille stayed in her own bedroom. It wasn't easy, and Seth often dreamt about one day making her his wife and making love to her.

All in good time. All in God's time.

A few weeks into Adam's recovery, Seth decided to bring Lucille in to officially meet his oldest son.

The two of them came to Adam's room at Seth's normal visiting time. Seth introduced them to each other, then explained why Lucille was present.

"This woman helped save my life." Seth's face beamed.

Adam looked skeptically at the beautiful blonde next to his father, so Seth tried to explain. "Adam, as I've tried to tell you, I had lost everything...you, your brother and sister, your mother, my parents, most of my friends, my business and finally my health. Most importantly, I started to lose my self-respect and will to live. I wanted to die. I was at the breaking point. I had all but run out of faith completely and just wanted God to take me.

"Lucille found me sick and freezing with a bunch of homeless people under the Summer Street Bridge right after I passed out from fever and dehydration. I could have died, but she brought me home to her apartment and nursed me back until I needed to be taken to the hospital."

Adam's skeptical look softened a little.

"Adam, I know what you're probably thinking, that Lucille is my girlfriend, that I've replaced your mom. That's not what happened. Your mom wants nothing more to do with me and she's made that abundantly clear. But I have to be honest. I have fallen in love with Lucille and I think she's starting to have feelings for me as well."

"Seth!" Lucille protested, rolling her eyes.

"Well?"

"Your father and I have become good friends." Lucille

approached Adam, who was sitting upright in a chair. He had gained the use of most of his muscles, and was learning to walk one day at a time. He had had to relearn many fundamental abilities, including how to talk, and had worked extensively with a speech therapist. Although he still could not talk like he used to, when he concentrated, he could slowly form words that could be understood.

"Thank you." Adam reached out his hand, which Lucille took it in her own after brushing away a tear.

"I've heard so many good things about you Adam, and I know you've been through so much. I only want what's best for you and your father, and I hope one day you and I can get to know each other better and become friends."

Adam looked at her with tears of gratitude in his eyes, and nodded. "I…would like…that." He then looked at Seth with a question in his eyes.

Seth read his mind. *He wants to know where we go from here.*

He hadn't told Adam that he had also lost the house to foreclosure and that he was temporarily living with Lucille until he could find a way to make ends meet. He had been in contact with Michael and had asked for a small loan so that he could find his own apartment where he could live with his son. He would hate to part with Lucille, but there was no way the three of them could fit, much less live together, in her tiny apartment. It wouldn't be right.

"Adam, I know you're probably wondering where you… where we will be living after you leave here tomorrow."

Adam nodded, his pensive expression turning into one of relief.

He's still so much like a child. The thought tugged at Seth's heart. *A child that still needs his father.* "Adam, you have nothing to worry about. I have a place, an apartment, all set up where the two of us…" he used his finger to point from himself to Adam to make himself perfectly clear, "…where you and I will live. A friend of mine who also happens to be my and Aaron's attorney helped with all of the arrangements. Speaking of which, I need to give him a call…"

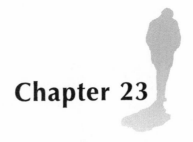

Chapter 23

Michael had worked non-stop investigating the tainted caviar debacle and he had finally found out the source of the Perfect Place restaurants' downfall.

A thought had come to the young attorney in the middle of the night when he couldn't sleep, which had become a normal habit of late as he tried to figure the whole thing out.

He waited until a week later, after he pored over medical and autopsy reports and talked to a dozen health and nutrition experts, before calling his partner to tell him his epiphany.

Jerry Rogers picked up the phone from the office, where he sat buried in paperwork. He and the other attorneys who worked at Rogers and Powers, along with several hired temps, had worked overtime for months taking over the burgeoning caseload left to them when Michael started devoting almost all of his time and energy into helping Seth Jacobs get his business back. Michael had told Jerry it was some sort of calling, something God had asked him to do.

Because he was doing the work pro-bono, Michael couldn't ask Jerry or any of the other attorneys or even legal aides in the firm to help. They had more than enough work to do for the paying customers, especially since he had to take a leave of absence.

Michael's voice came over the receiver in a frenetic rush. "Jerry, I think I might have the clue to setting this whole Perfect Place investigation on the right track!"

Jerry listened while his partner spilled his idea over the phone. "Didn't we find it odd that Senator Caine was the only fatality among the hundreds of people who became ill from the bad caviar?"

"Sure, I even told Seth that when I went to his house way back to talk to him about declaring bankruptcy to try to stay solvent. But it was just too difficult to investigate at the time, given the fact he was out of money."

"And at the time, I just accepted it at face value, I guess. But in reviewing this whole catastrophe and trying to make some sense of it all, I've spent hours looking over the senator's autopsy report trying to find something, and then it hit me. There may be nothing to refute that Robert Caine did die from the tainted caviar, but what if someone *planned* that he die that way? What if someone set it up so that he would be one of the hundreds of people to get food poisoning that night, knowing he would die from it?"

"Seems to me there would be an easier way to kill somebody."

"But think about it. If a person wanted him dead, would go to any lengths not to get caught, and made it look natural so that it couldn't be traced…it's possible, right?"

"Sure, I guess."

"And if the suspect could blame the whole thing on the restaurant…and not just any restaurant, but one of the most famous restaurant chains, owned by the most famous restaurateur in the world, a man so famous that the blame of such an incident would cast such a huge spotlight on him that it would leave the real culprit in the shadows…it would be the perfect plan."

"But how do you even begin to prove it?"

"The more I looked at the report, the more I asked, 'why would the senator die from the caviar while the rest only got sick?' I looked into Caine's medical history, and that of his entire family. None were allergic to caviar, which would make sense given the fact that the senator willingly ate it. But one of Robert Caine's uncles was highly susceptible to a rare infection by the bacteria Vibrio parahaemolyticus. He had once gotten extremely sick and almost died from ingesting something that contained V parahaemolyticus. Turns out the bacteria is only found in raw seafood."

"Wow." It was all Jerry could think to say. "Go on."

"This uncle had apparently not been close to his nephew Robert, so there was no way his nephew could know of this predisposition. But perhaps certain members of the Caine family would know. And perhaps one might want him dead."

"Hmmm…It's certainly worth a shot." Jerry looked out over the mountain of stuffed manila folders that engulfed him. "But please hurry, Michael, we need you back here soon, before I drown in paperwork or die of a stress attack."

Michael spent a huge chunk of his savings to hire a private investigator and his team to follow several of the late Senator Caine's relatives.

It didn't take too long before he got the call he had been waiting for.

The Caine family was notoriously similar to the famous Kennedy clan. In fact, it was rumored they were related to the neighboring Hyannis Port family somewhere along the old, old roots of the family tree.

Just like the Kennedys, several of the Caines had political aspirations, including Robert, who had just put his hat in the ring for the Presidential nomination shortly before the night of his death at the Perfect Place.

It was not widely known that one of his cousins, Geoffrey Caine, had always been jealous of Robert. That envy had apparently run much deeper than anyone had suspected.

Michael Powers sat in disbelief as the head of the private investigation team informed him that the extremely wealthy Geoffrey Caine was not only a huge contributor to his cousin's opponent, but also the son of the late John Caine, Robert's uncle...the same uncle who almost died many years ago of a bacterial infection that he got shortly after eating tainted caviar.

Instead of calling his partner this time, Michael Powers went directly into Jerry's office. Without knocking, he barged excitedly into the plush room, causing his partner to nearly spill his coffee on some already coffee-stained files.

"Michael! What are you doing here? You look terrible!"

Michael hadn't looked in a mirror, or he would have seen he had a scruffy beard starting to emerge on his face, dark circles, and a wild look in his eyes, not to mention he was not dressed in his usual attorney attire but in jeans and a rumpled sweatshirt. No wonder the other employees in the office had looked at him strangely as they greeted him with surprise.

"Happy New Year." Jerry Rogers' tone was sarcastic. He looked anything but happy, sitting tensely at his desk, his hands cupped around a huge mug of coffee.

Michael looked confused. "It's almost Valentine's day."

"I know, but you haven't been here since Christmas." Jerry looked tiredly at his partner. "I've tried to be understanding, Michael, but it's wearing on me."

"I know, and thank you. I'm so close. Just a couple more weeks, and I'll be finished with what I have to do."

"I just don't understand why you're going so far out on a limb to help Seth Jacobs. I know he's a good friend of yours, given you lots of business in the past, and he's been through hell and back. But as far as I can see you're not making a dime off him right now, and you're putting a big strain on the rest of us in the firm."

Michael sat in one of the leather chairs across the desk from his older partner. They had started the practice fifteen years ago and had been through a lot together. Most partners wouldn't have been nearly as understanding, Michael realized, but Jerry had a big heart. After a deep sigh, he tried once again to explain.

"I know it sounds totally crazy, but after Seth got his life back, I had this bizarre dream in which God asked me to work as hard as I could and to do whatever it took to help him get everything else back too. I was told it would be my mission until it was completed. Now I'm not super-religious as you well know, but how do you say no to God?"

"You got me there."

"Which is why I need your help."

"Whoa....wait a minute. This is your calling, not mine."

"I know, but this time, I think somehow we'll be rewarded. Not to mention, once I get this whole thing over with, I can come back to my normal work here at Rogers and Powers and you, my friend, can take a vacation."

Jerry leaned forward on his elbows. He still had a look of skepticism on his face, but he was now listening intently as Michael brought him up to date on what the private investigators had found out.

"So how are you going to help Seth now that you suspect who was behind the bad caviar?"

"First, I'm going to let the State's Attorney in on my theory and poor old Geoffrey Caine will be arrested on a whole slew of charges, including conspiracy and murder. Then I'll work with my prosecutor friends to cut Mister Caine a plea bargain in return for paying restitution for his wrongdoing and helping Seth out of the poorhouse.

"So why do you need me?"

"You're the best civil litigator around. I'm sure you can

come up with a reasonable settlement agreement once we bend good 'ole Geoffrey's arm."

Jerry frowned, still looking unconvinced.

"What, you think that's nasty?" Michael raised his eyebrows in mock innocence. "He brought down Seth's restaurant dynasty, so it would only be right that he build it back up again, don't you think? Besides, the man is loaded, so I'm sure he won't mind parting with a few mil to fix the damage he's done. Let's see, a third of that would be…" Michael punched his fingers in the air as if figuring it out on a calculator.

"Now you're talking." Jerry smiled. "But I probably would have helped anyway, out of the goodness of my heart."

Michael extended his hand and the partners shook on it.

"Well, no time to waste, we've got work to do."

Jerry let out a moan.

"Hey, remember, it's God's work."

"If you say so."

It took only about a week before the paperwork was signed.

Once Jerry told him that a settlement had been agreed upon in the case of *The Perfect Place Restaurants versus Geoffrey Caine*, Michael called Seth and invited him over to his brownstone. He had to tell him the good news in person.

They sat in the same family room where they had sat just months before, Michael the burdened, ungracious host and Seth a depressed, dejected, dying man.

Only this time, they were changed men.

And one of them was in for more changes.

Seth looked around as he sat on the couch while Michael went to the kitchen. The place looked cleaner, brighter to him now. *Maybe Michael painted or got more lamps or something. Or maybe it's just my new outlook.*

He didn't have a chance to ask about interior decorations, because Michael came back into the room with a flourish, brandishing an open bottle of champagne and two long-stemmed glasses. He filled them and handed one to Seth. With gusto, he clinked his glass with Seth's and said, "Cheers!"

Seth looked at him quizzically. *He must be congratulating me on my newfound health and my son Adam coming out of his coma*, he thought. "Thank you, Michael."

Michael smiled at him, looking bemused. "Congratulations!"

Now Seth looked even more puzzled, frowning. "You mean on my son Adam getting better? Or my getting better?"

"Yes, yes…and because I've got more good news for you to celebrate." Michael beamed.

He's looking a little crazy, Seth thought, still frowning with concern.

"You're rich!" Michael drank down the champagne in one gulp and gave Seth a huge grin.

Seth contemplated the words for a moment. *Of course I have my health back…and Adam came out of his coma and was going to recover just fine. And I'm in love with the most beautiful woman in the world. Of course my life is rich.* "Okay." The word came out of Seth's mouth sounding a little leery, because Michael was still smiling crazily, looking like he was going to start bouncing off the walls.

"No, I mean really, stinking, filthy rich." Michael fished his hand into his pocket and pulled out a slip of paper, handing it to his friend still seated on the couch.

Seth looked at it in shock. It was a check made out in his name for ninety-million dollars. *Ninety million dollars.* After staring at the check for a few minutes, he looked up at

Michael with his mouth open, his eyes glazed. Michael's smile had widened, if that was possible, his eyes gleaming with sheer delight.

"All yours, my friend. A little over one million for each Perfect Place restaurant that you lost as well as some more added in for residual losses, pain and suffering, et cetera. You can read over all the documents when you get a chance. You deserve every penny."

Seth saw through the tears in his eyes that the check was issued by Geoffrey Caine, cousin of the late Senator Robert Caine. Michael had filled Seth in on the investigation as it took roots and blossomed but Seth had had no idea what the outcome would ultimately be.

"He agreed to the restitution as part of a settlement Jerry worked out with the state prosecutor to avoid the public humiliation of a long, drawn-out jury trial. His family wouldn't approve of all that negative publicity you know." Michael strutted around like a peacock. "But don't worry; he'll still be sitting in prison for a few years as well."

Geoffrey Caine...the same man who caused the death of the senator, the death that was pinned on me and started the avalanche of my career and my life into the pit of hell... Seth let his mind and his feelings wander only for a few moments before he reminded himself that he had come to terms with all of this and had to keep working on letting go of the past.

Part of his new outlook on life, part of his new life, in fact, was to seek to forgive others who had wronged him. That included Maria, Judge Henry, his friends, even Geoffrey Caine. Seth had had a chance to tell the world what he thought of Geoffrey Caine when the media contacted him following Caine's arrest. It would have been his chance for public vindication. Yet he had declined, choosing to pray for him instead. *Jealousy really was a deadly sin, eating him alive,* Seth thought. *And now the man is paying in spades for what he has done. No need for me to play a part.*

Michael saw his friend's face lost in intense thought trying to sort out the information he had just imparted. "Michael, I don't know how to thank you…"

"Let's just say I've received my reward from the 'Man upstairs', who guided me to do the right thing."

Seth continued to stare dumbfounded at the glowing attorney. Then he thrust the check forward, trying to put it in Michael's hand. Michael cocked his head quizzically. "Seth, it's your money."

"I know, but I want to give it to you for…"

"Jerry and I agreed to handle this case pro bono. I'm sticking to that, but if you want to pay Rogers and Powers a commission, I'm sure they'd appreciate a small stipend."

"That goes without saying, but I want to pay you…"

"Seth, this is your money." Michael interrupted again. "To put you back in business. To restore to you what was taken away and is rightfully yours."

"I have a better idea, Michael. I want you to take half and…"

"No way, buddy. Way too much."

"No, hear me out." Seth took a deep breath. "Listen to me for a minute. I want you to spend half, or whatever it takes, and use it to pay yourself and a team of attorneys to find a way to get my son Aaron out of jail – and then find my daughter."

Michael groaned and sat down on the couch, holding his head in his hands. "You had to go and burst my bubble, didn't you?"

Seth smiled. "You'll do it then?"

"Sure. But I'll only spend what it takes to get the job done."

Seth crossed the room and hugged his friend. "You're the best."

"Yeah, yeah, yeah…" Michael waved him off.

Seth stared at Michael, his eyebrows knitted with concern. "What's wrong?"

"I'm wondering when the old Michael left the room and the new one came in." Seth smiled. "Humility never used to be part of your package."

Michael laughed. "I know, I know, I would normally take credit for all of this, and have no problem being paid a fat sum on top of it. But I read somewhere that pride is right up there with envy and the rest of the deadly sins, so I'm trying to remain humble, despite myself."

I guess I'm not the only one who has changed, Seth thought, and smiled through his tears. "I have just one favor to ask, Michael. Can we keep this between us? I just don't want to be bothered by the media anymore and I have some ideas about what I want to do with the rest of the money, but I need some time to figure it all out."

By the grace of God, Judge Henry was on vacation in Europe the day of Aaron Jacobs' new trial.

Michael and his team of lawyers, legal aides, researchers and investigators reopened the case files, probed all the witnesses, took countless depositions and did a thorough sweep of the prison, including background checks on all of its employees.

They found a series of cover-ups, denials and negligence that started with the lowest prison guard and went up the ranks to the prison doctor, the warden, the state prosecutor and finally, ended with none other than Judge Henry himself.

It turned out that one of the prison guards on duty during the fight that broke out between Sanchez Dominquez and Aaron Jacobs had never been asked for his side of the story. If he had been allowed to make a statement at the time, he would have told the police and prosecutors that Aaron had only used enough force to take the wind out of Sanchez. The guard had been shocked that the Latino had died, but when he went to express that sentiment and ask questions, he was told to keep his mouth shut, or else.

The prison doctor had flat-out lied. In trying to fix Sanchez up from the fight, he had prescribed the wrong amount of medication, giving him what ended up to be a lethal dose that made him hemorrhage. The warden, not wanting to suffer a lengthy investigation or media exposure of the prison's inadequate medical staff, which would surely cost him his job, covered up the malpractice. The police, who were tight with the warden, didn't dig any deeper, taking the medical report at face value, and the state prosecutor relied on the police report. That way the case would be open and shut, a sure win, which would look good on his record and that of his boss.

And his boss, the State's Attorney, had told him they had to nail this Aaron Jacobs. After all, it had fallen on his office to investigate Seth Jacobs and the Perfect Place in the death of Senator Caine and they had gotten nowhere at the time. Surely a win against the son might help their office look better since they had failed thus far in the case against the father. Plus the State's Attorney and Judge Henry were best friends, and the judge wasn't a big fan of the Jacobs family anyway and would most certainly lean the prosecutor's way during the trial.

Seth's middle child, Aaron, stood at the defense table next to Michael, dressed in a modest suit coat and slacks which his father had provided. He looked ten years older somehow. Aaron turned to give his dad a smile, raw hope in his blue eyes.

God, he really does look just like me, Seth realized.

Then Aaron's expression brightened like clouds parting to let the sunshine through when he saw his brother Adam sitting next to his father on the courtroom bench.

"Oh my God!" Aaron's voice emerged as a whisper. "You're…"

"Okay." Adam whispered the word back and smiled at his brother. "It's okay. Good luck!"

Michael also looked back at Seth and Adam with a smile. Determination was in his dark brown eyes.

"All rise." The honorable James McIntyre was presiding, sitting in for Big H. Aaron and Michael turned back to face the judge and face the music.

The entire trial took only fifteen minutes. Once the mounting evidence had started to flood the State's Attorney's office, thanks to Michael's investigation, the prosecution had readily and hastily agreed to drop the charges.

Aaron was free to go.

Chapter 24

Jonathan Mosha had been kneeling a very long time in the back pew of Temple Israel, the same pew where Seth had knelt and prayed as he had encouraged him to do. Encouraged him to repent, to make things right with God.

The rabbi was kneeling alone in the dimly lit temple. Then, without any apparent reason, he bolted up out of his pew and headed for his office to use the phone. Jonathan flicked on the light, dialed Massachusetts General Hospital and asked for Doctor Benjamin Grason.

His voice came out in excited, rapid fragments. "Ben, it's Rabbi Jonathan Mosha. I need your help. I've been tormented lately with guilt over the fact that I never really helped Seth in his plight, and I was wondering if you could give me some advice. I know how you helped with Seth's cure, and, well… Ben, I know this is going to sound crazy, but…did you talk to God at all during this whole cure thing?"

Ben's voice was calm, reassuring. "It's not crazy at all, Jon. Yes, I felt like God spoke to me in the middle of the night, encouraging me to help Seth the best way I knew how, to stop lecturing him and worrying if or how I was helping, and to just take action. And somehow, I just knew what I had to do. A little scary, I know. Why, are you getting the same message?"

"Yes, and I've prayed and prayed but no answers come. I'm so frustrated I'm driving myself crazy."

"Why don't you try talking to Michael Powers? He helped Seth recover his business and free his son Aaron. I'm sure he had some divine guidance. Hey, I gotta run, duty calls. Good luck."

The rabbi hung up, sat in silence for a minute, then picked up the phone again and called Rogers and Powers. Michael was in his office and told the secretary to let the call come through.

"Hey, Jonathan, how's it going? Have you heard all the good news about Seth and his sons?"

"I just talked to Ben, and yes, congratulations, Michael."

"Thanks. I gotta tell you though, it wasn't just me coming up with all these brilliant solutions. I think the Big Man upstairs had something to do with all of this. I'm definitely not an agnostic anymore." There was silence on Jonathan's end. "Jon, you there? I thought you'd appreciate that."

"You have no idea, Michael. I was actually calling to ask you whether you somehow got some direction from God. I asked Ben the same. And I'm hearing from God myself, only I'm not Seth's doctor or his lawyer and I'll be darned if I know how I can help as his rabbi."

"I think I can help you. The only thing...or person...still missing from Seth's life is his daughter Angelica. Seth asked me to spend some of his settlement money trying to find her. Maybe that's your calling."

And the rabbi's face suddenly shone as if a light bulb had exploded inside his head. "Thanks, Michael. I think God is talking to me right now through you."

Seth had told Jonathan that his daughter was living in Syria with her new husband Caleb Elia and his family, and that she was expecting a child sometime in January, which if everything went well, meant she would have a baby close to two months old by now.

Jonathan had been born in Israel in the harbor town of Haifa, then just a tiny fishing village. As he understood from old friends and relatives still living there, it was now a bustling harbor city full of life, industry and culture perched on the magnificent hills overlooking the Mediterranean.

Damascus, the capital of Syria, was about as far from Haifa as Boston was from Providence. Not that far.

After hanging up with Michael, Jonathan made a long distance call to Haifa. His old friend, Simon Hirsch, was a rabbi who still lived in Haifa and taught in Jerusalem. Simon had climbed the ladder of importance and power, Jonathan had heard, and might have some connections.

Minutes later, Simon was on the line, and Jonathan explained how he needed to find the Elia family in Syria. More specifically, he needed Simon to find Angelica Elia and her newborn baby.

Since Caleb's father worked for the Syrian government, which was headquartered in Damascus, Simon suggested it shouldn't be too hard to find them. "What do you want once we locate her?" Simon asked his old friend.

"The goal is to get them out of there." Jonathan explained that his search needed to be kept a secret, that the young woman's life and her baby's were possibly at stake. "The father of the girl wants her to come home badly, and has reason to believe she wants to come home too. But her husband and his family probably don't want that to happen, and if that's the case, they'll do what it takes to stand in the way of their departure. I take it that men still dominate most affairs in Syria?"

"Yes, and right now the borders have been fortified, so that it's not so easy to get in and out. Whether or not I can bring a woman and child back with me is a huge gamble. I can try though."

Two weeks later, Jonathan heard from Simon that he had found the Elia family. Angelica had given birth to a baby girl in a hospital in Damascus, then brought her back home where she lived with Caleb and his parents on the capital's outskirts. They lived in a well-off but conservative, old-school Muslim village where women still hid their femininity and were considered subservient to men, and boys were definitely the gender of choice when it came to their offspring.

"Perhaps they won't mind parting with the baby, then?" Jonathan sounded hopeful as he spoke to his friend.

"I'm afraid that isn't the case here," Simon replied. "A wife leaving her husband and taking his child from him, even though it's a girl, would be considered a disgrace, a crime, and would be punishable by force or prison or both. I'm sure there is no way the Elia family will give Angelica their blessing for her to divorce her husband. The only way is for her to lie and say she is merely taking a temporary leave to visit her father and show him his granddaughter. But the husband will probably want to come with them. Even if he didn't, and he allowed them to leave, the Syrian borders with Iraq, Lebanon and Israel are extremely volatile right now with the continuing turmoil in the Middle East. I don't see how this can happen right now, unless…"

"Anything you can do, Simon. I'll come over there myself if I have to."

"No, that would be out of the question. The U.S. Embassy is sending Americans home, not allowing them into the country. There's only one way I can think of to get the mother out of Syria, and that's to sneak her out across the Israeli border into my country, then deport her by boat out of Haifa. Since she's Jewish, Israel will welcome her. But it will still be very dangerous. There's no telling what could happen to Angelica if she's found out."

"What about the child?"

"Angelica will most likely have to leave her if she really wants to get out of Syria. I don't see any way that the father will let his child go. I will leave it up to her how much she wants to risk."

Seth was elated when Jonathan told him he had a baby granddaughter. Jonathan said he didn't have any details on the baby, or on the plan to bring mother and child home. The rabbi didn't tell his friend that the plan was highly dangerous and there was a possibility that in order to bring his daughter home, his granddaughter might have to stay in Syria. The news would break his heart and he had already been through so much.

Seth was home playing chess with Adam while Aaron was out shooting hoops with some guys in the neighborhood when the phone call came.

It was Jonathan Mosha, telling him he needed to meet him the next day at Logan International Airport. His daughter Angelica was coming home.

Jonathan waited for Seth's shouts of joy to die down before he imparted the very bad news.

"I am really sorry to tell you this, Seth, but your granddaughter won't be coming home. The baby died of a sudden fever brought on by some rare disease. Her name was Serena. Seth, I'm really sorry…"

He listened as Seth cried into the phone, praying for God to comfort his friend.

Seth was deeply saddened that he never knew his first grandchild. But the news that his daughter who had been lost to him was finally coming home took some of the sting out of the news and reminded him to try to stay grateful.

Angelica was coming home tomorrow.

Seth, Adam, Aaron and Jonathan were sitting in the waiting area for military flight six-forty-seven from Jerusalem to arrive. While they waited, Jonathan filled them in on the fact that Angelica had promised information to the Israeli military on Syrian terrorists which she had gleaned from her husband. It had given Simon a bargaining chip in helping gain her freedom.

Angelica's father and brothers sat together with Jonathan Mosha, nervously silent, lost in thought.

Seth had worried over the past forty-eight hours that some crazy turn of events would somehow prevent his daughter's arrival. *What if Caleb or another member of the Elia family intercepted her trip to Haifa, or found out about her escape and somehow shanghaied her boat while it was bound for Jerusalem, or managed to stop her from getting on the plane?*

Jonathan offered some comfort to his friend as they sat waiting. He reminded Seth that the last thing he knew for sure was that Simon had safely brought Angelica across the Syrian-Israeli border. The rest was kept secret to minimize the risk of her escape route being discovered. Seth knew the rough game plan, but didn't know when or how it was being carried out.

Stop! Seth willed himself to be calm, praying for faith, hope and strength. *God, please let her come home safe to me.*

The minutes ticked by slowly until they finally heard the announcement that flight six-forty-seven from Jerusalem had arrived.

The four men jumped to their feet and stood waiting. Angelica would have to go through customs and the accelerated security that had been in place over the years due to terrorist attacks.

Still, they couldn't sit. They all paced and waited and leaned against the wall, and then waited and paced and waited some more, craning their necks to see past the international flight exit where passengers slowly started trickling through.

They almost didn't recognize her when she approached them. Her hair, which had been long, thick and black when they last saw her, was now short and red, and she was thinner and paler than she had been when she left.

It wasn't until she stopped five feet away, dropped the bag in her hand, and quickly walked toward them that they realized it was Angelica.

She would have run, but she carried a bundle in her other arm.

They saw it was a baby girl.

The most beautiful baby, except for his own daughter, that Seth had ever seen. Her eyes were large, inquisitive and dark chocolate brown and her pudgy, pink cheeks were framed all around by black ringlets.

"Daddy?" Angelica slowly approached her father, then looked on either side to see both of her brothers.

Jonathan had sent Simon a letter from Seth to hand deliver to Angelica telling her all that had transpired with her family since she had been gone.

Still, she looked as if she was in shock to see Adam and Aaron standing before her. Seth wasn't sure who was more surprised—her or them.

Angelica gently handed the baby to Aaron, who stood awkwardly with Adam, both of their mouths agape, then bounded into her father's arms, sobbing.

"Shhh, it's alright, my baby girl." Seth tried to control his own emotions in order to comfort his daughter, but the tears escaped nonetheless and fell down his cheeks and nose as he held her tight, rocking her, stroking her hair. "You're home with your family now. You're home."

A loud wail escaping from the baby that Aaron still held tentatively in his arms interrupted Seth and Angelica and turned their weeping into laughter.

Angelica held out her arms and took the baby from her brother, then gave both Aaron and Adam a big hug, which caused the baby to cry louder.

"Daddy, Aaron, Adam, this is Serena." Angelica unwrapped the blanket from the crying infant and comforted her until she quieted down, staring at her new grandfather and uncles with wide-eyed curiosity.

Seth grinned and stroked the baby's cheek. "She is beautiful, Angelica. This is truly a miracle. We thought she was, well, um…"

"I know, Daddy; I'm sorry. Simon told me we had to pretend she had died to save her life. It was the only way to get her out of there. It's a long, awful story but I can tell you in the car ride. Right now, I better feed her or she's going to start screaming again. And I'm pretty famished myself." She flashed her brothers a huge grin. "You have no idea how great it is to see both of you. All of you. Now that's a miracle."

Jonathan stood quietly on the sidelines of the scene before him, smiling as he witnessed the joy of this miraculous family reunion.

Seth put his arm around his friend and brought him into the family circle. "Angelica, you remember my friend, Rabbi Jonathan Mosha? He's the one who started the chain of events that brought you home."

The rabbi extended his hand, which Angelica brushed aside, giving him a big hug instead. "Thank you so much, Rabbi."

"You can call me Jon. And welcome home, Angelica, and you too, baby Serena." He took the baby's tiny fingers into his larger, worn ones and playfully winced as the baby squeezed tight. "Just like her momma, a fighter."

Seth laughed and then became serious. "Jonathan, did you know the baby was coming home?"

"No, I didn't know much more than you. This is such a relief! I guess I did okay, yes?"

"More than okay." Seth smiled, grateful that his friend had helped bring his daughter and granddaughter back to him.

The car ride was full of animated chatter as Seth drove the reunited family home to the cottage house on the outskirts of the city where he now lived with Adam and Aaron. Serena slept in her car seat, so they tried to keep their voices down despite all they had to say.

"So what's with the red hair?" Aaron said from the back of the car, where he sat with Adam on either side of the baby's car seat. He playfully reached over the front passenger seat and tousled his sister's red bob. After just a half hour in the car, the warm, comfortable camaraderie they had had in the past blanketed them all, fortifying the bonds that had never really been broken.

"I know, it's awful, isn't it?" Angelica pulled down the visor in front of her and looked in the mirror, sticking out her tongue at her reflection, which caused her brothers to laugh. "But Simon said I needed to totally change my looks just in case Caleb..." She paused, swallowing hard. "It's still hard to say his name out loud." Tears pooled in her eyes. "In case he was looking for me. That's why I had to make up a big lie about Serena. That was the worst part of all. Knowing you all thought she was dead, and being without her for a whole week while we pretended to have her funeral...it was awful."

Angelica explained that she had to tell Caleb and his family that while she was shopping at the market, the baby had started to choke, and by the time she rushed her to the hospital, she was dead. When her husband and in-laws asked to see her body, a man planted by Simon at the hospital to masquerade as a doctor told them the child had been cremated at the mother's request. Angelica received a slap in the face for that, but she withstood it knowing her daughter was still alive. She lied, telling Caleb she couldn't bear to see her daughter's tiny body lying in a casket, and wanted to preserve her in ashes instead.

Angelica had been forced to secretly start weaning the child to a bottle so she could be fed without her. Then Serena had been whisked away from the hospital to a safe house in a tiny village on the Syrian border. The baby was then picked up by Simon, who brought her to live in his small house next to the temple in Haifa. Meanwhile, Simon had found help from a local woman who had lost her own child to take care of the baby girl.

"That must have been really hard." Adam touched his sister on the shoulder, comforting her.

"You have no idea." Angelica turned back toward her brothers and tearfully smiled. "But I just kept holding onto the thought that soon the two of us would be back in America with all of you. When I got Dad's letter telling me the two of you were back home, and that all of you were safe and well, I couldn't wait to see you. And when Simon called offering his assistance to bring me back home, I knew right away that it was what I wanted, needed to do. But I told him there was no way I was leaving without Serena. So we came up with our secret plan. I was scared to death, but it worked." Her smiled broadened.

"But don't you miss Caleb at all?"

"No." Angelica's response was immediate. "He turned into a completely different person when he was in Syria.

His country, his parents, even his aunts, uncles and cousins eventually seemed to come before me and our marriage. It was like he was married to Islam and because I wasn't a Muslim, I couldn't fit in. And the thought of bringing Serena up as a second class citizen made me sick. I vowed that once she was born, I'd find a way to bring her to America. Thank God for Jonathan and Simon."

"Yes, my friends have been very helpful." Seth glanced at his daughter as he drove and smiled at her. "There is one friend you haven't met yet who helped me tremendously…saved my life in fact."

Adam and Aaron quietly exchanged knowing looks in the back seat.

"Her name is Lucille." And with that, Seth pulled the car into the driveway of their Cape Cod home. Lucille was waiting inside.

Seth turned toward his daughter and took her hand, looking into her eyes. *She has eyes just like her mother.* He couldn't help himself from thinking that every time he gazed into them. This time he felt a mix of sorrow and resolve. "There's something more I have to tell you that I didn't write in the letter I sent. I wanted to tell you in person. I know I did write that your mother and I were divorced. I didn't explain the whole thing, and I will some day, and I think your brothers will help you understand because they're just starting to understand themselves." Seth took a deep breath and continued. "I grieved over your mother leaving, but when I got so sick, I was focused just on staying alive. Actually there came a point in time when I wanted to die and end my misery. Lucille found me close to death under the Summer Street Bridge and literally saved my life. She helped me to want to live again, helped me to have faith and hope again. And she helped me to love again. Somehow I've fallen in love with her in the process. She doesn't feel the same yet; she wants to keep everything professional since I'm her patient. But I know she'll come around one day."

"Does she live with…"

"No." Seth interrupted her question. "It's just the boys and I living here for now. I made a promise to myself and to all of you that you will always have a home here with me until you're ready to move out on your own. But Lucille does visit often and, bless her heart, cleans up the mess we three bachelors sometimes make. And she's here today waiting to meet you."

All four of them sat quietly for a minute. Angelica finally spoke.

"But what about Mom?" Tears welled up in Angelica's dark eyes. "I really miss her. I've gotten a few letters from her, but she didn't say much in them. Only that she loved me and regretted that she had to leave us, but felt it was the only thing she could do at the time to keep her sanity. She told me she was living in Los Angeles and that she was trying to start a modeling or acting career, and that she hoped to see us all soon. I couldn't even tell her about Serena being born because of the dangerous state I was in, not to mention I couldn't get a letter out at that point. I wonder how she'll feel about being a grandmother."

Seth watched his daughter's brow furrow in pain. Angelica turned from her brothers and faced forward, staring out the front windshield, her eyes tearing up, her hands in her lap. *For all of her bravado and growing up into a woman and mother, she is still my little girl,* Seth thought.

"Oh, honey, I know she'll be thrilled to hear about Serena and once she sees her and holds her…" He took her hand in his. "Your mom was under the impression that the baby had died too, so she may be shocked at first but I'm sure she'll be overjoyed just like we were. She knows you're flying home today and told me she wants to see you as soon as she can. We'll call her when we get inside and I'm sure she'll get on the first flight here. While she may have stopped loving me, she never stopped loving you and your brothers."

"We miss Mom too." Aaron added. "We've only seen her a few times ourselves since we've been living with Dad. When she heard about Adam coming out of his coma, she flew home to see him, and then came home again when I got out of prison." Aaron's voice softened. "She couldn't face Dad so we met her at her hotel in Boston. She said she still loves us and cares about us and I believe her. She did ask about dad too. I'm not sure how she feels about him anymore. But I think she's ashamed about everything. "

"What do you mean? I swear I've been so cut off from everything and everybody!" Angelica's defiant nature surfaced.

"I should probably let her tell you her story herself," Aaron said slowly. "I mean, she has been living a life she's not proud of and she regrets her decision to leave dad, to leave us. She made a few poor choices to try to get ahead out there in Hollywood, like you hear a lot of budding actresses do…hooking up with the wrong people, partying too much, you know. But I think she's done with all of it now. I know she'll want to hear about you and Serena."

"How could she hurt you so much?" Angelica's voice cracked as she looked at her father, tears in her eyes. Seth reached his arm around his daughter and held her.

"I don't know, but I've forgiven her, just like you'll need to do. And I know you can because I know my daughter and her big heart and kind soul."

"Dad has helped us too," Adam said from the back seat.

"I love you, Daddy." Angelica squeezed her Dad tight. "I just don't know if I can be as forgiving as you."

"Give it time, sweetheart. Just remember, now you're a mother yourself with your own little one to take care of. And I know, if you want her to, Lucille will help. Now we better get in there before she wonders what happened to us."

"Dad, I think you've suffered long enough. If this

woman…Lucille, makes you happy, then I'll be happy for you if it all works out. Besides, she must be a saint to clean up after the three of you!"

Seth breathed out a sigh of relief. "I know she can never replace your mother, but I also know you'll find her to be the sweetest, kindest, warmest woman you'll ever know. I'm going to head inside and let her know we're here."

Angelica let go of her father's hand as he got out of the car to head into the house. She turned around to look at her brothers, her eyebrows raised.

"She really is great, sis." Adam spoke up.

Just then, as if on cue, Lucille opened the front door and waved.

"Wow, you didn't say she's also beautiful," Angelica said, stealing a quick look at her possible future stepmother as she helped Serena out of her car seat.

Lucille, with Seth just a step behind, crossed the expanse of front lawn to greet the weary travelers. Upon seeing the baby, her face lit up with joyful surprise. Seth proudly introduced her to his daughter and his new baby granddaughter, the newest light of his life.

"Welcome home, Angelica." Lucille uncertainly extended her hand.

"Thanks. You have no idea how great it feels to hear that." And, instead of taking Lucille's hand, Angelica wrapped both her arms around her.

The phone ringing prompted them to go inside.

Chapter 25

The two women stopped abruptly in the foyer when they saw Seth appear from the kitchen. His face was drawn, almost ashen, looking as if he had just been told his cancer was back again.

"Seth, what's wrong? Who was that on the phone?" Lucille dropped the small piece of luggage she was carrying and went to him, concerned. Angelica stood still, frozen. Seth had received so many ominous phone calls over the past few years that they were afraid for him.

"It was Maria."

"Is she alright?" Angelica sucked in her breath, her question escaping in barely a whisper.

"Yes, she's fine." Seth moved away from Lucille and started to pace the foyer. "She's taking the next flight out here to see Angelica. It takes off from LAX in an hour. I told her about Serena and she started to cry but I heard the joy and excitement in her voice. But here's the strange thing – she said she also wants to see me. That she needs to talk to me. That it's important. She sounded…different."

"Different how?" Angelica asked.

"Not angry or bitter. She sounded…soft, nice…maybe even humble." Seth looked at Angelica. "She wants both of us to meet her at the airport." He turned and gazed at Lucille for a reaction and got none. "If it's okay with you?"

"Of course." Lucille's voice masked any emotions she may have been feeling. "I'll help you get the baby ready."

Seth and Angelica nodded, both apparently lost in their own thoughts.

What could Maria want with me now? Seth wondered. He looked at Lucille again for guidance. "Are you sure?"

"Go to her." Lucille smiled reassuringly.

The reunion of Seth and Angelica with Maria at Logan Airport was charged with mixed emotions.

Angelica had told Maria about the baby before bringing Serena with her to see her grandmother for the first time. Still, Maria put her hand over her mouth to stifle a sob of happiness as she ran toward them, bags in hand. She dropped the bags and hugged Angelica, and then Seth, tears streaming down her face. Serena was lying wide-eyed in a carrier on a seat in the airport lobby next to where Angelica stood. Maria knelt down and touched a finger to her cheek. "She's beautiful, an angel, just like her mommy."

Angelica brushed away tears. "Would you like to hold her mom?" She gently picked up the baby and placed her in Maria's eager arms.

Seth looked at Maria holding their baby granddaughter and in that instant of pure joy a year of grief slipped away for a few moments. Maria smiled at Seth and he couldn't help returning it.

"Why don't we go get some dinner?" Seth picked up Maria's bags. "We have a lot of catching up to do."

Over dinner in the airport hotel where Maria was staying, Angelica filled her mother in on all of the events leading to her arrival with Serena back in the U.S. Seth was quiet most of the dinner, and caught Maria glancing his way a few times with a smile of gratitude.

Maria sympathized with her daughter on all she had gone through, and told her how sorry she had been to add the strain of the divorce to the situation. She started to explain where she had been and why she hadn't been there for all of them, especially Seth, when Serena started wailing.

"I guess she's just really tired, since she just ate," Angelica said. "I'm sorry, but I think we better call it a night. But mom, we need to finish…"

"That's okay, I'm here for a few days actually." Maria interrupted her daughter with reassurance. "I would like to see each of you again, individually if I can, to spend more time with all of you, and of course my sweet little granddaughter. And to, well, try to make an amends." Maria's words caught Seth completely off guard. He hadn't known what to expect from her visit, but had never considered spending time alone with her, much less getting an in-depth apology.

She told them both she'd be staying several nights at the airport hotel and asked if Angelica and her brothers could come and visit the next night, and then Seth the following night. "I just have so much to tell you." Her eyes probed Seth's for a long moment. He wasn't sure what he saw in them, but decided to grant her request.

Two nights later, Seth showed up for dinner again in the hotel restaurant, this time alone. He was seated at the table nervously waiting when Maria appeared, dressed in a cranberry-colored, sleeveless dress.

It had been an unusually warm day for Boston's early spring. Her arms and legs were still shapely and tanned. *She looks good*, Seth thought, despite the turmoil that wracked his heart. He couldn't deny the trace of hurt and anger that still lingered upon seeing her face, still beautiful with pouty lips that matched the shade of her dress. And he still felt an uneasy tug at his heart. *Is it…can it still be attraction after all of this time, and all of the pain she's caused? No, that's impossible, isn't it?* He almost felt like he was betraying Lucille in even thinking this way.

Seth stood, unsure how to greet her, but Maria decided for him, hugging him and allowing him to pull out her chair and help her be seated.

When the waiter came by for drink orders, Maria asked for a club soda.

"No wine?" Seth was surprised. Maria always ordered wine before and during dinner.

"No I gave it up, along with a few other things that I had a little too much of in LA."

"So what do you have to tell me?" *Brace yourself, this might be rough,* he told himself. *She probably wants a ton of money and doesn't realize I've given most of it away. That should spark some fireworks.*

"I'm sorry, Seth." Tears trickled down Maria's face, smearing her mascara, making her look like a vulnerable little girl.

And that simple apology, the last words Seth expected to hear from his ex-wife's mouth, began to erase the old, faint scars of hurt and anger that still lay unseen inside.

Seth tried to stammer out, "it's okay," but Maria went on.

"I'm sorry for a lot of things…for being selfish and angry, spiteful and hateful. For blaming all of the misery of my life on you when in fact I allowed myself to become miserable.

"I tried to escape from my old life by searching for what I thought would be the perfect career. I landed some modeling jobs and a few minor acting jobs in commercials. I wanted to be a star and forget all of you.

"I worked crazy hours and when I wasn't working, or looking for work, I partied. But it was never enough. It got to the point where I needed valium to fall asleep and Quaaludes and cocaine to get me through the day. I drank a lot and smoked a lot and was a mess. And the worst part..." Maria took a deep breath and swallowed, "...well, I hit bottom when I did what I told myself I'd never do. Just like you hear about all the time, there were some sleazy agents and directors who said if I slept with them, or at least did a sexual favor for them, they'd get me a big job, make me famous. And I finally got so desperate; I gave in to one of them." Maria took a tissue from her purse and dabbed her eyes, trying to stop the tears, but her voice was choked with them.

"It makes me sick to this day. But it made me realize I was done. That I didn't really want to be a star, or even be a model or actress anymore. I hated LA, I hated my life and most of all, I hated myself and who I had become. Part of me just wanted to die, but I was too scared to kill myself. I guess I still believed in God. I didn't know what else to do, so I went to confession, to this little old priest at a small Catholic Church downtown. He suggested I go see a counselor, so I took what little money I made and went for a few sessions. Somehow I saw I was being selfish and needed to let go of the anger and fear pent up inside, and especially my pride. Most of all, I realized I just wanted to come home. I missed the kids. And I missed you.

"My heart went out to you as I watched on the news about your getting cancer. I wanted so badly to call you or write, but I was just so beaten down by then, so ashamed. I felt so sorry for myself that I couldn't rise above it for a long time. When I came to visit Adam, and then Aaron, it was all I could do not to see you. I still couldn't bring myself to talk to you. I was so afraid you wouldn't want to listen, wouldn't care."

Seth looked into Maria's eyes and saw the pain there and his heart broke for her. He knew she was telling the truth, and he could relate to what she had said. *I wanted to die too,* he remembered. *Only I had someone reach out and help save me. She had to reach out herself. That took a lot of courage.* Seth reached across the table and took her hand in his. "I missed you too."

Maria smiled through her tears. "I know you've made a life without me now. And I know I have no right to ask you for anything. All I know is that I want to stay here in town for awhile, and if it works out, try to get a job and move back so I can spend some time with the kids. I've actually done some soul searching about what I'd like to do for work, and it keeps coming back to me that what I truly love is gardening. So I was thinking that maybe a job with a local florist would be good. What do you think?"

Seth realized his mouth was hanging open a bit. *Who is this woman?* "I think that sounds...good."

Dinner arrived and the two of them ate, sticking to small talk about the children and baby Serena, which wasn't too difficult, as so much had occurred.

After dinner, silence enveloped them for a few moments, each of them lost in their own thoughts. "Seth, there's one more thing." Maria cleared her throat, and gave him a small smile. "I can't help saying this. I need to say it. I...I still love you."

Seth found himself fighting to not get lost in those huge, smoky, charcoal gray eyes. He looked down at his plate, trying to find the words. After a few agonizing moments, he found the courage to look at her again. "Maria, all you've said...well, it's pretty amazing. I've forgiven you long ago. But thank you. I don't know how I feel." *And what about Lucille?* he reminded himself.

As if reading his thoughts, Maria said, "I know you have become friends with a woman named Lucille. She was in the photos of you at the press conference. At first I hated her, thought she was just a dumb blonde clinging onto you, hoping to get something out of your big cure. But I asked the kids and they said you were just friends, that she was your counselor. Although when I pressed them for more information recently they said you seemed to be attracted to her. Are you...do you have feelings for her other than friendship?"

Seth winced but knew he had to be honest. "I do, but we've kept our relationship platonic. And she has kept it professional on her end since she's been my counselor and believes it would be crossing the line to be anything more than my friend. But I'd be lying if I said I don't love her."

Maria looked down at her plate and was quiet for a few moments.

"Well, she's much smarter than I was, to treat you with compassion, and I'm grateful to her. And as much as it hurts to say it, I will be happy for you no matter what you decide or who you end up with. I'm just asking you to search your heart and see if there's still a tiny piece that can find its way back to loving me again."

Wow. Seth wiped the tears that stung his eyes. Strangely enough, his wedding vows rang in his head. *For better or worse, in sickness and health, 'til death do us part. Could it be she really has begun to change? Is there still a piece of my heart that belongs to her? Or did I wall that part off, leaving it to grow cold, harden and die, giving the rest to Lucille? What about Lucille? Haven't I fallen in love with her? Isn't she my saving grace, my new life, my angel?*

Maria noticed the frown on his face. "There's no need to answer. I'll be staying here for two weeks doing some job-hunting, spending time with the children, and of course, our new baby granddaughter. And if you want, I'd like to spend time with you too. After that, I'll just see how it all works out, one day at a time." She got up from her chair, walked around the table, bent down and kissed him on the cheek. "Thank you for dinner, and for seeing me after all I've put you through." And then she forced a smile, waved and walked away.

Since it was late and he was exhausted, Seth decided to stay the night at the hotel. He had told Lucille ahead of time he may be getting a room – of his own of course – and called her now to tell her his plans. He left a message on her voicemail, checked in and after watching a few minutes of mindless television, fell asleep on the hotel bed.

That night he dreamed he was drowning in Boston Harbor, and an angel came to rescue him from the icy water, grabbing his arm and lifting him up and out. She had long, flowing blonde hair and sky blue eyes and looked just like Lucille. Then another angel came and took his other arm. She too had long hair but hers was the color of bittersweet chocolate, and her eyes were a smoky, dark gray. It was Maria.

He wasn't sure if they were fighting over him or just both trying to save him. Then they were gone and he was left alone, lying cold and wet on the pier.

Seth couldn't get back to sleep but didn't want to watch more television, especially at four o'clock in the morning. He sat up in bed, found the Bible in the nightstand drawer, and read until the sun came up.

He had just opened the book randomly, hoping to find a passage that would soothe him. It had been a long time since he had bothered reading the Bible or Torah. The page that appeared before him was out of Genesis. It began: *"So the Lord God cast a deep sleep on the man, and while he was asleep, he took out one of his ribs and closed up its place with flesh. The Lord God then built up into a woman the rib that he had taken from the man. When he brought her to the man, the man said: 'This one, at last, is bone of my bones and flesh of my flesh. This one shall be called 'woman,' for out of 'her man' this one has been taken.' That is why a man leaves his father and mother and clings to his wife, and the two of them become one body."*

Seth got on his knees next to the hotel bed and prayed for a long time. He reflected on what he'd read, the conversation with Maria the evening before, and all of the crazy events that had befallen his life over the past two years. *God is certainly full of contradictions and surprises.*

Up until this point, the pieces of his life had somehow fallen back into place, thanks to the grace of God. *And now this.* He meditated on all that had transpired over the past two days, wondering if there really were any coincidences in God's world.

Seth spoke to God, asking Him to help him sort his thoughts. *It seems like it would be fair to tell Maria she's made her bed and now she has to lie in it. Or that it's too late...we're divorced and I've fallen in love with another woman. Haven't You put Lucille in my life for a reason? Even though we've maintained our relationship as friends, I feel in my heart that it could be more. That I want it to be more. I've felt the attraction between us. And I think she feels the same way too. Why are you now throwing this monkey wrench into the mix?*

Seth tried to remember every day to pray to do God's will, usually unsure what it was, but praying to do it anyway. *And yet, I have my own free will,* he mused as he prayed now. That had to be one of life's greatest ironies – one of the great contradictions he would never understand.

He had a choice. He had to choose. He only hoped he chose God's will for him.

Chapter 26

Angelica Jacobs puttered around the huge, stainless steel kitchen of the Perfect Place restaurant on Rowes Wharf, peering over the shoulder of one sous chef, giving last minute instructions to another.

She had grown her hair back to its long, black tresses, which she had knotted up in a bun while she cooked.

She had also resumed her maiden name. Angelica had changed her name to a fake new one on all the paperwork upon embarking for America to throw Caleb off as much as possible from finding her, but she didn't have to be in hiding for too long.

The change back to her real name became official when she became a widow just a year after her arrival home.

Seth and Angelica had kept in touch with Rabbi Simon Hirsch; he had informed them that Caleb had died while fighting with the insurgent army serving the new governing faction of Syria while it was trying to preserve its tenuous foothold among political turmoil. Simon told them he received a posthumous medal of honor, and that Caleb's father was one of the leaders of the new government.

The rabbi also told them Caleb had tried for several weeks to locate the wife who had abandoned and shamed him. The word on the street was that he would have her publicly humiliated, jailed, and possibly executed. But once his father's star began to rise and he became one of the leaders of the fledgling army with a lot of responsibility, he gave up the fight to find his disobedient wife. Meanwhile, Angelica had worked to have the marriage annulled.

Now, twenty-five years later, Angelica had nothing but business on her mind. She hadn't had the time or desire to remarry. On top of raising Serena, Angelica had eventually taken over as part-owner and president of the Perfect Place. The former conglomerate now consisted of only five restaurants, including the one in Boston and those in New York, Los Angeles, Chicago and Washington, DC.

Seth had done a lot of soul searching about how to spend the money he had been awarded in the Caine settlement. Rogers and Powers had only used up two million in working on Aaron's case. Seth had a hunch Michael hadn't taken a dime of it.

The restaurateur had briefly considered buying back all of the Perfect Place restaurants, even adding a few more. But the more he thought about it, the more he realized he no longer needed to rebuild his empire, or prove himself, and his former employees had long since found other employment.

No, not the more I thought about it, but the more I prayed about it, Seth reflected now, as he swept the floor of Over the Bridge, a homeless shelter he had built with a chunk of the money from the settlement.

It was an attractive red brick building on the corner of Summer and Dorchester Streets, just a few blocks from the place under the bridge where he had stumbled upon the homeless people huddled around the garbage can fire. *Where someone saved my life.*

As he swept, Seth pondered all of the changes in his life that had occurred over the past twenty-five years.

He and Lucille worked weekdays at the shelter: Seth ministered with his culinary skills to make delicious meals that drew hundreds of people off the street, some of whom kept coming back until they were able to make it on their own; Lucille headed up the counseling department, staffed with a variety of experts who offered help on many levels, providing twelve-step programs for various addictions and spiritual, emotional and mental healing.

Even though it was a Saturday, Seth had come in early this morning to spend an hour or so cleaning up a bit, knowing his wife probably had a big day planned for Monday, his seventy-fifth birthday.

He smiled to himself. He had chosen Maria to be his wife again. *And I think God was okay with that.*

When Seth had returned the day after that fitful, fateful night twenty-five years ago when Maria had apologized and asked for him to come back into her life, he had come home feeling more confused than he ever had in his life.

Lucille hadn't been there; just his three children and granddaughter.

They had explained that Lucille had received a phone call early that morning from her boss in Social Services, asking her to come into the office to discuss heading up a new adoption program. The project would require her to fly to a few foreign countries to start investigating various adoptive possibilities for childless parents in America as part of a United Nations effort to find homes for unwanted children across the world.

Lucille had been in the spotlight for her efforts on behalf of the world-renowned Seth Jacobs, who had been cured of cancer, and she had been selected along with several other prominent social services workers in the U.S. with similarly stellar resumes.

She immediately accepted, and had called Seth later that

day to explain that her time over the next several months would be jammed with traveling abroad and work on the new project. She said she hoped he would be alright with it and she would see him when she returned.

While he was disappointed she had to be gone for so long, Seth felt he couldn't possibly stand in her way. Still, it had been extremely hard for both of them to say goodbye.

Over the next several days Seth had grudgingly accepted the fact that Lucille would be gone for awhile. Days later he called Maria and asked her to stay in town longer than the two weeks she had originally planned. *She needs to spend more time with the children, and get to know her new baby granddaughter,* he had reasoned. Yet deep down he knew he wanted to figure out if the small piece of his heart that had once belonged to her was still alive, and could possibly grow.

They got together, tentatively and awkwardly at first, as reacquainted friends, walking Serena in her stroller through Boston Commons, sharing a meal here and there with the kids, and occasionally, just talking, the two of them. And eventually they reached a warm and comfortable place again that somehow felt like home.

Maria had truly become a new person. Or rather, she had found her way back to her authentic self, the person she had been before all of the tragedies in their life befell them and swallowed them both up, spitting out only shells of their former selves. *Her old self, only better,* Seth realized.

And over the next few months, Seth fell in love with her all over again. He still loved Lucille. But Seth and Maria had a family together and a past, like a rich tapestry that time dulls a little but never unravels. They had rediscovered that tapestry, brushed off the dirt and lovingly added new stitches until it shone more colorful and beautiful than before.

Lucille had come to understand and over time, Seth and

she had reinvented their relationship into a deep, unconditional friendship that they knew would last forever. And eventually, they had become partners in the shelter, while Maria had opened a successful floral boutique and landscaping business.

Beams of sunlight shone down through the ceiling's skylight, dancing through the floating dust particles and making them shine. Seth smiled again as he heard pots and pans clanging in the industrial-sized kitchen.

He was occasionally envious that he wasn't running the show in there, but sometimes he found comfort in menial chores like sweeping. *Gives me time to converse with God, to reflect on all the good things in my life, to be grateful*, he thought.

It had taken him a while on this journey called faith, but Seth had eventually stopped questioning why God had tested him during his period of misfortunes, or whether it was a test at all. Seth had come to discover that perhaps, instead, it had all been God's tap on the shoulder, letting him know his life was starting on a new path and he needed to make the journey, no matter how rocky and long. He just trusted in God's plan, praying for faith each day that he could fulfill it.

Seth had thought he had all the faith he needed for most of his life, but looking back, realized he had been sorely lacking. *How easy it is to have faith when everything is going your way*, he had come to know. He now also realized that it wasn't possible to ever achieve perfect faith; that he had to grow in his faith every day. And, like Jesus said, *without works it is dead*. Seth had been through so much that his faith had been split wide open. He now believed that there was room for Judaism and Christianity in his heart and that he and Maria could grow together in their faith.

Of course, many years ago he would have argued that he was working his faith, giving to others. He knew now that, in fact, he had been making token gestures to make himself feel better.

Seth had actually thought he had it all back then, before it all started slipping away, but he realized today it had all been an illusion. *I thought I had planned out my life so perfectly, and for a while, it was all working out according to plan*, he mused, bending over with a dustpan brush to gather a small pile of dirt. *Before it all fell apart, spinning out of control. The control, the plan, the perfection…all illusions. I never stopped to think that a man can never reach true perfection along the path of life and that one can ever be fully in control. Maybe I had to go through all I did to see the truth; that we each only have today. And once I accepted that the plan for my life was in God's hands and not my own, He restored it to so much more than I could ever have planned.*

Seth no longer looked at success as an accumulation of material wealth, or power, or prestige like he did long ago. And he no longer considered happiness to be a measure of what he could get out of life.

Happiness isn't getting what you want, but wanting what you have. He had heard that somewhere and now he really believed it. *I truly have all I need*, he knew.

Both of Seth's sons had returned to Harvard to finish college. Adam had gone on to medical school and then took an internship at Massachusetts General under the tutelage and watchful eye of Doctor Benjamin Grason. He now had his own practice downtown as a neurologist and often was called in to the hospital to assist on highly specialized brain trauma cases and surgeries. One had involved the separation of a set of four-year-old Siamese twin girls, the success of which had met worldwide acclaim. Yet Adam had also managed to raise a family of two girls and a boy, who were now all teenagers and gifted in their own rights.

Aaron had followed in his attorney's footsteps, becoming one of the country's most renowned defense attorneys after freeing an innocent man from death row. After working his way up the ladder at Rogers and Powers, he had become a partner with Michael once Jerry Rogers retired. Aaron and his wife had four sons, all strapping football players and all smart yet ornery like their dad had been growing up. Aaron would always jokingly lament at family gatherings how God was paying him back "in spades" for the grief he had given his own parents.

And Angelica was living her dream; she had worked side by side with her father, learning everything she could until he retired, and ended up taking over the family business. Meanwhile, Serena had grown up to be a lovely lady, had married and had given Seth and Maria a great-grandson.

After giving it much thought and spending a lot of mornings and nights on his knees, Seth turned over the Perfect Place legacy, albeit much smaller and more manageable, to his daughter.

He and Maria had purchased a modest home on a few acres on the water just outside Boston where they were visited often by their family. Seth put several million away in trust funds for his eight grandchildren. Then he donated twenty million dollars to build Over the Bridge and the rest – still many millions – he contributed to "Keep the Cure for Cancer Alive," a fund he set up under the auspices of Massachusetts General Hospital to continue the research in hopes to spread the cure to all nations, even the poorest of the poor.

"What are you smiling about?" Lucille startled him out of his trance, approaching him from the hallway where her office was located. She was dressed in her business attire, slacks and a blazer.

"Just how lucky I am."

"And don't you forget it, mister." Lucille wagged her finger impishly.

He stopped and gave her a hug. "It's amazing how quickly life goes by when you stop planning it and take it one day at a time, relying on God's plan. Who would have ever thought I'd be standing here in a homeless shelter, finally with a purpose to my life? I never thought at seventy-five years old I'd have so much to be grateful for."

"I bet you thought I forgot your big birthday coming up."

"It hadn't crossed my mind. I was kind of hoping everyone might forget. I can't believe I'm going to be seventy-five. I still feel like fifty…well, most days." Seth stopped and leaned on the broom. He did get tired more often these days, but it was nothing an occasional nap didn't cure. His cancer had stayed in remission and his last physical had shown he was in great health for his age.

"Of course I wouldn't forget, silly. Does Maria have anything special planned?"

"It's still not for two more days, but you know her, the consummate party planner. I'm sure she's dreamt up something."

Just then Maria walked through the shelter's front door.

"Alright, I heard my name mentioned. What are you two talking about behind my back?"

"Nothing, dear." Seth walked up and kissed his wife on the cheek.

"Well, if you were wondering about your birthday, I've got it all taken care of."

Seth laughed, and Maria gave Lucille a knowing wink. "I know it's not until Monday, but since today's Saturday, I figured we should celebrate tonight and sleep in tomorrow.

I went out on a limb and made reservations at the Perfect Place."

Seth's eyes lit up.

He loved sampling the work of his daughter because he knew she loved creating it. Seth had teased her many times that she could never be the culinary wizard he was, but he knew her talents surpassed his own. She was a natural.

And now her skills were being put to the test today for the most stressful event she had ever hosted: Seth Jacobs' seventy-fifth surprise birthday party.

Maria, along with help from Angelica, Aaron and Adam, had planned the whole affair, hoping to fool Seth into thinking just the family was celebrating with him at an intimate dinner.

The guests numbered two hundred and twenty, all the restaurant could hold without putting them in serious danger of breaking fire code regulations.

The big night had finally arrived, and Angelica glanced at her watch in horror. She flung off her apron and darted for the swinging kitchen door, yelling orders and a thank you over her shoulder to the kitchen staff.

She almost banged right into her brother Aaron.

"Hey, slow down, sis!" Aaron caught her with his beefy arm before she fell backwards.

"I can't. I've got to get ready. Look at me! I'm a mess!"

"Well, if you just get this parsley out of your hair and this flour off your face…" Aaron started picking at his sister's hair, pretending to find disgusting bits of food hidden there.

She glowered at him, swatting his hand away.

"Hey, I'm just kidding, you look great. I'm here to see what I can do."

"Stay out of the kitchen, for one thing." Angelica took a sweeping look over the huge dining room where the guests would be seated. The chandeliers and Italian marble floor sparkled. Fresh linens and flowers adorned each round table and a decorated head table sat between the indoor waterfall and an ice sculpture of a large number seventy-five. "Why don't you go check on the orchestra leader over there in the corner and make sure he's all set to go?"

"Will do."

"And of course, start greeting any early guests once they begin arriving."

"Hey, that's not fair. Won't you be back in time?"

"I'll certainly try. Call Adam on your cell and get him to come down here and help."

"Yes, master."

Angelica stuck out her tongue at her brother, just like in the old days.

The guests began arriving at five-thirty and helped themselves to platters of appetizers and flutes of champagne served by waiters who floated expertly around the room.

Aaron and Adam and their wives greeted the early arrivals as they came through the French doors. Angelica joined them a half hour later.

With her light blonde hair and floor-length white gown, Aaron's wife stood in stark contrast to his sister, who wore her dark hair swept up to the side and a tea-length black dress. Adam's wife dressed the most conservatively in a navy satin gown but looked elegant as usual, her honey brown hair perfectly coifed around her delicate features.

Angelica got along well with her sisters-in-law because she knew her brothers adored them and wouldn't have it any other way. Fortunately, they were both pretty likeable. And they had given Serena a whole host of cousins to play with over the years.

They all sat around a table in the corner of the cavernous dining room now, laughing and joking with each other and admiring the adorable, three-year-old boy who was showing off his latest dance steps. He had the dark, black curls of his mother, and sea blue eyes of his great-grandfather.

Serena and her husband Matt beamed with pride at their son, Dillon, who was loving the attention he was getting as he performed in front of his seven second cousins, whom he called his "aunts and uncles."

The room quickly started filling up with noise. A huge belly laugh caused even self-absorbed Dillon's head to turn.

It came from Henrí, who had entered the room and was being hugged and fawned over by Seth's children.

They had been told the story of the night when, in this very room, more than a hundred people had gotten sick all over the place, causing an uproar that had left the maitre d' blubbering like a scared little boy.

Angelica had just mentioned there would be no caviar on the menu, but if Henrí would like some, she could have it flown in special for him.

"Oh, but I did make a scene zat night!" Henrí wiped his eyes, which had tears in them from his laughing so hard. He was bald and overweight and still the jovial, likeable man he had been twenty-five years ago. And although he walked with a cane now, he was healthy and happy and traveling the world as a single man with various lady friends. A gorgeous redhead was on his arm this night. Henrí made the appropriate introductions, gave each of Seth's children a hug and kiss, then lead her to their table.

Bill Brown and Miss Carla came in right behind them. Bill's wife had been sick with the flu, and when he found out he was coming alone, he offered to be Carla's escort. The beautiful singer had remained single, traveling the world to perform once she left the restaurant business to become a famous recording artist, although she travelled a little less often now that she was in her sixties.

"I hope we talked you into singing something tonight?" Aaron took Carla's hand and kissed it.

"Why, Aaron Jacobs, you are just as devilishly charming as your father." Carla beamed from the attention. "I think I can manage to make these old vocal chords cooperate."

"Don't let her fool you." Bill Brown put his arm protectively around his friend of forty years. "She can still belt it out. And there's nothing either one of us wouldn't do for your father."

"It would be my honor." Carla curtsied.

Michael Powers and Lucille entered a few minutes later, a very attractive husband and wife who appeared very much in love. They had married a few years after Seth had remarried Maria.

After saying hello to Seth's children, Michael and Lucille slowly walked together along the long photo table, where Angelica had arranged a variety of pictures and photo albums of her dad and his family and friends spanning the past seventy-five years.

They both stopped in front of the two framed photos in the center of the table with a small sign that read, "With us tonight in spirit."

The photos were of Rabbi Jonathan Mosha and Lucille's mother, Rosie O'Hanlon. Both had died of natural causes in their late nineties.

Michael gently picked up the photo of Jonathan. "He was a good man."

"And a good friend." Ben had walked up behind the couple and put his hand on Michael's shoulder. "We all went through a lot together, but I wouldn't change a thing. Thanks to Seth, I not only became a better person, but found three new friends in the bargain." Michael and Lucille both turned and hugged their old friend.

"Just don't go expecting free doctor's visits." Ben smiled.

"That's fine, as long as you don't go expecting free legal advice."

Ben shook Michael's hand. "Done."

"And no free counseling either," Lucille chimed in, making them laugh. The three of them headed back to join Ben's wife at their table.

Angelica nervously checked her watch. "Oh my God, it's almost seven o'clock. Dad will be here in fifteen minutes!" There were still about a dozen people in the lobby, waiting to come through the receiving line. She started giving out orders. "Adam and Aaron, without being rude you get these people to their tables, I'll go check on the kitchen, and if you two could just make sure everyone gets seated and is happy," she motioned to her sisters-in-law, who nodded and went off in different directions.

Adam and Aaron stood erect like soldiers and saluted.

Angelica glared at them, half menacingly, half smiling at them, and headed toward the kitchen.

Soon the room was hushed, filled only with whispers and the tinkling of glasses, and the lights were dimmed. The orchestra played softly in the background.

A limo pulled up and Adam, who took his cue from the maitre d' stationed at the front entrance, signaled to the room that Seth and Maria were arriving.

After shaking the hand of the maitre d', Seth led Maria into his favorite restaurant in the whole world. As they walked out onto the first step that led into the main dining room, suddenly and simultaneously the lights brightened, the orchestra struck up a loud version of Happy Birthday and two hundred and twenty people shouted "Surprise!"

Seth almost fell backward, but Maria was there to support him, both physically and emotionally; after the initial shock wore off, her husband began to cry.

He quickly wiped his eyes as he and Maria descended the steps onto the dance floor, where he was met by his friends and family who warmly greeted him, hugging and kissing him, shaking his hand, patting him on the back, wishing him well.

Angelica took the microphone and welcomed everyone, then raised her glass toward her father, who was now seated at the head table with Maria, their sons and their wives and children, and Serena and her family.

"This will be the first of many toasts tonight, I'm sure, so I'll make it short and sweet." She smiled radiantly at her father. "To the most incredible father a girl could have... happy birthday, Dad."

When she saw her father start to wipe his tears again, she added, "And you all better enjoy the food tonight. Or else." Her last comment caused the room to erupt in laughter.

Following a sumptuous feast of broiled lobster, braised veal, filet mignon and various accompaniments, Ben Grason approached the microphone stand.

The lights dimmed. Again the noise fell to a hush.

"My good friend Seth Jacobs, you have come so very far," he said, his voice choked with emotion. "You deserve all the riches here tonight. And to honor you, I have a special surprise. I'd like to bring out two very special people who want to wish you a happy birthday in person."

A woman in her mid-forties and a man in his mid-thirties approached the microphone.

Seth vaguely recognized the woman, who spoke first.

"Hi, my name is Jennifer." Seth felt a stab of familiarity

jab his heart. It was the strange mixture of relief and anxiety a person might feel welcoming a long lost distant relative thought to be dead or gone, who came back into one's life after twenty-five years of nothing. Mostly relief the person was alive and well. And a small pang of anxiety at not knowing what to expect.

"Twenty-five years ago Doctor Grason brought in a fellow cancer patient to visit me. His name was Seth. I had ovarian cancer, which took away my ability to have children of my own. But I told Seth at the time I'd like to adopt, if I survived the cancer and lived long enough to raise them." Jennifer paused for a moment and smiled and Seth remembered. She had drastically changed. When he had met her, she had had no hair and she was thin, pale, ghostly looking. But her green eyes had still sparkled with hope back then and she had smiled. It was those eyes and that smile which caused him to remember her now.

Her smile broadened, gleaming on her tanned face, framed by wavy, shoulder-length, auburn hair. "Thanks to Doctor Grason, and his colleagues at Massachusetts General – and most especially, thanks to Seth – I am the mother of two wonderful teenagers from the Czech Republic whom I adopted with my husband. They're home in California where we now live, and where I work as a writer on one of the soap operas." Applause and cheers erupted. "But I wouldn't even be standing here today if not for the grace of God and a special man celebrating his birthday who risked his life to find a cure. Thank you, Seth, and happy birthday."

Seth stood and Jennifer walked over to him. They embraced to more applause and cheers.

Then Seth sat back down as a young man approached the microphone. "Hi, my name is Joe," he said.

Seth's lip started to quiver. He hadn't recognized him,

but knew who he was now after listening to Jennifer speak. *I don't know if my old heart can take this*, he thought, dabbing his eyes with a napkin.

Ben and Lucille secretly smiled as the rest of the room listened in curious wonder. "I was only ten when I met Mister Jacobs." The young man cleared his throat and smiled. "I mean Seth. They told me I only had a few weeks. I was dying of lymphoma. But like Jennifer, I too was offered the opportunity to live when Seth took a chance for all of us and sacrificed himself to find a cure."

Now the room was silent, tears falling quietly all around. "I'm thirty-five today, I live in Michigan with my wife and five-year-old son, and I'm a graphic designer and painter. So if you need to add some art to your homes, look me up on my website. A third of all I make goes to the "Keep the Cure for Cancer Alive" fund. But I'm sure most of you have already contributed," he winked and smiled, nodding toward Seth. "And by the way, buddy, you still owe me a game of Texas Hold 'em. Of course, when I win, I'll donate my profits to a good cause."

Seth stood and this time, he crossed the short distance and walked toward Joe. Fresh tears broke out across the room as the two men hugged and thanked each other.

Ben grabbed the microphone. "Alright, that's enough crying. It's time to celebrate! I heard Miss Carla is in the house!"

Everyone clapped and cheered as Carla walked up to the orchestra, leaned over to whisper something to the band leader, then took the tool of her trade in her hand and said, "Happy Birthday, Seth Jacobs. This song's for you."

Seth took Maria's hand and led her to the dance floor as Miss Carla sang a beautiful rendition of "Unforgettable."

The two of them didn't notice as the dance floor filled

with people around them. They were lost in their own little world.

Seth looked deep into his wife's soft gray eyes. "You knew about all of this, didn't you?"

"What if I said I did?" Maria teased, sliding easily along the floor to Seth's lead.

"I'd say I'll have to spank you later when I get you alone for being a bad girl."

"Alright, then, I confess." She smiled playfully, then rested her cheek on his shoulder as they danced.

Seth closed his eyes for a moment, smelling the vanilla scent of Maria's perfume, hearing the melodic sweetness of Carla's voice as it drifted across the room, seeing in his mind's eye the people who had brought him so much joy tonight.

A slight tug on his pants leg brought him out of his rapturous reverie. He looked down and saw a little mop of black curls and brilliant blue eyes staring up at him.

"Grampa!"

He reached down and lifted his great grandson into his arms. "Yes, Dillon?"

"Happy Birfday, Grampa."

And with two tiny arms wrapped around his neck, and his wife's strong arms wrapped around his waist, Seth felt safe, secure and loved.

He thought there must be no man on earth who felt as happy as he did this very moment. Seth silently whispered a prayer of thanks.

Life is good.

About the Author

Michele Chynoweth (pronounced shun-ó-with) has worked in journalism, advertising and marketing prior to becoming a published author. She has won several awards for her work including first place in the drama category of the Maryland Writers Association fiction contest. She is a graduate of the University of Notre Dame, is remarried, has five children and lives in her native Maryland.

Michele believes that the stories in the Bible's Old Testament are compelling, but because they were written so long ago, readers today have difficulty relating to or comprehending them. She believes she has been called to "re-imagine" these Bible stories through modern-day novels filled with the same drama, suspense and romance, yet written so that today's readers can easily see themselves in the characters and hear what God is saying.

Her stories will not only grip you, taking you for a wild ride that will leave you hanging on until the end - they will inspire you to search your own heart for God's Will in your life and find a deeper faith in God's Plan.

Also from Michele Chynoweth

Chessa's husband, U.S. Senator Darren Richards, is a behind-the-scenes, narcissistic alcoholic. None of that changes when he becomes the leading Democratic candidate for President of the United States. Chessa's worries about her husband reach a fevered pitch as he closes in on winning the nation's highest office. How can she support his candidacy, even if it will mean becoming First Lady?

Darren's opponent, Leif Mitchell, is selected from his more humble life as a horse rancher and country rock singer to run for political office. His charm and leadership pave the way for him to become a national hero and a real threat as the leading Republican presidential candidate. A rich and powerful Darren will stop at nothing to bring Leif down, causing Leif to reconsider his "high road" approach to politics.

When Chessa finds out Leif is preparing to seek revenge on Darren in an attack that will not only destroy her husband's candidacy, but will probably cost other innocent lives as well, she is suddenly faced with a decision: Should she preserve peace at all costs, protecting those who would otherwise become collateral damage as a result of the ensuing battle—and in default, her husband—in turn sacrificing her freedom and risking her own life? Should she try to stop Leif, which may ruin his chances but save his soul?

The Peace Maker is based on the story of David and Abigail in the Bible's First Book of Samuel – a story of adversity, struggle, courage and faith that God will lead his people if they but let Him.

Ellechor
PUBLISHING HOUSE

W W W . E L L E C H O R P U B L I S H I N G . C O M

Enjoy an excerpt from The Peace Maker...

He stood and offered his hand to help her out of the booth, then held her coat for her. He waved to the bartender and patrons who recognized him, then opened the door and led her out into the blustery night and quickly into his sleek black sedan. Chessa was nearly as impressed with the car as she was with the man. She looked around its interior, admiring the soft leather seats and new car smell, which mingled nicely with the scent of his cologne.

The ride seemed to go by too quickly, and within minutes the sedan pulled up along the circle in front of Chessa's dorm. She thanked the senator as he opened her car door and again offered his hand to help her out of the vehicle.

"You know, Miss Reynolds, this has been the most delightful interview I've ever had, and I've had a lot of them," he said, holding her hand in his. "Perhaps I could have the pleasure of your company again soon? Could I get your number and give you a call next time I'm in town? I have to go to D.C. for the next few weeks on business, but I'll be back in New York for the holidays, and I'd love to take you out to a much nicer place."

Chessa's heart hammered in her chest as she wrote her number on a page in her reporter notebook, ripped it out, and handed it to him. *Can he really be interested in me? He's a man of the world and I'm just a schoolgirl, just a...*As if to answer her unasked question, Darren leaned over and kissed her on the cheek, bidding her goodnight.

She smiled as she walked dreamily to her dorm room. *Amy won't believe this one.*

Being a reporter and writing for the paper was Chessa's second love. Her first was her mission to help underprivileged women who were victims of domestic violence or abuse.

She wasn't sure how she'd developed her career goal. Perhaps it started around the time her parents divorced when she was twelve. She remembered attending group counseling sessions for students in her grade school in Greenwich Village who were children of divorced or widowed parents, and admiring the woman who had led the group, thinking she'd like to be a counselor like her someday, helping others.

Chessa recalled the intense anger she had felt when her alcoholic father left her mother for the last time. Even though Stephen Reynolds had walked out the front door dozens of times over the years after the many shouting matches he had with his wife, he always returned. Sometimes it would take a day or two, but he always came back. Until the last time.

Often Chessa would try to intercede between her parents when they argued, if the argument wasn't too intense or violent. She would play peacemaker by standing in between them and trying to divert their attention, asking them for a snack, to help with homework, anything she could think of. One time she even brought home a stray cat and hid it in her bedroom until she heard the yelling start, and then brought it out to show them. That time, the yelling only got louder, and the cat was booted out the door and she was sent to bed early.

Theresa Reynolds got full custody of Chessa in the divorce proceedings. Chessa was never asked her opinion and later in life she would wonder if her father ever argued for custody, but was too afraid to hear the answer.

Her father would pick her up at the door on his obligatory semi-monthly visits and take her to the movies or the park, bowling, fishing, or out to eat. Often she had wished her dad wouldn't take her anywhere but just sit in the car and talk to her. They always had a good time, but she just never really felt like she came to know him that well. He was never the hugging, affectionate type.

Still, she had adored her father and like most children, blamed herself and her mother for his leaving. *If only I had been a good girl,* she had chided herself. *If only Mom had loved him better.*

Chessa vowed that she would marry someone just like Stephen Reynolds one day and that she would love him enough so that he would never leave her.

The self-pity she wallowed in for years as a teenager had waned some when she eventually became wrapped up in the lives of those less fortunate whom she read about in the news while doing research for her sociology paper in her sophomore year. She had read about rape victims in the Congo, some not even teenagers yet, who were held hostage and often violently abused by enemy soldiers, sometimes whole armies of them. Some were so severely sexually abused that they ended up physically and emotionally scarred for life, unable to bear children, or were forced to become prostitutes or sex slaves.

While feeling sorry for these girls halfway around the world made her feel less sorry for herself, Chessa also struggled with her faith. She would weep for hours after reading the stories, lying on her dorm bunk bed unable to sleep at night, wondering why humans inflicted such pain on each other, trying to make the torment of those mental images go away.

Chessa had always believed in God, although her parents rarely took her to any formal religious services growing up, but she started to wonder how a God who was all-loving and all-powerful could allow suffering of such magnitude. The only thing that helped her cope was her decision to do something about it. She hoped to graduate from Columbia's School of Social Work and become a counselor. Perhaps she would never get the opportunity to visit the Congo, but she realized she could at least help on a local level. She knew that women in the United States, right here in Manhattan, suffered abuses, perhaps of a lesser degree, but painful and degrading all the same. She felt in her gut that she was meant to help.

Between her studies, her job at the paper, and volunteering at the local women's shelter, she had little time for anything else, including a boyfriend. Chessa had only had a few dates since she had attended Columbia, and she had made just a few close friends.

Her best friend was Amy Darlington, who had been assigned as her roommate freshman year.

Chessa remembered the day she met Amy as if it was yesterday.

The two girls had just stared at one another that first day in their dorm room on campus—the tall, skinny white girl with long, light-brown hair and green eyes, and the short, heavyset black girl with short, curly, raven-black hair and black-brown eyes. The first one smiled shyly and said hello. The second one just kept staring in disbelief.

Amy didn't like most white people very much. Her parents' agenda was to get ahead, get their fair share when she was growing up as a child, and white people seemed to be the 'enemy.' So Amy was wary of whites, even at an early age, and she figured Chessa Reynolds was no different than the rest.

Chessa hadn't liked Amy at first either, but it wasn't because she was prejudiced. Being raised in Greenwich Village by parents who were middle-class bohemian scholars, Chessa had grown up open-minded about a lot of things, and had been taught to be tolerant and nonjudgmental about other races, creeds, nationalities, and the like. But Chessa had detected a negative vibe and defensiveness almost immediately upon meeting her roommate. It was an imperceptible feeling that turned into the discovery that Amy felt she had something to prove as a female African American.

She had tried, introducing herself with a big smile and an outstretched hand that fateful day.

But her hand was left dangling.

"This is just great," Amy had said sarcastically, walking right past Chessa to head out of the room. "I'm going to have to make a change."

Chessa was hurt but persistently optimistic. "What's wrong?"

Amy stopped in the doorway, turned around and looked at Chessa with a scowl. "Well as you can see we're totally different."

"Is it because I'm white or because I'm beautiful?" Chessa folded her arms defiantly.

"Hah, you wish!" Amy crossed her arms too and they both glared at each other for a moment longer before bursting into laughter. "Well, no one else will probably take you in so I guess we can give this a try." She held out her hand to Chessa, who shook it, and then gave her a hug.

The two had somehow learned to like each other over time despite their differences. Amy's judgmental attitude would often infuriate Chessa, but when she did her dead-on comedic impressions of other students or teachers, or used her exaggerated "poor Negro" tone, or even sometimes when she got really angry, Chessa would laugh so hard that the two would forget what made them mad in the first place.

Eventually they came to love each other as friends.

Chessa helped Amy become more tolerant and patient. Amy helped Chessa become more outgoing and confident. They balanced each other out in a good way, and found out they had more in common than they'd originally thought, including a mission to help the oppressed. Amy also worked at *The Spectator* and wanted to become an investigative reporter when she graduated.